"I'm sorry."

"I'm not." Disappointment filled Sophia's face. "Don't you dare say you weren't into that kiss, because I'll call you a liar."

"I wanted to kiss you or I wouldn't have," Ace answered.

"Buuuut...?"

"You're tired, Sophia. Hurt. Scared. Trapped, most importantly. There are a lot of things impeding your judgment. I'd rather shoot myself than take advantage."

"So this is you being noble."

"Trust me, this is not the time to be jumping into something we can't take back."

"Wow, I really freaked you out, didn't I?"

"Sophia, I work for you. I'm trying to help you find the treasure your father may have buried while keeping an unknown number of bad guys from killing you. The last thing you can afford is for me to be distracted. And that was already a pretty big issue before you kissed me."

His speech seemed to be sinking in. She nodded, a gleam in her eyes making him incredibly nervous.

"I get it. The timing is off. So we table it for now. But once we're out of this hole and back at the house, all bets are off."

Dear Reader,

I'm so happy to be writing to you again with the publication of my second book for Harlequin Romantic Suspense, *Undercover Cowboy Protector*. It's the first book in a new series that takes place in a real Texas town called Gun Barrel City. I have long thought it was a great name to use in a book, and you are finally holding it in your hands!

As you read, you'll be whisked away to the intriguing world of Hidden Creek Ranch, where danger and romance intertwine as a treasure hunt heats up. Our hero is Ace Madden, a former SEAL turned private security agent, whose unwavering dedication makes him the perfect guy to go undercover to ensure his employer stays safe after a break-in. Sophia Lang, who recently inherited the ranch, is thrust into a web of secrets and danger that threatens everything she holds dear. Soon she's falling for her cowboy protector, but what will happen when she finds out he's not the ranch hand she thinks he is?

I loved writing this book and dropping the seeds for the other two Lang sisters' stories too. I learned a lot about Maya artifacts (yes, it's *Maya*, not *Mayan*—the things you discover while researching a romance novel...), so I hope you learn some things as well while reading about the treasures from Pakal the Great's tomb. Happy reading!

PS: I love to connect with readers. Find me at kacycross.com.

Kacy

UNDERCOVER COWBOY PROTECTOR

KACY CROSS

ISBN-13: 978-1-335-59401-3

Undercover Cowboy Protector

Harlequin Enterprises ULC
22 Adelaide St. West, 41st Floor
Toronto, Ontario M5H 4E3, Canada
www.Harlequin.com

Printed in U.S.A.

Kacy Cross writes romance novels starring swoonworthy heroes and smart heroines. She lives in Texas, where she's seen bobcats and beavers near her house but sadly not one cowboy. She's raising two mini-ninjas alongside the love of her life, who cooks while she writes, which is her definition of a true hero. Come for the romance, stay for the happily-ever-after. She promises her books "will make you laugh, cry and swoon—cross my heart."

Books by Kacy Cross

Harlequin Romantic Suspense

The Secrets of Hidden Creek Ranch

Undercover Cowboy Protector

The Coltons of New York

Colton's Yuletide Manhunt

Writing as Kat Cantrell

Harlequin Desire

Marriage with Benefits
The Things She Says
The Baby Deal

In Name Only

Best Friend Bride
One Night Stand Bride
Contract Bride

Visit the Author Profile page at Harlequin.com for more titles.

To the hero of my own story, Mr. Cross, because you don't think it's a burden to do all the housework while I write. I am truly blessed.

Chapter 1

Sophia could feel the new ranch hand watching her again. And not in the I'd-like-to-buy-you-a-drink kind of way she was used to.

That, she knew how to handle. In two languages. She could send a midlevel exec in a suit packing before he'd even rounded the bar with that expectant, hopeful expression on his face.

This ranch hand business was something else. Something she needed to figure out how to handle. Stat. Especially since this was the third time and he'd just started yesterday.

Plus, she was technically his boss. As soon as she figured out how to boss cowboys, she'd be the bossiest boss in East Texas.

As she walked toward the barn, the back of her neck heated, then the warmth spread right down between her shoulder blades. Jeez. Had this guy come equipped with lasers instead of eyes? The skin on her arms prickled and all her senses blipped into high alert.

Whipping around, she let her gaze flit along the scarlet siding that made up the barn, searching for the now-familiar battered hat the color of beach sand. Sure enough, the cowboy her ranch manager had called Ace leaned against the split-rail fence, casually looping a rope with gloved hands.

His eyes stayed locked on his task. This guy was good. But he was faking it, plain and simple, because she *knew* he'd been staring at her five seconds before, while she'd skimmed the report her accountant had emailed her.

The fact that she could never catch him in the act made not one bit of difference. He had a lot of practice hiding his avid interest in his boss, that was for sure. Why he chose to study her on the sly—that was the million-dollar question.

Maybe he was quietly plotting whether to use an ax or his bare hands to murder her. He had that hard, dangerous look about him. As if he'd seen things people didn't talk about in polite company. Perhaps he'd done some of those things too.

Or, more likely, he was just a regular ranch hand trying to reason out why a woman wearing a designer dress was running a place like Hidden Creek Ranch. For the record, because she didn't have any other type of clothes to wear while running this ranch. *Run* being a generous term, especially if you didn't look too carefully behind the curtain.

If she'd known the nebulous verb called *ranching* would be so difficult, she might have reconsidered this cockamamie idea of turning Grandpa's property into a luxury dude ranch. Folks who paid a lot of money to hang out for a rustic weekend expected horses to be a part of their experience. Horses meant ranch hands.

Ergo, Sophia now employed ten or twelve of them. She'd lost count, but the number was part of a long list of details that woke her up in a cold sweat at night.

She couldn't do it all. That was what she kept telling

herself, even as she continued to spread herself thinner as the clock crept toward midnight, then turned over to a new day. A day where she still didn't have anyone she could lean on when it all got to be too much.

That's fine. It was fine. She could handle this and anything else life wanted to throw at her.

"Jonas," she called as she caught sight of the ranch manager and double-timed it across the hard-packed earth that led to the barn's south entrance. "How highly recommended did that new ranch hand come?"

Jonas's face resembled a statue 90 percent of the time, and the other 10 percent didn't count because you couldn't tell what he was thinking anyway. The man never registered a blessed thing in his expression, a trick Sophia would like to learn. So, if he thought the question was weird, she'd never know.

Jonas spat on the ground, but she refused to jump as she assumed he meant for her to. It was no secret that her ranch manager didn't truly consider himself her employee. He let her act like the boss and accepted the paycheck that her accountant issued, but that was the extent of his concession toward the illusion that Sophia was in charge of Hidden Creek Ranch—a name she was still testing out in her head but liked.

"Didn't come recommended at all," Jonas finally said after an eternity of silence that she suspected was meant to scare her off.

Except she didn't scare easily. If she could shoulder the probing stare of Ace, the Ranch Hand Who Had Zero Recommendations, she could handle Jonas.

"Curious why you hired him, then." She crossed her arms in a show of stubbornness—the same flaw that had gotten her into this situation in the first place. "I thought I made it clear that you could only hire experienced ranch hands."

"You didn't ask about his qualifications. You asked if he came with a recommendation."

They stared at each other for an entire sixty seconds. Which she knew because she counted. It was a trick she'd learned at a corporate retreat, where you use the rhythm of counting to soothe yourself before you blew up at an employee.

It didn't work.

She caved first. She had to. The to-do app on her phone beckoned, the one she never closed because she was always doing something on the list while rushing to get to the next item down. When cell service worked. Which wasn't always.

"I don't have time for semantics," she informed Jonas frostily, wondering yet again if that was his first name or last. "That guy bothers me."

Unlike Ace, the ranch manager had come recommended by her housekeeper, who knew everyone in Gun Barrel City. Sophia had hired Jonas on the spot, too pressed for staff to be choosy. So far, he'd done a stellar job getting the rest of the personnel lined up.

Ace notwithstanding. And the irony didn't escape her that she'd yet to learn the name of any of the other ranch hands. The rest of the nondescript guys in cowboy hats roaming the place barely registered with her.

The back of her neck prickled again but she refused to glance over at the sandy-colored hat or the face underneath it.

"If he's bothering you, I'll fire him," Jonas said blandly as if it didn't matter to him one way or the other.

Guilt. Okay, that was her least favorite emotion and it tasted sour in her throat. Jonas made it sound like Ace had cornered her in the barn and made inappropriate comments. In the corporate world, yes, that was grounds for termination. And probably on a ranch too.

But that wasn't the situation. You couldn't fire an employee because you had a feeling that he'd checked you out a couple of times. Could you? Besides, what if he had a family he was trying to feed with this job? She'd be taking food out of a baby's mouth all because a ranch hand had her spooked.

"No, it's fine," she ground out through clenched teeth. "He hasn't spoken to me. It's just...keep an eye on him for me. I don't trust him."

To be fair, she didn't trust anyone. But Jonas didn't have to know that Sophia was a recovering control freak who had burned out as an ad executive and then grasped the lifeline of this inherited ranch, determined to remake herself into a luxury destination resort owner. Along with that, she planned to be Zen all the time and forget how to spell the word *stress*.

Obviously, that was going well.

Jonas tipped his Stetson in her direction and waltzed away in his funny one-two step that she'd decided meant he'd spent a lot of time on the back of a horse. He was exactly the kind of person she needed running this ranch. She'd do well to remember that delegation was her friend before she questioned him again about his hiring decisions.

Sophia turned on her heel and strode back toward the Victorian-style house that she still thought of as Grandpa's but really belonged to her, legally and everything. Out of the corner of her eye, she noted Ace's head swivel in her direction, his gaze no longer on his rope. She ignored him.

Maybe he was attracted to high-strung women working on their second career before the age of thirty-two. It wasn't a crime and she had too much else to worry about to pay much attention to the hard-edged cowboy who didn't know how to talk to a girl.

When she hit the paved part of the sidewalk that curved around toward the back entrance of the house, it occurred to her that she'd completely forgotten her original reason for heading down to the barn. Dang it. Distracting ranch hands would be the death of her.

What she needed to do was inspect the new riding equipment that she'd noted on Becky's accounting report—that's why she'd been on her way to the barn. The saddles and other horse-related paraphernalia had cost her over $25,000, according to the line item. Naturally, she'd wanted to see the stuff herself because surely it had been handcrafted out of solid gold, then encrusted with diamonds to warrant that kind of price tag.

Just as she started to turn around again, she noticed the back door leading to the kitchen wasn't closed. Huh. Had she really been *that* distracted on her way out a few minutes ago?

Sure, part of the appeal of Hidden Creek lay in the fact that folks swore you didn't have to lock your doors in this part of East Texas. A born-and-bred city girl like Sophia needed more than a few days to be cool with reversing a lifelong habit, but the door was *open*, not just unlocked, and she'd have sworn she'd pulled it to.

Maybe someone else had left it open. Except her housekeeper had gone to the grocery store, her blue four-door still conspicuously missing from the circular drive in front of the main house where she always parked. Everyone else lived in the bunkhouse down at the other end of the paver stone walkway or, in Jonas's case, in the manager's quarters.

Something heavy settled in her stomach.

She shook it off with a laugh. First, she got riled over a ranch hand checking her out and then panicked over an open door. It might have a faulty latch for all she knew. She'd only been living at Grandpa's ranch for less than a week.

She'd never been this paranoid in Dallas, and while she'd lived in a pretty upscale part of the city, crime wasn't unusual. Generally, if you kept your head down and didn't go out after 10:00 p.m., nothing bad happened, though.

Nothing bad was happening here, either. Sophia herself had left the door open on her way to the barn. Plain and simple. The stress was really getting to her.

But when she reached out a hand to grab the doorknob, intending to pull it shut for real this time before heading back down to the barn—*again*—she saw the faint scratches on either side of the keyhole. As if someone had inserted instruments of the long, thin variety into the slot and then jiggled them around to spring the lock.

Sophia's pulse leaped higher than a frog introduced to firecrackers for the first time.

Someone had broken in.

Someone was inside who wasn't supposed to be there.

Someone who probably thought she'd be away from the house for a bit longer.

This someone had vastly underestimated Sophia Lang

and her tolerance for people taking things that didn't belong to them. This ranch had been left to *her.*

Without hesitation, she flung the door open and called out, "I know you're in here. Come out and play nice, and I'll handle this situation civilly. Otherwise, I'll start dialing the cops."

That's when the sheer distance to the main road wormed through her adrenaline-laced brain. It took eight minutes to drive to the edge of Grandpa's land, for crying out loud. How long would it take a police car to arrive from town? A vague idea formulated that maybe they didn't even have a proper police department in Gun Barrel City—it might be more like a sheriff's office.

So she'd be handling this situation herself.

She needed a weapon. She glanced around for anything that would do in a pinch. Umbrella? No. Something heavier would be better.

The housekeeper, Jenny, had a line of cookbooks set up on the kitchen counter, held in place by an iron bookend shaped like a pineapple. That would do.

She hefted the iron weight to shoulder height and crept past the island where the housekeeper had left a giant bowl covered in a dish towel. Good, Jenny would obviously be back soon. Sophia would feel much better with a wingwoman.

Man, she needed to get back to the gym. This weight was *heavy.*

The door to her office stood ajar. No way would she have been distracted enough to skip closing it. She liked her privacy and liked to maintain the fantasy that she had her ducks in a row. The chaos of her office told a different story, one that starred a tornado wrapped in a hurricane, which frankly described her life over the last two months. Since she didn't want everyone to clue in that her ducks were more like squirrels in a mosh pit, she kept the door closed. Always.

The thief must be in her office.

A thin film of wrath turned her vision red for a moment.

No one touched her stuff. Of course, Grandpa had left the whole ranch to Sophia in his will, so technically everything on this side of the office door belonged to her too, but the things inside she'd brought from her corner office in the Hathaway Building. It was all she had left of her previous life, all she had to remind her that she'd conquered the Dallas advertising space. Promoting a luxury destination resort should therefore be a piece of cake.

The office was like a giant motivational poster. No one got to invade her sanctuary.

Peeking through the opening where the hinges met the frame, she spied a man in dark clothes rifling through her desk.

"What do you think you're doing?" she screeched as she flew into her office, bookend raised.

The man glanced up, clearly not feeling all that threatened, his expression growing hard and focused as his gaze landed on her. A stranger. She'd have remembered if Jonas had hired this guy. Faces, she committed to memory, even if she didn't always remember names.

The guy dropped the notebook he had in his hand as if it had burned him, then skirted the desk. Toward her. With intent. Fast. As if he meant to tackle her.

She didn't think. She reacted, swinging the bookend toward the intruder.

She missed. He hit her shoulder with the brunt of his weight, knocking her against the wall.

Pain exploded across her clavicle and down her arm. The thief twisted her bookend-wielding arm up over her head, shaking it. No, pushing it down in the direction of her face.

He was trying to force her to hit herself with the bookend! She fought back, screeching a litany of nonsensical words, but her brain wasn't exactly functioning at top speed. His fingernails bit into her shoulder as he pushed her back against the wall.

All at once, the pressure on her arms vanished. So did the guy, in a whirl of dark colors and a blur of motion.

Someone had pulled the intruder away from her, and the two men grappled with each other for a few heart-rending seconds. Then her attacker broke away to race out of the door, her rescuer hot on his heels.

Ace. She'd recognized him instantly. The ranch hand's hat hadn't even been knocked askew. Her lungs certainly had. She couldn't catch her breath.

She was still standing there in that same spot when Ace returned, his expression taut and searching as he met her gaze for the first time. Unflinchingly. Yeah, this was not a guy who was afraid to talk to a woman.

Holy cow. His eyes were gorgeous, the color of the ocean in a storm when it couldn't decide what color it wanted to be, and all of them were fascinating.

"Are you okay, Ms. Lang?" he drawled, his voice honey as it flowed through her, coating all the bruised places inside. Even the righteous indignation of being victimized.

"I think so." Dropping the bookend, she stretched out her arm, rolling the shoulder that had hit the wall. "The more important question is, are you? Don't women in movies put a steak or something on the guy's hand who punches their attacker?"

The ranch hand's mouth twisted up into a half smile so unexpected that it dazzled her for one crazy moment. Why had she never noticed his dimples and magazine-worthy cheekbones? The eyes she could be excused for missing, given his avoidance issues, but the rest? She needed her vision checked if she'd missed how hot he actually was.

He bobbed his head. "I'm fine, thank you. I'm not one to waste a woman's offer of a steak on my hand."

Okay, she absolutely should not be so charmed by someone she'd labeled untrustworthy not too long ago, but she got a pass given the circumstances. Anyone who played the part of a white knight had earned the right to a second first impression.

"I guess I don't have to ask how you knew I was in trouble," she said ruefully, figuring it was better to call a spade a spade. As closely as he'd paid attention to her all day, it was no mystery.

The ranch hand raised an eyebrow. "I heard you yelling all the way down at the barn. I figured it was my civic duty to investigate. Just to make sure you were all right."

Dulcet tones she did not have, a fact that she readily acknowledged. But really? That's how he wanted to play it? As if she'd made up the whole idea that he'd become her number one fan and he just happened to be there, ready and willing to jump into a fray that included an intruder who had attacked her.

She quirked a brow right back at him. In this case, it had worked in her favor to have earned his interest and obviously he'd saved her instead of being the one to come after her with his bare hands.

But neither did he actually appear to be as reticent as she'd first thought. What was his story, then?

"Well, I appreciate the assistance regardless. You're a real hero."

Ace scrubbed the back of his neck where his skin had turned a mottled color that had nothing to do with the sun he worked under for hours on end. She'd embarrassed him. Adorable.

"Well," he drawled with a faint accent she couldn't place. "He got away. Maybe save the praise for next time."

"Oh, goodness, let's don't assume there will be a next time, okay?" She shuddered, suddenly aware that he had a valid point.

The guy had escaped. *Without* whatever he'd been searching for, presumably, since she'd interrupted him. Why wouldn't he come back? Maybe at night when alert ranch hands would be asleep.

"I don't assume anything," he said grimly. "What do you think he was looking for?"

She threw up her hands. "I have no idea. I've barely been living here a week and there's so much I don't know about this place."

"If you're okay, I'll contact the local sheriff's office." He jerked his head toward the door. "I'll give them my statement about this situation. Ask for them to send a regular patrol around, just to be safe."

Heroic and thorough. If this guy kept exceeding her expectations, she'd have to figure out how to keep from switching places with him—and then she'd be the one checking him out on the sly. The hard edges she'd noted certainly weren't imagined and translated into a whole lot of very well-defined muscle.

After spending several long minutes in his company, she had the impression the drool-worthy cowboy hid behind that edge deliberately. What else was he hiding?

Chapter 2

The law enforcement in this backwater place left a lot to be desired, but Ace Madden didn't usually take no for an answer, and today wasn't looking like the day he'd start.

"Madden," he repeated into his phone, glancing behind him to make sure Sophia Lang hadn't materialized two feet away, as she'd been prone to do lately. "Look, I'm authorized to make this call by the property owner. I need you to send a squad car by so we can reassure her that the cops will keep the intruder away."

It was rare that Ace missed Afghanistan, but no one there ever questioned whether he had the authority to take care of business when the need called for it. On the plus side, he could opt to spare lives in his current profession and did. That was the important thing. He clung to that while repeating to the dispatcher once again that he'd happened upon his employer being attacked and pulled the intruder off her.

No one had to know that he'd learned that particular technique strictly so he didn't have to kill anyone. Deep inside, it felt like a gutless move, but that was the real problem, wasn't it? He had talent for violence, but he didn't particularly like having to get violent with anyone. And even if he was going after bad actors who posed a threat to innocent people, it was a paradox that had driven him from the navy into private security work.

At least he liked the cowboy hat. It was better than eighty pounds of gear and a HALO drop out of a helicopter over the Persian Gulf. In the dark.

Finally, the dispatcher agreed to send the sheriff to check out Ace's story in person.

"Thank you, ma'am, I appreciate that," he told her sincerely and hung up, shuffling back out of view before someone noticed him.

Jonas had too much going on to pay much attention to Ace, but some of the other hands were the good sort who liked to be friendly to newcomers, prone to chatting him up about the weather or throwing out a "How 'bout them Cowboys?", which he'd quickly learned meant the football team, not the ranch hands. Who were also cowboys, but paid considerably less, and no one wanted to talk about them.

Such was the enormous learning curve for being an undercover security operative tasked with keeping Sophia Lang safe without alerting her to his hired-gun status, as dictated by his employer.

Of course, he didn't even know who had hired him. A minor detail he cared not one whit about given the number of zeros tacked onto the end of the paycheck deposited into his business account. It hadn't covered all his sister's medical bills, but the second half, payable in one month, would nearly clear the deck.

While waiting for the sheriff, he texted the other ex-SEALs who made up the staff of the security company he'd formed, telling them simply that the job had just gotten interesting.

While there hadn't been any call thus far for McKay and Pierce to join him on the ranch, Ace had been on the premises for less than twenty-four hours, and he'd already scared off an intruder who may have been after Ms. Lang. This might quickly turn into a three-person job.

The sheriff rolled onto Hidden Creek property with his lights flashing. Ace's eyes drifted shut in disbelief. And maybe in hopes of some fortification.

Obviously, he should have told the dispatcher to instruct the sheriff to come in a little less hot. Of course, he'd have to explain the presence of a squad car to someone eventually no matter what, but it would have been nice to do so with a little less fanfare.

Nothing to do for it now. Ace strode forward to clasp the sheriff's hand, introduced himself and flashed all his fancy new civilian identification. In the end, the sheriff just nodded at the dog tags peeking out from the V of Ace's shirt.

"I'm a vet too." The sheriff tipped his Stetson to the back of his head. "What branch?"

Finally, something was going Ace's way. "Navy. Served in Afghanistan mostly. You?"

"Army. Saw a lot of Gulf War action but that was way before your time," the sheriff acknowledged with a belly laugh.

Ace smiled, relieved that he'd managed to score an in with the sheriff his first week on the job without even trying. That couldn't be a coincidence and he took a moment to thank his lucky stars.

"Not that much more before my time," he countered lightly as a courtesy toward the older man, who did seem to be graying at the temples and carried a lot more weight than he likely had when he'd been active duty. "About my intruder..."

The sheriff took his statement, nodding absently when Ace brought up the idea of sending around regular patrols in case the intruder made a repeat appearance.

"We're a small department," the sheriff explained without sounding apologetic at all. "We'll come by as we can."

Ace checked his eye roll. Obviously, whoever had hired him knew the local cops weren't going to be much use. Fine. He'd keep Ms. Lang from being attacked again. That's what he got paid for, but it would have been great to keep doing it on the down-low while the police did the heavy lifting.

The sheriff went up to the main house to have a word with Sophia Lang, whose statement wouldn't sound much different than his, no doubt.

When he turned around, Jonas was leaning against a fence post, chewing on his tobacco with a laziness that didn't fool Ace for a moment. "What was that all about?"

Couldn't a guy get even a second to conjure up a plausible cover story?

"Oh." Ace ducked his head, shrinking himself down as much as possible in a likely futile attempt to blend into the background. "Nothing major. Helping out Ms. Lang."

Maybe if he left it at that, Jonas would too.

The ranch manager nodded, if you could call that slight head tip a nod. "Uh-huh. That fence on the back pasture fixed?"

"Will be," he promised and hightailed it out before Jonas could ask any more questions.

Unfortunately, the back pasture's proximity lay out of sight of the main house. In the last twenty-four hours, he'd followed his initial plan of lying low and getting a feel for the environment, but that strategy wasn't going to work anymore now that a very real threat had made its presence known.

Therein lay the difficulty of this job. He didn't quite know what to expect since the assignment had few details. All he knew was that Ms. Lang had inherited the ranch and someone wanted to ensure her safety. From what, he'd had no clue until today. That guy would be back, no question. And the intruder might have friends lurking in the shadows of the trees ringing the ranch property.

Once Ace had the fence repaired, he took a long walk around the perimeter of the tree line, just to familiarize himself with the layout in case the knowledge came in handy in the near future. It also couldn't hurt to look for places someone might hide out with the intent to spy on Ms. Lang or any of the other ranch personnel.

Truthfully, it wouldn't be difficult to infiltrate the population of the ranch. He'd done it, almost without trying, and no one had looked twice at his made-up résumé that swore up and down that he'd worked on a ranch before. He hadn't.

But this seemed to be a pretty chaotic period in the life of this ranch. Lucky for him. If things settled down, there might be more scrutiny over his lack of cowboying skills.

A flash of dark against the lighter-colored ground caught his eye.

The color and shape didn't belong. But he couldn't tell what it was from here.

Fading into the trees, he circled around behind the area. No need to open himself up for his own surprise attack.

Ace shimmied up one of the taller trees without breaking a sweat, even though his cowboy boots worked as well at gripping bark as oil would help him hold on to an eel. He was used to less-than-stellar conditions and assignments that pushed his creative and physical limits, though. Cowboying was child's play in comparison.

Silently, he surveyed the remote spot, noting it had a good view of the ranch goings-on but didn't seem to be visible from the barn. Hard to tell from here.

Quick surveillance revealed no one was hiding in the trees. The dark thing was a tarp, stretched out over the ground, ready for someone with binoculars to spread out on. Unless he missed his guess, that's exactly what Ms. Lang's attacker must have done.

But alone or did he have a partner?

Well, he wouldn't be letting his guard down either way. And he realized he'd been away from Ms. Lang too long. After giving the area a quick but thorough search, he headed to the main buildings.

When he got back to the barn, he scouted around for another task to keep his hands busy and settled on helping Rory Montgomery feed the horses. A never-ending job, but Ace didn't mind it too much. It had a good view of the house, and since his primary objective was keeping an eye on Sophia Lang, he'd gladly feed horses all day long if they'd let him.

Except the joke was on him. Ms. Lang wasn't at the house. She'd stepped out the door and started down the long path on a straight line right toward him.

He put his head down, praying it did actually give him a less noticeable vibe, but at six-two, it was hard not to be one of the tallest guys around.

"There you are," she said brightly, her voice carrying across the open expanse. "I've been looking for you."

He bit back the urge to shush her. First the sheriff and then Ms. Lang seemed bound and determined to point a bunch of arrows at his face. This was his first undercover gig and might be his last, based on his inability to keep a low profile thus far.

Montgomery, who had that look about him as if he'd been born and bred in East Texas, let a slow grin spill over his face. "Madden, did you get crossways with the boss already?"

Not likely, but given what she'd most certainly sought him out for—a recap on his meeting with the sheriff—he'd prefer a dressing-down due to some ranch duty infraction.

"Not at all," she corrected, tucking a long strand of dark hair behind her ear, one of many that had escaped her tight hairdo. The real mystery lay in why she bothered to put it up.

"Could you excuse us for a minute?" he mumbled in Montgomery's direction.

Ace gave the dude credit for flicking his gaze in his boss's direction and waiting for her to nod before heading off. At least most of these boys had manners drilled into them at some point.

"I wanted to thank you," Ms. Lang said. "For earlier. I didn't get a chance to tell you how grateful I am that you came to my rescue."

Normally, Ace was a fan of grateful women. Especially one who looked like Ms. Lang. This was not the time to segue the touch of "my hero" shining from her bright gaze into a little more of a mutually satisfying thank-you.

"No problem." He lifted his hat, edging backward a bit to give her the impression he had to get back to work. "Anyone would have done the same."

"No one else was paying attention," she said wryly. "Only you. I have to admit, it came across as a little questionable at first, but in retrospect, I'm pretty happy to have been the subject of your interest."

Dang, she'd noticed him watching her? Here he thought he'd been a lot more subtle than that. Damage control time. Better to err on the side of looking like a flirt than a one-man surveillance crew. "You caught me. Sorry about that. My mama really did teach me better, but in all honesty, I think she'd agree you're pretty pleasing on the eyes."

"Well, I wasn't expecting you to come clean," she said, her eyes wide and her smile warming up things nicely.

So she'd not only taken the bait, the idea of him finding her attractive didn't seem to be too unwelcome. And that part wasn't a lie, thankfully. Sophia Lang might be one of the prettiest women he'd ever seen, but he'd never expected to admit that out loud—in fact, he'd have laid odds on keeping that fact all to himself.

Distractions of the female variety, he did not need. Especially one who had The Job slapped all over her. Distance between them worked better.

On the flip side, it was nice to be able to speak the truth for once. The number of lies required to maintain his undercover status bothered him. It was so much easier in a lot of ways to drop into a firefight wearing fatigues and black paint on his face, fingers curled around an M4A1. Everyone who saw him knew what he'd come there for.

No one knew what he'd come to the ranch for, and he needed to keep it that way.

"I'm an open book, Ms. Lang," he told her with a dose of false cheer.

If only he'd met her under different circumstances, and he had the latitude to flirt with her for real.

She wrinkled her nose. "Call me Sophia, please. Listen, when you talked to the sheriff, did he say anything about sending out more officers to do an investigation?"

"He didn't mention it."

In the sheriff's mind, the hard work was done—he'd taken their statements. What more was there to do? Such was the mentality of many small-town law enforcement departments.

The tarp in the woods lay fresh on Ace's mind, though. That signaled intent and planning on the part of the man who'd gotten away. And worse, it meant the threat still loomed.

He couldn't tell Sophia any of this.

Worry sprang into her eyes. Wouldn't it also be nice if he could reassure her, let her know that he was on the job and he wouldn't let anything happen to her?

"Figures." She hmphed. "I asked him about it, and he brushed me off. He could have at least dusted for fingerprints or something, to see if the guy has a record. That's what they always do on *CSI*."

He grinned. "Want me to call him back and mention that?"

"No. I'm sure he's doing what he's supposed to."

That made one of them. Just because the sheriff and Ace had the armed forces in common didn't mean they were both competent at their post-service professions.

All at once, he realized that his current plan of keeping Sophia at a distance wasn't going to work. Surveillance only made sense if you were searching for an active threat. He'd found one.

Time for a new strategy. Especially one that set her mind at ease. “If you like, I can make it a point to keep an eye on things. Circle the house a few times during the night. Set up some floodlights around the doors and windows.”

Curiously, she eyed him. “You’d go without sleep on my behalf? You really are a white knight.”

He ducked his head, a reflex that had become more common than he was used to, but the number of times he’d been put in the spotlight lately had become alarming. And slightly embarrassing. “No, far from it. You’re my boss and anything you need done is part of my job.”

“What if I needed a sounding board?” she suggested with raised eyebrows. “Someone who clearly has keen hearing, eyesight and a secret ability to scare people off without blood or flashy weapons.”

“You mean me?”

Her smile broadened. “Yes, you. That guy was looking for something. What? I don’t know anything about running a ranch or horses or even cowboys for that matter, but I do enjoy your ‘aw, shucks, ma’am’ routine. More than I thought I would. So maybe your paycheck could extend to helping me figure out what was so interesting in my office.”

He stared at her for a moment. Never in a million years would he have expected Ms. Lang herself to come up with his next move—and for it to be such a perfect way to keep close to her without raising suspicion. “You bet. Anything you need.”

“That was easy. I’ll clear it with Jonas.”

That got a hearty *yes, please* from him.

“It’s not a routine, by the way.” Which wasn’t at all important to clarify in the grand scheme of things but he felt compelled to mention for some reason. “I’m just a guy who has a healthy respect for women, especially if they are the ones signing my paycheck."

"Stop, you had me at 'pleasing on the eyes,'" she told him with a laugh. "I've never been called that before and let's just say it's my new favorite compliment."

So, Ms. Lang had a bit of her own flirting game going on. He couldn't rightly say he objected. "You're welcome, then."

"Come by the house in about ten minutes after I've had a chance to explain your new duties to Jonas."

She sauntered off, leaving him a bit dumbfounded. And trying to sort through the distinct feeling that Sophia had asked him to help her not because she really needed another set of eyes. But because the attacker had spooked her, and she didn't want to be alone.

If so, why hadn't she just come out and said she'd like to repurpose him as her temporary bodyguard?

Chapter 3

Sophia risked another sidelong glance at her companion because *hello.*

Ace Madden—last name now known thanks to the other cowboy—was very easy on the eyes. *How* had she missed that before? And his voice. That was the secret star of the show. It was the kind of voice made for close quarters with low light and no other people.

This time, he caught her mid-perusal, but he just smiled. "Wondering what a guy like me is doing in a place like this?"

She had to laugh. He didn't exactly fit into her ergonomic desk chair. In fact, most of him spilled over the edges and into the surrounding area.

Okay, maybe not physically, but he had this presence that she found both affecting and oddly comforting, despite knowing very little about him. What she did know counted though—he missed nothing, with a sharp-eyed gaze rivaling a bird of prey and an alertness that said nothing would get past him.

If someone had told her back in Dallas that she'd suddenly find alertness attractive, she'd call it ridiculous. But after nearly being brained by her own bookend courtesy of this unknown assailant, she'd quickly revised her understanding of basically everything. Especially the mysterious circumstances around her inheritance, which she'd been ignoring thus far in favor of her enormous to-do list.

It was time to change that.

"Maybe you should be asking me that question," she advised him and picked through the contents of the second desk drawer.

Ace lifted his brows as he glanced up from his own drawer on the left-hand side. "What is a girl like you doing in a place like this?"

Touching her nose, she leafed through the papers Grandpa had left behind. "That's the one."

"To be followed by the more pointed question—if you don't know anything about running a ranch, why are you here?" he asked. "Assuming you don't mind me asking since you brought it up."

Yeah, she had. It hadn't occurred to her that admitting such a thing to one of her ranch employees might not be the best way to instill confidence in her ownership of Hidden Creek. All she'd been thinking at the time was how to get a desperately needed second set of eyes, preferably ones used to evaluating ranch-type details.

And maybe she wanted to spend a few more minutes in the company of the man she'd stumbled over in her backyard. It wasn't hurting anything.

"The ranch was supposed to be a family venture," she said, struck by how bitter it tasted in her throat to say so. "My sisters and I were each left one-third ownership, but they both bailed on me. I can't afford to buy them out, not yet, so they basically gave me a year to get this place profitable or they want me to sell and split the proceeds."

"That's rough," Ace said with what felt like genuine sympathy. "No pressure or anything. The original owners were your parents?"

Somehow, she'd assumed Ace Madden hailed from Gun Barrel City and thus would know the ranch's history. It was interesting to learn that he wasn't a local in this roundabout way. "No, my grandpa. Billy Lang. He ran a stud farm that was pretty well known for producing quality horses, but my dad wasn't interested in following in his footsteps. As my grandpa got older, he had to let the business go."

All delivered with an even voice that belied none of the horribleness that had represented her childhood. Two sentences to encapsulate a decade and a half of listening to her parents fight about moving to the ranch. Sophia's dad cared nothing for horses, never had. He cared about one thing and one thing only: treasure. Rumors of treasure, stories about treasure, searching for treasure…anything and everything that even hinted that something valuable might be there for the finding.

And he'd finally left his family over it.

She hadn't seen her father in over fifteen years. Last she'd heard, he'd been headed to Bolivia with his partner in search of some obscure Incan artifact rumored to be buried in a tomb near Lake Titicaca. As far as she was concerned, David Lang didn't exist.

But Hidden Creek Ranch did, and she had a more than fair share of indignation at her dad for abandoning not only his wife and daughters, but his father, and the legacy left behind.

Ace glanced at her. "Pardon me for saying so, but it seems like a tall order to get a breeding program up and running in a year. You know, because the horses have to have time to breed and such."

"That would be a fair statement if I planned to resurrect the stud farm. I'm opening a luxury destination resort instead," she told him and swallowed back the sheer panic that rose up as she contemplated all the work left to do and the very small amount of time to do it in. "You know, like a dude ranch? With trail rides and cabins along the creek."

"That sounds like a fine idea," he said immediately, earning major points by not listing all the reasons it wouldn't work, like her mother had done.

"Really?" she squeaked out before she could stop herself, but she'd become desperate for validation and apparently not very picky where she got it from. "You don't think it's a dumb idea? The smartest thing to do would be to resurrect the breeding program by contacting my grandpa's old clients. The records are all here somewhere."

Ace's mouth curved up and she didn't mind at all that he noticed she'd stopped rifling through the papers in favor of watching him.

"Smartest things and decisions of the heart are rarely the same," he said simply and lifted his hands in a lazy shrug. "I always figure it's better to be happy than it is to do what might seem to make the most sense."

Boy, if that wasn't the solid truth. If she'd intended to do the smartest thing, she'd have stayed in Dallas and gone to therapy to work through her burnout, then kept on climbing the ladder in the advertising industry. Instead, she grasped the lifeline of this inheritance, plunking it down as the path to a happier, healthier life.

"Thanks for that," she said sincerely. "I needed to hear

that someone doesn't think it's silly to completely convert a stud farm into a resort."

Though, she had just met this someone. And he was an employee. Who until recently, she'd mistrusted. Had she jumped the gun on reversing her opinion of him for no other reason than because he'd come to her rescue? After all, he could theoretically be in cahoots with her attacker in a good cop, bad cop routine.

But she didn't think so. Up close, Ace had this warm vibe that made her comfortable, not edgy. Sure, he still had that hardened exterior that he presented to the world, but that's what had saved her bacon earlier. The man knew how to command a tense situation, had obviously used his skills before, many times.

Honestly, that dichotomy intrigued her. *He* intrigued her as a whole. Plus, she had extra incentive to keep him talking. She had a feeling she'd be hearing his voice in her sleep tonight.

"So, you think maybe there's some valuable information about your grandpa's breeding business in here?" Ace asked as he resumed glancing through the papers she'd pointed him toward.

Sophia sat back in her borrowed kitchen chair, the slats hard against her spine. She'd given Ace the larger padded chair behind the desk out of courtesy—she was a head shorter than him and never until this day considered whether she'd fit into a chair or not. Ace clearly had to worry about that often.

"I mean, I guess that makes the most sense," she said slowly, trying to recall how the breeding logistics worked from the many conversations she'd overheard as a kid. "I do know that the baby horse is less valuable without the lineage paperwork."

"I think they're called foals," Ace said with a tiny smile that wasn't the least bit patronizing despite the correction.

"See, this is why you're here. I need someone who knows the lingo and understands what they are looking at. Otherwise, I might not know that I've found what the attacker was searching for."

Task solidified, they worked side by side for another hour, carefully paging through her grandpa's old files. Her mother had pushed to have this all cleaned out after the will had been read, but Sophia had resisted, largely because she had a mile-long list of things to do to get the ranch ready for guests. Paperwork had been the last thing on her mind.

"I found a list of all the stallions my grandfather owned." Sophia held it up, reading off the first few. "Franklin, Kennedy, Reagan, Lincoln. He named them after presidents."

"Keep that," Ace said decisively. "That could be useful later. I have a stack of vet bills. I can't imagine that would be helpful, but just in case, hand me a paper clip and we'll be sure to keep them all together."

Sophia did as asked, and frowned at the envelope she'd just uncovered simply labeled "David." Her father's name. Probably something her grandfather had intended to give his son, but since no one knew where he'd gone, never had the chance.

She reached toward the trash, intending to throw it away—after all, her father hadn't even bothered to come home for the funeral—but at the last second, slid it back into the drawer. Just in case. A stupid, ridiculous notion that one day, her father might show up so she could give it to him. Vain hope.

She pushed that whole subject out of her mind. Or tried to anyway.

Jenny, the housekeeper, finally back from the store, kept making excuses to walk by the office, obviously curious about the cowboy Sophia had brought into the house, as if she'd rehomed a feral cat and let it make a nest in the corner.

Okay, yes it might be a bit unorthodox to have one of the hands sprawled across her desk chair, but this was Sophia's house, wasn't it? She could do whatever she wanted to do.

But after ten minutes of second-guessing herself, she'd finally had enough. "I think this is a lost cause."

Ace glanced up from his sheaf of papers, his lashes low in an affecting way that put butterflies in her stomach. Oh, man. This was not good. She had no latitude to be thinking about him in any way other than as an employee. It was unprofessional. Besides, she needed him to be doing cowboy things to help prepare Hidden Creek Ranch to become a tourist destination. Period. That was the only thing she should be focusing on right now.

She stood, determined to put an end to whatever this interlude was.

"We didn't find anything," Ace reminded her.

"We might not ever, either. We have no idea what that guy wanted. For all we know, he might have been a random thief who hoped to find jewelry or money in my desk. I'm probably making too big of a deal out of this."

In a flash, the hardened side of Ace appeared, his expression becoming one she'd bet scared a lot of people into doing whatever he said in no time flat. She stared back at him, curious what had flipped that switch.

"I don't think we can make a big enough deal out of it,"

he finally said, his arms crossed. “No random guy breaks into a house with ten ranch hands a stone’s throw from the back door. A run-of-the-mill thief would start in the bedroom. That’s where people keep jewelry. He targeted this room specifically. I’d like to know why.”

“This is why the sheriff should be the one doing the investigating,” she said wryly. “How do you know so much about what a thief would and wouldn’t do?”

“It’s not because I have a history of running on the wrong side of the law,” he said, his mouth tugging up into a half smile. “It’s common sense.”

“Well, be that as it may, I have some pressing things on my agenda, so I’ll let you get back to your day.”

Ace didn’t move from his sprawl. “Why do I feel like I’m being dismissed?”

“Because you are?” she said with raised brows and crossed her arms in kind to match his, hating that he probably saw it as the barrier that she’d meant it to be.

But she didn’t know how to trust him all at once and that wasn’t his fault. She had issues with all men, thanks to her father. And yes, she was quite aware of how silly that sounded, thanks. Knowing about her mental blocks and removing them were two different things.

Besides, it was better to depend on Sophia Lang only. Then she never had to worry about whether an unexpectedly sexy cowboy had her best interests at heart or was the type to be eyeing the door behind her back.

Well. She didn’t have to worry about that anyway. She was his boss. Nothing else.

Maybe the one she really didn’t trust was herself.

“I should stick close to you,” he argued, clearly not picking up on her skittish vibe. “In case that guy comes back. Or has friends.”

“Plural? I might have to worry about more than one other guy out there who’s planning to break into my house?”

His expression softened all at once and something inside her chest did too. Against her will.

“You don’t have to worry about it at all, Ms. Lang,” he said. “That’s my hope anyway. Let me be the eyes in the back of your head and you do your boss stuff. I promise I won’t let anything happen to you.”

“You can’t promise that,” she countered, wishing that he could, wishing she could melt into that promise and roll around it in, safe from harm.

The problem was that while he might keep her safe from another attacker, who was going to keep her safe from Ace himself? Obviously, he excelled at rolling right through her man-shield.

“Try me.” His voice had pure steel running through it.

That’s when he stood, towering over her with his trademark combo of authority, command of every situation and extremely cut body.

What, exactly, he was challenging her to try got lost in the shuffle as she stared up at him. Hard-edged cowboys with warm, gooey centers were not her type, and everything inside was demanding to know why.

“I’ll go,” he murmured. “Since obviously I’ve done something to make you uncomfortable. But I’ll be on the other side of that door, making sure nothing comes through it besides folks you choose.”

Including himself. He’d solved her problem in one fell swoop. He wouldn’t come inside unless she invited him.

Even though he'd already clearly expressed his attraction to her as a woman.

That spoke volumes to her. This was a principled man who had readily volunteered to watch out for danger without her having to ask him. Without forcing her to admit she was scared. Without pressing his advantage, which he easily could do while they were alone here in her office.

Before she could figure out which direction she planned to waffle, a deafening crash reverberated outside.

"What in the world was that?" she said.

Ace didn't blink, even as people started yelling. "Sounds like it came from the direction of the barn. You should stay here."

"Not on your life. This is my property."

The wall of man in front of her didn't move. "There are a lot of people employed on this ranch, most of them new. Any of them could be a threat. It would be safer for you to stay in the house."

Impasse. And she had a feeling he wouldn't budge until she did. "Fine, I get it. But I need to see what's going on."

"Look from the window. But stay to the side."

What, like someone might take a shot at her as she peeked through the blinds? Ridiculous. Right? But anxiety and the sheer stress of the day had taken its toll on her will to argue. Besides, she'd be a fool not to heed the advice of someone who clearly knew a thing or two about dangerous situations.

She dashed to the east wall of the house and louvered the plantation blind open so she could survey the barn area.

It was chaos. Half of the back section of the building had collapsed on itself in a pile of scarlet siding and dark roof tiles. Men scrambled like ants. Hand to her mouth, she watched as Jonas and some of his cowboys heaved together to move the debris in erratic motions.

Her barn. It was half-gone. The other half wobbled unsteadily like it might come down any second.

Ace materialized at her back, silently taking in the scene from over her shoulder.

“Is someone…trapped under there?” she asked, pulse hammering in her throat. “Is that why they’re so frenzied to get that pile of siding moved?”

She glanced back at Ace, who jerked his head in grim acknowledgment, his lips flat. “It’s likely.”

“You should go help,” she decided instantly.

That was one of her employees under the heavy beams and wood walls that had once held her barn together. They would need all the strong backs available.

“I should stay here,” he corrected. “Because the odds of that having been an accident are low. It was meant as a diversion. Fortunately, I wasn’t outside when it happened, so you’re not left here alone. Which I am pretty certain was the intent.”

Sophia’s stomach squelched as she processed what Ace had just thrown down between them. He was saying the barn collapse wasn’t an *accident*? Someone had done that on purpose? Surely not. He was making way too big a deal out of this.

She crossed her arms. Tight. “I’m not going to be a prisoner in my own home.”

By way of answer, he pulled her out from in front of the window and positioned her well away from it, his hands on her shoulders. “Until we know what we are dealing with, you should consider all of your activities risky.”

“Ace, I’m in the middle of renovating this property to

be a dude ranch," she burst out. "I don't have time to play a nervous woman afraid of her own shadow."

And then it hit her that the barn had just collapsed. One of her employees might be hurt or worse. The expense and the time alone would be a prohibitive blocker to opening on time, but the potential loss of one of her people—that weighed heavily on her heart.

Because it was her fault. Either way. Someone had done it deliberately to get to her. Or it was an accident, due to faulty construction of a building she owned.

Someone banged on the back door.

Sophia's whole body jerked in involuntary fear. Her heart hammered painfully against her rib cage.

Ace put one finger to his lips. *Shh.*

Sure, like she intended to yell out, *Here I am, come and get me*. Besides, his other hand still lay on her shoulder, holding her in place. Comforting her, even.

Ace Madden was here, and he was more than willing—and capable—of standing between her and whatever threats might be about to spill through that door.

She'd just about reached the point where she saw the wisdom in letting him.

Chapter 4

Somehow, Ace got Ms. Lang—Sophia—to agree to stay in her office with the door locked while he did a sloppy recon job to figure out who stood outside the house trying to get in.

Sloppy only because he didn't know the house that well and he was used to having a lot more tools at his disposal, like a SOCOM satellite feeding him an on-the-ground livestream of the enemy's position. But he'd get this job done despite the less-than-stellar circumstances because that's how he did things—efficiently and thoroughly, even if he had to improvise.

Stealthily, he maneuvered to the window near the door and peered outside. Jonas. It was the ranch manager standing on the back doormat. Ace breathed a little easier. As far as he knew, Jonas was on the up and up, a solid guy who worked hard and expected the same of others.

But when he swung the door open to face the man who might have fifty pounds on him, Ace realized that he'd put himself in a tenuous position as Jonas swept him with a look.

"What're you doing answering Ms. Lang's door?" Jonas asked, his gruff voice laced with suspicion that didn't bode well for the rest of this conversation.

He ducked his head but making himself smaller wouldn't take the spotlight off him. "I was helping her out with some files in her office. She said she cleared it with you."

The expression on the other man's face spoke volumes. "There's a big difference between helping a lady move boxes and answering her door like you got privileges."

Ah, dang. That was a wrinkle he hadn't expected.

Ace met Jonas's stare head-on, refusing to back down or respond to the implied slight. It was no one else's business if Sophia had invited him into the house to go through papers, bake a soufflé or strip him naked and have her wicked way with him. Though it was obvious Jonas had the idea that Ace might have been the one taking liberties.

As if he'd even remotely consider seducing his boss to gain favor above the other staff.

"Did you need something?" Ace asked coolly. Because right now, he was the one with privileges, namely the right to protect Sophia from all harm, and until he determined the state of things, she was staying in her office.

"There's been an accident. Ms. Lang needs to know what's going on." Jonas glanced behind Ace as if he hoped to spot her hovering in the background, maybe wearing a filmy robe that would lend credence to the idea that the manager had interrupted something illicit.

"We saw. What's the status?"

Jonas shifted from foot to foot. "I'd rather talk directly to Ms. Lang, if you don't mind."

"I do." Ace crossed his arms. He wasn't ducking his head now and Jonas had to look up to him to meet his gaze. Not an accident. "She can catch up with you later. For now, tell me the status. Did you call in the fire department? They should have contacts who can bring in some cranes."

Nodding, Jonas appeared to at least accept the status quo whether he agreed with it or not. “Yeah. They’ll be here. Lost half the barn. We pulled Hanes out from under a beam. Broke leg, looks like, but he’s breathing, so that’s something. They’re sending an ambulance. Horses were all out to pasture. Mostly all the tack is okay on account of it being stored in the standing half.”

It sounded like the best possible outcome, but he’d let Sophia be the judge of that. Since Ace had stood in the open door for a good three minutes now with no issues, he’d downgraded the situation from critical to serious. But he wasn’t the target. Anyone could take a shot at Sophia as she stood here listening to the manager give the rundown. That might have been the end goal for whoever set up the barn to collapse.

“Deliberate?” he asked Jonas, curious if the man would even have the slightest clue where to start that determination. And if he did, would he be up-front with Ace about it?

Jonas jerked his head. “Couple of the support posts were sawed through. Hanes noticed it right before the roof came down. What do you know about it?”

“It was a guess.” An educated one. “Barns don’t just fall over.”

“True enough.” That seemed to be all Jonas had to say, to him at least. “Tell Ms. Lang I need to see her.”

“Noted.”

Jonas stalked off, and Ace watched him go, his gaze casing the perimeter by habit, but all activity on the grounds seemed centered on the barn. He took a half second to look for sunlight glinting off long-range surveillance equipment, but the woods around the place seemed clear as well.

He knocked on the office door. “Ms. Lang, it’s me.”

She immediately opened it as if she'd been on the other side waiting on him. "What's going on? I heard Jonas's voice."

Deep strain marks edged her eyes, the kind that would age a woman who wasn't as delicately beautiful as Sophia. As it was, seeing them just made him want to smooth them away with the pads of his thumbs. Or something else that would be more boss-employee appropriate. Which didn't exist.

He stuck his hands in his pockets. "Yeah, that was him at the door. Barn's a loss, which I'm sure you expected. One of the hands broke his leg. Ambulance is on the way."

"You're hedging." Her gaze flitted over his with shrewd attention. "What are you not telling me?"

"It wasn't an accident."

"That's confirmed?" When he nodded once, she let out a long breath. "And you think it was meant to be a diversion. So the intruder could finish what he started."

Not to put too fine a point on it. But whether the intruder had meant to harm Sophia or had merely intended to draw her out of the house, he wasn't sure. He didn't like being unsure, not when he had a job to do. Two jobs.

"We need to talk about how to handle security around here," he told her flatly. "Jonas was a little too keen to get a handle on what my presence at your door meant. I'm going to apologize in advance for not thinking that through when I insisted you stay out of sight."

"What?" She bristled, hands on her hips. "What are you saying, that he insinuated I'd lured you into my clutches so I could oil you up and chain you in my basement?"

Well. Someone had a vivid imagination. He filed that information away for later. Much later. Like when he needed a laugh. It would never be appropriate to think about Sophia with a bottle of oil in her hand in any way, shape or form.

Too late.

Annoyed with his lack of control, he flushed the entire slew of provocative images out of his mind. It took a lot more effort than he'd like. "I think it might have been more the other way around."

Her brows rose. "He pegged you for the one to be chaining up women in the basement? He has met you, right?"

This bizarre conversation actually put a spark of heat in his cheeks. "No one is being accused of activities involving oil or chains. But the point is that my presence around you will raise questions. I don't want you subject to that kind of scrutiny. It might be best if I handled it a little more discreetly."

"Why don't we just tell everyone that we're dating. Isn't that what they do in the movies?"

When she crossed her arms and leaned on the doorframe, he had the distinct impression this whole scene amused her. Which made one of them. "I'm not cut out for fake dating. Sorry."

Fake cowboying seemed to be his hard limit. And there was enough half-truth and playacting that went along with that to have him second-guessing why he'd ever thought that was a good idea.

He couldn't even imagine how difficult it would be to fake date a woman as beautiful as Sophia Lang.

"You could ask me out for real. Then it wouldn't be fake."

The challenge hung there between them, the space heat-ing with the spark she'd set. One he needed to put out quickly. But that die seemed to have been cast.

Since he'd already admitted to her that he found her attractive, he had to tread carefully here. "That sounds like the worst idea I've ever heard."

Okay, so he wasn't going to be known for his smooth moves around Sophia Lang. Noted. Fortunately, she laughed.

"Just what every woman wants to hear from a hot cowboy," she said with a flat expression he couldn't read. "I didn't mean actually go on the date. I just meant…you know what? Never mind. It is a terrible idea."

Great. That comment certainly fixed the awkwardness and inability for him to get his wits about him. No less than he deserved, though, after telling her she was pleasing on the eyes and setting all of this up to be one big flirt match.

"I'm sorry," he said and then shook his head to jar loose some words that worked in his favor. "Maybe we could stick to business for the time being. You need someone to keep you safe and we also need to keep all of this on the down-low so no one else suspects there's anything going on."

She clapped her hands like a little girl at a birthday party with ponies. "Ooh, I love secrets when I'm the one keeping them. But why all the cloak-and-dagger stuff? The more people who are aware that Intruder Man might come back, the more eyes we have to alert us."

The way she dropped *we* into that sentence shouldn't have warmed him as dangerously fast as it did. But he clung to it for a brief moment. It was as much of this woman as he could allow himself to take.

She didn't know him. What he was capable of. If he told

her, she'd run very fast in the other direction. Which he couldn't afford at the moment, given his assignment. Neither could he stomach romancing a woman under false pretenses. She thought he was a cowboy. A simple guy from a good family who could sweep her off her feet with pretty phrases and still have energy left over to take out bad guys.

At least it seemed as if she'd moved on from the cover story that had apparently cast him in the role of the romantic bodyguard hero. He wasn't who she thought, nor was he capable of romance. Better to let all these sparks die out and leave the ashes on the floor.

"Intruder Man might be working with someone on the property," he explained, adopting her term because he liked it. "Easier to keep everyone on the suspect list than to try and weed out the bad apple. Plus, you're hiring people left and right. We can't trust your existing guys not to do their amiable cowboy routine and accidentally tell the wrong person we've got surveillance going on."

Sophia's gaze zeroed in on him a little too closely. "You've worked in law enforcement before. Is that why you talk like that?"

This was where he should be aw shucks-ing and ducking his head, but it was starting to hurt his neck. Maybe it was better to just be as much of himself as he could be. No one had ever told him he couldn't be truthful about his background, and it wasn't like he'd intended to keep it a secret.

"Former military. It's in the blood."

Or in his case, the thirst for excellence had been in his blood since the beginning. He'd gotten very good at being a weapon for the United States Navy and they'd pulled him out of their toolbox often.

By the time he'd quit, the blood he had spilled made up most of his résumé.

Dawning understanding lit up her features as she swept him with an appreciative once-over. "That explains a lot."

Hopefully it explained why she needed to listen to him and stop dropping hints that she found him attractive right back. "So, are we agreed that I'll keep an eye on things, you'll keep this between us and neither of us are going to talk about dating?"

She made a face that didn't hold any real heat. "Fine. I have too much to do to argue."

Now he was just being reckless for the sake of being reckless. "Well, if you wanted to argue with me about whether we should date, I have a few minutes."

Also known as not letting the sparks die. Idiot.

Laughing, she shook her head. "No, you were right about that. Business only between us. I meant arguing about keeping quiet. Silence is not one of my skills."

"You don't say," he muttered, which also got a grin out of her.

Points in his favor, though. At least she wasn't still upset about the intruder and the worry lines were gone from her face. Looked like he'd managed to soothe them away, after all.

"So how is this going to work?" she asked. "Are you going to follow me around?"

Actually, it would work a lot like it had been already, where he watched her from afar, except this time he had the benefit of her being aware of his attention. And he could speak to her when necessary.

That part was key. Because he needed the distance from Sophia—Ms. Lang. Fast. "Why don't you let me worry about how it works, and you do what you do best. Run the ranch."

She rolled her eyes and pulled out a phone from the pocket of her off-white dress and handed it to him. "As long as one of us thinks that, I'll take it. My to-do list is beckoning. Enter your number so I can text you if I need to."

Dutifully he did so, understanding the wisdom. But it felt more intimate than it should. As if he really did have those privileges Jonas mentioned.

She called him and hung up, so he'd have her number in his missed calls.

"I best get back to work," he told her and exited the house as fast as possible.

He made a mental note to find his phone and keep it on him. Maybe get an industrial-strength case to protect it from ranch life. He'd never gotten used to carrying one in the first place since he never took a phone on a mission and cowboying didn't lend itself to something solid in his back pocket.

But for Sophia's sake, he'd work it out if it made her feel safer. Ms. Lang. Dang if he didn't need to tattoo that to his hand so he'd remember she was his boss, not a woman he could pursue, no matter how much he liked her. This was a job and he needed to figure out how to do it without compromising the whole thing.

Quickest way to do that would be to make good on his sudden strong desire to text her something inappropriate and non-work-related.

The first thing he did when he found his phone was save Ms. Lang's contact information with the label Limpet. It was a particularly nasty magnetic mine he'd used a time or two to take out al-Qaeda destroyers. And every time he saw the name come up on his phone, he'd be reminded what would happen if he ever told Ms. Lang the truth—any warm feelings she had toward him would die in a fiery explosion.

Chapter 5

The designs the contractor had emailed Sophia for the pool were all wrong.

She fired back a bullet point list of the nine missing elements she'd requested and the fifteen—scratch that—sixteen blatant errors in the details, willing away a monster headache. How hard was it to take notes during their conversations? For that matter, how hard was it to look at a CAD drawing and see that the spa feature sat off-center?

Like everything else she'd had to touch around Grandpa's ranch, Sophia was about to become an expert in pool design. As if she totally had time to do other people's jobs, especially when she was paying the company six figures for the pool and cabana that would overlook the back pasture.

Okay, mentally blocking the headache wasn't working and now her arm hurt from being propped up over the keyboard since it still hadn't healed from when Intruder Man twisted it. Sophia poured out two ibuprofen pills from the bottle that seemed to have made a permanent home in the corner of her desk and popped them into her mouth, swallowing with the glass of water next to it.

Could you manifest a new stomach lining? Because she

might need one by the time the ranch renovations were completed.

Creak.

She jerked her head, breath stalling in her lungs. What was that?

After several seconds of tense silence, she finally exhaled shakily when no dark shape appeared at her office door to finish the job Intruder Man had started yesterday.

Rubbing her arm, she tried to focus on the paperwork in front of her. But man. Her nerves were shot. Where was her nicely built cowboy who had promised to keep her safe? She could use a distraction with great biceps.

He'd earned her trust the old-fashioned way, by showing up, keeping his word—and she couldn't stress this one enough—not taking advantage of her offer to get cozy while playing the part of her bodyguard.

Ace had made it clear that he was not interested in anything fake.

That idea had been born out of sheer lunacy. A brain scramble that was part terror and part curiosity. And he'd shut it down while making her feel good about it. That took some skill. The whole scene had done nothing more than intrigue her further. Ace was obviously a complex guy and she wanted to peel back another layer in the worst way.

But true to his word, Ace had been doing his surveillance things from the split-rail fence surrounding the barn. Not that she'd scoped out the situation a time or twelve, peering through the slats of the blinds in the kitchen like a woman scared of her own shadow.

The scenery was nice. Anyone would agree that having a man who looked like Ace in easy viewing distance didn't suck. But the reason for it—that was what had kept her up all night long, imagining she saw Intruder Man's face at the window over and over.

And if she'd spent some time dreaming about Ace's hands on her shoulders as he impressed upon her the importance of staying clear of the window, no one had to know.

Her phone buzzed, rattling against the teak desktop.

Ace. No. Jeez. What was wrong with her? He could walk fifty feet and knock on the door if he wanted to talk to her. He wouldn't call her unannounced, like a heathen. Only one person did that.

"Hey, Charli," she said dryly, opting not to mention yet again that prearranging a time to call before hitting the button wasn't that hard.

Honestly, she appreciated the interruption. For once.

"What's wrong?" her sister demanded, sirens wailing in the background.

Sophia did not miss city noises one little bit. She settled back in her chair, absently tapping a pen against her paper notebook where she kept a written to-do list of "maybe" tasks that she transferred to her phone as they became real jobs. "Is that the standard greeting you kids are using these days?"

"Ha, ha. Wait until I pull out some real slang, O ancient one. You'll be lost."

"Doubtful."

Charli was only three years younger than Sophia but it felt like ten sometimes. Her sister spent twenty-four/seven putting the "free" in free spirit, mostly because her bank account found new and exciting ways to register a zero balance. That's why it was so baffling that Charli wouldn't want to start fresh at the ranch, working alongside Sophia. It was a sure thing, a solid, guaranteed job. They'd be partners.

But neither of her sisters had jumped on the offer. Sore spot. For all three of them.

"Seriously," Charli said, sounding as if she might be getting comfortable on a couch, possibly even in her own apartment, though that wasn't a given. "You sound like you could use a spa day. Meet me at Solange this weekend and we'll splurge."

Oh, man. What did it say about the state of everything that Sophia actually thought about it for a moment? Even though she knew it was ploy to get her to pay, it was still tempting. "You know I can't. If you loved me at all, you'd be here at the ranch picking up half my to-do list so I could make time for a spa day."

Sophia could hear the face her sister was making. Unexpressive, Charli was not.

"That's what I was waiting for," her sister said with a laugh. "When you didn't start on me immediately, I was concerned. Glad to hear everything is normal."

"I don't ride you about your decision." Very much. "You don't want to work at the ranch. I get it. It's a tough job, far from the city. That's what makes it great, though."

"Hard work. No fun. Nothing but dusty, dirty ranch people. And you wonder why I said no." Charli and sarcasm were old friends.

But Sophia did wonder.

Because it felt like a betrayal, even as much as she really did get it. This wasn't the life Charli or their baby sister, Veronica, wanted and sometimes, Sophia had just enough energy to wonder why it mattered so much to *her*. Especially after Intruder Man had broken the quiet sanctuary she'd been building here.

What had he been looking for anyway?

Since Charli had been the one to call, Sophia figured it was a sign she should at least work the angle to see if her sister knew anything.

"Do you remember Grandpa at all?" she asked her sister.

"A little, sure. Is it weird being at the ranch without him there?"

Sophia had to pause for a minute to check in with herself on that since she hadn't actually thought about it. "No, not really. It might be different if we'd spent a lot of time here as kids. But now, it mostly just feels like a home."

That part, she had thought about. A lot. This place felt right, as if it had been here waiting for her to show up and settle into turning the ranch into something new and different. Something luxurious, yet down-to-earth, sustainable, a large employer for the area. Lofty goals, sure. But if anyone could check off a to-do list in record time, it was Sophia Lang.

As long as she didn't keep flinching at harmless creaks and groans. Ace would be here in a heartbeat if something happened. She had total faith. She did. It was just… She was used to being in control of her own destiny, not feeling like this freaked-out, shuddery version of herself.

"Well, that's good, I guess. I can barely recall what the grounds look like. You should send more pictures," Charli said with a laugh.

"Really? You've never seemed all that interested." And maybe Sophia had censored her texts to her sister out of hurt. If Charli didn't want to do this ranch project with her, there was no reason to share any of the high points or even low points.

But maybe that was a petty way to look at it.

"I'll send you some. The dusty people you've turned your nose up at are basically cowboys and there's not a lot there to hate."

"Ooooh," her sister squealed, making Sophia immediately sorry she'd opened her mouth. "Are they hot? They're hot, aren't they? If you tell me there's even one as tragically beautiful on a horse as Kasey Dutton, I will be on the next plane."

"This is not *Yellowstone*," Sophia commented wryly. "No one is tragically beautiful. There are just a lot of guys in hats and boots doing physical labor within sight of my kitchen window. You can draw your own conclusions as to why that might be of interest to a red-blooded woman."

Honestly, she'd put Ace Madden in a sexy cowboy contest with the actor who played Kasey in a heartbeat, and she was pretty sure Ace would win. Not that she was biased or anything, but that other guy was playing a cowboy. Ace was one. There was a huge difference between walking the walk and spending hours in wardrobe to shoot a three-minute scene, then strolling back to your trailer for an espresso.

She had a feeling Ace would do a lot of non-job-related things with his unique blend of intense precision and authoritative capableness. Things she should definitely not be thinking about as his boss, particularly after he had made it so clear that it should be business only between them.

The problem was that knowing she should steer clear wasn't the same as being able to unring the bell now that she'd imagined what a thorough kisser Ace must be.

Sophia fanned her face. Well, she'd wished for a distraction. She'd found one. And it wasn't her sister.

"That sounds oddly specific," Charli mused. "Are you watching one in particular, by chance? Is this an announcement that you've met someone?"

"Of course not. Don't be ridiculous. We're talking eye candy only. They're my employees." It was almost like Charli could read her very unprofessional thoughts.

"What's that got to do with the price of tea? Like, forty-five percent of all relationships are made up of couples who met at work. Do you have a no-fraternization rule at the ranch or something?"

That set Sophia back a bit. It had never occurred to her that she could make up the rules. That was not one she wanted to put in place all of a sudden for reasons she'd rather not examine. "Totally not the point. I'm not the type of woman who can handle being the boss of someone I'm seeing. Maybe other people can but keeping things on a professional level is something that makes sense to both of us."

The slip had already left her mouth before she realized her mistake. Charli pounced on it.

"Aha! I knew there was someone. And this someone is important enough that you've already had a conversation about the rules. Tell me everything."

The way Charli emphasized "the rules" put a hitch in Sophia's throat. Was that what had happened? Ace had laid down the rules and planned to stick to them?

That was fine. Totally fine. Great. Exactly what should have happened. The last thing Sophia needed was a hot cowboy taking up all her head space while she desperately tried to focus.

"There's nothing to tell," Sophia muttered. "Besides, that's not what I wanted to talk about. I found a bunch of Grandpa's papers, ones from the breeding program. Did you ever talk to Mom about that? Or Dad?"

She threw it out casually as if they talked about their father all the time when in fact, this was the first time she'd brought him up in years.

"Why would I talk to Dad about anything?" Charli's tone dripped venom.

"I don't know. I was just asking. The paperwork is... odd," she threw out lamely, cognizant of the fact that she wouldn't do herself any favors if she flat out told Charli about Intruder Man.

Not if she had any hope of her sisters eventually changing their minds about partnering with her on this place. No one would be swayed if they thought the place was dangerous. Plus, if she told Charli that someone had broken in, word would get back to Mom and then Sophia would be spending umpteen hours arguing with an upset woman about whether the ranch was in fact safe for her daughter.

"My advice—throw all the paperwork away. No one needs it any longer, least of all you."

Sophia frowned. That wasn't a bad point, as much as she hated the idea of throwing away something that might be a clue. But if she cleaned out the office and made a big show of putting all the papers into boxes at the curb for bulk pickup, maybe that would get back to Intruder Man. He wouldn't have any reason to come around again.

"I might do that," she said and glanced at the clock mounted to the wall above the fireplace that didn't work, nearly yelping out loud at the time. "I have to get back to work. I have an appointment with the decorator in a few minutes."

"Sounds delightful," Charli said with heavy sarcasm. "I still want to hear about this mystery guy. But I'll give you a pass for now. At least until you figure out why you're so set on throwing down the boss card. It sounds like an excuse to me. Before I let you go, tell me that you're happy out there in the boondocks."

"I'm happy," she responded immediately, gratified to feel the truth of it in her bones.

The other truth Charli had forced her to reconcile—that being Ace's boss felt like an excuse—wasn't sitting so well with her. Because she wasn't the one who had thrown that card down. He was.

Chapter 6

Ace found excuses to hang out near the split-rail fence with the best view of the house for as long as he could get away with. It wasn't the best angle, but someone had seen to clipping back the shrubbery ringing the wide porch, so no one was getting past his eagle eye.

Not even Sophia. He'd hoped to catch a glimpse of her this morning, even from afar. But she hadn't left the house. For the best. He couldn't keep an eye out if she took off somewhere.

His luck ran out at midday when Jonas strolled by with that look in his eye that meant Ace was about to be set on a job no one else wanted to do.

"Madden."

It was as close to a pleasant greeting as he would get. "Fine day, Jonas."

"Ain't seen you lift a finger on that barn yet." The ranch manager set his hat back on his head, which was what he did when he expected a fight.

Since a skirmish was the last thing he had the time for, Ace shrugged. "Seemed like there was plenty of folks already on that. I didn't want to get in the way."

"Sent Pokney and Thomas over to the south pasture.

Seems like there was something going on over there." Jonas spat on the ground, a nasty habit that was definitely Ace's least favorite thing about cowboys.

"Yeah?" he said noncommittally because he still wasn't sure where Jonas was going with this.

"Fire. Looked like someone built it while camping on the property overnight. Least ways whoever it was put it out."

Fortunate, yes, but not unexpected, given that Ace had his suspicions about who the squatter might have been. If he was right, burning the place down didn't suit Intruder Man's goal.

Ace didn't like the way Jonas was eyeing him. "One of the hands sneak out there last night?"

"Well, I don't rightly know. That's the thing I'm looking to find out. You know anything about it?"

Ah, so *he* was the cowboy currently under suspicion. Whatever Jonas thought was going on between Ace and Sophia—Ms. Lang, and he'd do well to remember to think of her formally—had crawled up his backside and sat there, festering. Ace didn't mind extra scrutiny most of the time. Live your life right and you never had to answer for anything.

But this wasn't the military, and he wasn't following Jonas's orders, as much as the man might like to think Ace was. Extra scrutiny wouldn't help that situation.

"Don't know a thing about your fire," Ace told him, which didn't really count as a half-truth since he didn't know for sure if Intruder Man might have been the one hanging around. But it was a safe bet. "You want me to check it out?"

It would work out handily if Jonas would assign him

to that task, but he had a feeling that the ranch manager might not be letting Ace out of his sight much.

"Nah, that's what I sent those two boys to do. Asked 'em to check around and see if they could figure out if we have a trespasser or something else going on. Meanwhile, need you at the barn. Clear away that back section where the hay bales were stored and see what you can salvage."

Grunt work. No less than he'd expected. Ace nodded and kept his thoughts on the matter to himself. It wasn't too far off the main path to the house, so his view would only be partially blocked. If Jonas would mosey off to do something else, Ace could still stroll by the house occasionally to make up for the decreased visibility.

The collapsed barn was still a mess. Earlier today, they'd gone on and knocked down the rest with a tractor, using the front loader like a battering ram. The cranes hadn't made it yet, probably being shipped from Dallas or Houston, so they'd only worked on the parts that could be more easily managed with a strong back.

Except it was hot. And Ace hadn't done this kind of heavy lifting in a while, not since leaving the navy and his brutal workout routine behind. If it wasn't for his inconvenient principles, he'd be inside the house, lounging on a sofa or something while Sophia—Ms. Lang—worked.

Idiot. That's what he got for throttling back the dating idea she'd cooked up. Couldn't he have faked being her boyfriend for a week or two while making sure he had ready access to anyone who tried to get through him to her?

Obviously not. Instead, here he was lifting splintered boards out of busted bales of hay in hopes of salvaging some of it. He got it. Hay was expensive and any little bit they could save meant something to Sophia. So he'd do it and complain in his head.

"What's up, Madden?" Rory Montgomery strolled into view, pulling on his work gloves. "Looks like we both got the short end of the stick."

"You here to help?"

Montgomery nodded and dived right in, bless him. Ace had a fine appreciation for solitary work, but he'd been part of a team for too long to sneeze at an extra hand.

"Jonas is sore because I broke a pair of wire cutters trying to use 'em to fix a hinge on the back gate," he admitted cheerfully and grabbed a long board on top of the pile, trucking it by hand over to the dumpster that had appeared earlier this morning. After heaving it into the dead center, he dusted off his gloves. "This is supposed to learn me to use the proper tool for the job."

Well, Ace couldn't argue with that as a great life lesson. But that would mean admitting he was wasting his own skill doing menial labor when he could be acting like a proper bodyguard for Sophia.

But that would mean admitting he couldn't stop thinking about her. He'd always had a thing for dark hair on a woman and Sophia's was amazing. Plus, she had this birthmark high on her cheekbone that changed positions depending on how she smiled. He did like being the one to shift it.

Taking her up on her fake-boyfriend offer would mean having to temper his attraction to her while in the same room with her, and he needed his faculties about him. The job—the real job—mattered more than his intense desire to curl up with Sophia near that fireplace in her office and tease that wry humor out of her over and over again.

And maybe see whether she kissed with as much fire as she spoke.

"Don't you think so?" Montgomery asked, jerking him out of that fantasy at the worst time.

Best time. *Best.* He had to stop indulging in that kind of thing or he'd miss more than whatever his barn-clearing mate had been jabbering on about.

"Sure, I guess," he hedged, hoping he hadn't just agreed to partner with Montgomery at the next hot-dog-eating contest or greased-pig-wrangling event.

"Oh, come on. Even a straight arrow like you wouldn't sneeze at that much money."

Montgomery pulled a pretty good-sized bale from the pile that hadn't lost too much of its hay and set it aside, taking his sweet time to get to the rest of his point. Which now had Ace's full attention since it included an assessment of his personality.

So much for lying low.

"I like money as much as the next person," he commented mildly. "It buys stuff that keeps you from starving."

And paid medical bills. Eventually maybe Stephanie would be able to handle them on her own, but for now, he was happy to help.

"Well, whatever this treasure is worth, I can pretty much guarantee it'll do more than buy some groceries."

Casually, Ace pulled another board out of the pile, wiping the back of his neck with his bandanna as if it didn't matter to him one way or the other, but was meant to keep his mate talking. "That sounds like some treasure."

"Most folks in town say it's just a story, but there's so much land out here, it's not hard to imagine someone could've buried a treasure somewhere and no one would ever know." Montgomery eyed one of the splintered boards he'd yanked from the pile. "You don't think it was in the barn, do you?"

"The treasure?" Ace shrugged, doing his level best not to react to the huge possible clue Montgomery had just dropped to Intruder Man's presence here. "Seems like that would be too obvious. If you're going to hide something, it would be someplace that never has a lot of people around."

"That's true," Montgomery mused thoughtfully, as if he might solve the mystery right then and there. "Where would you hide it?"

Apparently, Ace wasn't going to have to do a whole lot to keep Montgomery talking. "Depends on how valuable it is. Are we talking pirate treasure or Knights Templar treasure?"

The look Montgomery shot him told Ace that the other man didn't read a whole lot. "Knights hid treasures in a temple?"

Ace flashed a brief smile. "Something like that. I'm asking if it's supposed to be like a chest full of gold pieces or a room full of gold statues. Big difference in where it might be hidden and how valuable it might be."

"Oh." Montgomery frowned. "I think it's both? Mr. Lang's son chased after it for years down in Mexico. Supposed to be some kind of famous emperor of the Mayans who had a bunch of stuff in one of those pyramids."

Mr. Lang? As in the former owner of the property? Montgomery must be talking about Sophia's grandfather, and possibly her father. Did she know about these rumors?

He shot a glance in the direction of the house, wondering if clues about the location of this mythical treasure might be what Intruder Man had been after in Sophia's office. Not horse records. A treasure map.

"This is legit? The treasure?" he asked, hoping he didn't sound too interested, but Montgomery seemed like the type who would readily talk someone's ear off without any encouragement.

The other ranch hand shrugged. "I don't know, man. Everyone talks it about. Has for years. Seems like Mr. Lang would have been driving a Ferrari or something if it really existed, but maybe he never found it. Wouldn't it be sweet to stumble over something worth a lot of money while doing nothing more than pulling pieces of barn from a pile?"

Indeed it would, but only because it might help him do his job. His real job. "Anything we found would belong to Ms. Lang."

"Sure, yeah, of course anything valuable would belong to the owner of the ranch," Montgomery agreed readily.

Sophia. He had to mention this to her. Possibly she'd already heard of the treasure and may even know if it had already been found. Or never existed in the first place. This might be a red herring.

But he didn't think so.

The same gut instinct that had kept him alive deep behind enemy lines kicked in. And he knew this treasure Montgomery had so casually mentioned played some kind of part in the presence of shadowy figures here at the ranch.

The big question in Ace's mind was why now? Had the death of Sophia's grandfather set something new in motion? Introduced some new players to the treasure hunt game?

Ace let the conversation drift, an easy thing with a guy

like Montgomery. So far, he'd learned his new friend grew up in Gun Barrel City, Montgomery knew everyone in town since there weren't that many residents, and that the town motto was "We shoot straight with you."

Sounded like a place Ace could appreciate.

After twenty minutes, Ace started scouting around for some earplugs. Man, could this guy jabber on about nothing and everything. They'd only cleared about 20 percent of what could be moved by humans, which lent further credence to the fact that Jonas had stuck his least favorite people on the job.

"I'm going to get some water," Ace finally broke in during the middle of a story about a tornado that had touched down in Ellis County, which, as best he could tell, was about an hour away. So it wasn't entirely clear why the tornado was of interest, but to be fair, he'd lost the thread of the story long ago.

"Bring me a bottle, would ya?" Montgomery took his hat off and wiped his face with his shirt.

Without his hat, he looked young enough to be carded at the beer store, but most of the hands did. With age, some of the romanticized parts about being a cowboy must wear off.

Ace strode across the packed earth, ducking into one of the buildings where the ranch hands lived so he could text Sophia without anyone noticing.

Need to talk. Let me in the front door in three minutes.

The answering text came immediately.

Limpet: Okay

Jeez. He tried not to read anything into it. She was obviously the type to carry her phone around in her hand. It wasn't like she'd been sitting there, waiting for him to text her, smiling as she saw his name pop up on her screen.

Though it was a nice little fantasy to imagine exactly that.

He didn't have time to waste answering her back with something else she'd have to reply to, just so he could watch her name pop up on *his* screen. It wasn't her name anyway. It was Limpet. On purpose. He should add an explosion emoji or something.

Circling the house via the woods so he could enter from the front where none of the hands—or Jonas—could see him took longer than he'd expected thanks to a squirrel who had forced him to freeze for an eternity behind a wide oak tree. He'd half hoped it would be Intruder Man, but it was better that it wasn't.

Sophia was waiting on him.

Literally, as it turned out. She swung the door wide before he'd even mounted the first step to the wraparound porch, then she stood there, one hip kicked out, framed by the eggshell-white doorframe, her dark hair escaping from the severe knot at her crown. A pink dress poured down over her curves, fitting her to a T both in style and cut.

She was stunning and he forgot to breathe.

He had a terrible, wonderful moment where he wished she'd thrown open the door to greet him at the end of a long day. As if she belonged to him and this place with her was his life that he'd earned.

Not in the cards for a guy like him. He swallowed against the catch in his throat.

Besides, Sophia Lang might be gorgeous, but she had

high maintenance written all over her. Not his type. And even if he thought for a moment he could make an exception, all of the other stuff that stood between them wasn't so easily dismissed.

"You rang?" she murmured with just enough irony to tease a reluctant smile out of him.

"I heard about something. A treasure," he said without preamble because this wasn't a social visit, no matter how much he might wish otherwise.

Her brows shot up. "Do tell."

That didn't sound like a woman who knew what he was talking about. "One of the hands mentioned it. Said it's common knowledge that Mr. Lang's son buried something on the property. You ever hear anything about that?"

The expression on Sophia's face went so utterly blank that he worried for a second that something had happened to her. He'd already taken a step toward her, hand outstretched to check for a pulse or gauge her pupil response, when she shook her head.

"My grandpa's son was a deadbeat. If David Lang ever found anything of value, you can guarantee he either lost it or sold it to fund his expeditions. He definitely never sent any of the money back to his family."

Her voice rang with enough certainty and grief that he didn't have to ask if they were talking about her father. "So you've never heard any rumors of a treasure? The ranch hand grew up here. He says the local folks have talked about it for years."

Sophia's expression never changed. "There's no treasure."

The alarm bells in his gut went off. He couldn't put a finger on what had tripped them. Something in her tone or her ramrod-stiff stance hinted at a fragility that contradicted the outward appearance of strength.

If there was anyone who understood putting on appearances so no one else could tell that a body was a mess on the inside, it was Ace. “Are you saying that because you’re sure there’s not one? Or because the alternative is unacceptable?”

That’s when her face crumpled.

Chapter 7

Crying in front of Ace was not happening.

Except Sophia's eyes seemed to have received a different memo and welled up at the same time her throat closed.

"Hey," he murmured, suddenly a lot closer to her than he had been, his hand warm on her shoulder as he peered down at her with equal parts compassion and confidence, as if he had every right to be the one right here when she fell apart.

"I'm fine," she said, the lie rattling in her aching throat. "I don't talk about my dad often. For a reason."

"I get it." He nodded but didn't move his hand and she hated how steadying it was.

Oh, she liked him touching her. That part wasn't in question. Her greedy insides had gobbled up the heat instantly and started sniffing around for more. But the fact that she needed someone to steady her—that was a problem.

She'd asked Charli about their father. That had gone fine. Mostly because Sophia took her responsibility for being the oldest sister—and therefore the one who managed everything—seriously.

This was one time she didn't have to have it all together, but it was fine. She could lean on someone else for a change. It was…nice.

She should step back. Her legs didn't obey her. Most of the rest of her seemed to think it was a fine time to sway forward, in fact. Closer to him. Where it smelled like man and grit and evoked thoughts of unspeakable things that were not on her to-do list.

But she very much wanted to do them.

Worst idea ever.

A man like Ace would be a shock to her system—wild, untamed and a little bit dangerous. None of which sounded like a cautionary tale all at once.

Too bad he wasn't interested in her. He couldn't have been clearer that there would be far more business between them than pleasure. As in a 100/0 split.

That was enough to dry up the emotion clogging her throat. "I'm sorry, I'm not normally this much of a mess."

His lips turned up. "If this is you being a mess, you should teach a class."

Dang, he wasn't supposed to be both kind and funny. She dabbed at her wet lashes, likely making her raccoon eyes worse. "I'm actually pretty capable and can handle myself. I promise. What you've seen so far is not at all representative of who I am as a person."

The light that came into his expression transfixed her for a moment as he cocked his head, evaluating her curiously. "But capable is exactly how you come across. As someone who makes no bones about being in charge. Who knows her own mind and speaks it. None of those things have anything to do with being broadsided by a memory that digs into places that don't have calluses. It's not something you should apologize for."

Her insides went liquid as she stared at him. "Are you

sure you can't ditch the cowboy stuff and follow me around all the time? You can be my motivational coach."

"Sure," he said with a shrug and another of those small smiles. "Since it was my fault you got upset in the first place. That sounds like a great plan. I stick my foot in my mouth and then figure out a way to take it back."

Good gravy this man could not be for real. Principled, hot *and* able to admit he was wrong without wincing. It was like winning the lottery and then misplacing your ticket. She couldn't have him and the sooner she got that message through to her brain, the better.

"Maybe we should start over," she suggested with an answering smile. "Hi, Ace, nice to see you. How was your day?"

"So far, so good," he said, instantly falling into the rhythm she'd set into place, as if they'd done this a million times. "I heard about this treasure from one of the guys and thought we could discuss it. Does that fit into your schedule?"

"Everything on my agenda has just been canceled. Would you like to come inside?"

She'd offered before thinking through how much more of Ace would be accessible behind closed doors, away from potential prying eyes. Or how he would fill the foyer as he swept past her on a wave of solid male.

"We can sit in my office," she said briskly because, come on. She wasn't a simpering sixteen-year-old at her first dance, for crying out loud.

Ace was just a man. Who was here because he'd heard something of note that he thought she needed to consider. Given that she'd been attacked in her own home and then someone had sabotaged her barn, she'd do well to remember that the only reason she had any interaction with Ace was because he'd agreed to keep watch for threats. That's it.

She crossed her arms and stood in the doorway as he sprawled in one of the chairs on the guest side of the desk. Which she appreciated. Last time, she'd let him have her chair and he could have taken that as permission to always sit there, as if he had some sway in her life. But he hadn't taken any liberties whatsoever.

A shame. She had a sincere desire to figure out what would set Ace Madden on simmer. Did he even let himself near a fire long enough to feel the heat?

Shaking her head, she dived into the matter at hand. "About this treasure. I don't think it exists."

"Oh, actually that's not true," a voice said from the hall.

Sophia spun to find the housekeeper, Jenny, standing behind her with a stack of folded towels in her hands. The elder woman paused in her mission to put the laundry away, clearly interested in the reason this subject had come up.

"You know something about a treasure?" Sophia asked cautiously, not sure she should be having a conversation like this in front of Ace. Not that she wouldn't immediately spill every detail to him later, but it didn't seem like the best plan to clue in other staff members that he had her confidence in what some might consider a private matter.

Jenny didn't seem overly bothered by the presence of the cowboy in Sophia's office, though. She nodded, her eyes brightening the way they did when she talked smack about other people in town, especially if the gossip was particularly juicy. "You better believe it. Everyone knows about the treasure. Your grandpa never told you he found a Maya coin in the flower bed? About five years ago, seems like."

Five years ago, Sophia would have been twenty-seven.

The exact age she'd been the last time she'd had any contact with her grandpa. He'd invited her to the ranch out of the blue, no reason given. But she'd been too busy climbing the corporate ladder in a sad cliché. Especially given that Grandpa had left the ranch to her after all, even though she hadn't made any time for him while he'd been alive.

What would he have said to her if she had come?

Shamed all at once, she bowed her head. Turning this place into a luxury dude ranch was her tribute to a man who had entrusted her with the property, and she *would* succeed at this thing she'd set out to do. Selling it to someone else sat wrong with her.

And so did dismissing this treasure that she'd never heard about. Until today.

"I'm sensing I should have asked you about this much sooner," she told Jenny wryly as she recalled that the housekeeper had come with the property, having been employed by her grandpa for many years. "I didn't know anything about the Mayan coin he found. What happened to it? Did he still have it when he died?"

Oh, goodness. Had he left it to Sophia in his will? Wouldn't that be a slick move, to discount the idea of a treasure, only to find out she owned a piece of it unwittingly.

"It's Maya, by the way. Your grandpa taught me that after he did some research. Mayan is only used to mean the language they spoke." Jenny shook her head, then. "To answer your question, no, he didn't still have the coin. He sold it. Always planned to use the money to start his breeding program back up again, but he got sick before he could. I think a lot of the proceeds went to medical bills. Your grandpa didn't have health insurance after he quit the horse business, so it was a lucky break he had that extra cash handy."

Lucky? Or something else? "He never found any more coins? One Maya gold piece doesn't sound like much of a treasure to me."

"I don't guess he ever mentioned finding more," Jenny mused. "But I always had the idea he thought that there was more. He just didn't quite know where to look for it. Seems like Mr. David wasn't too chatty about where he'd buried it."

Dumbfounded, Sophia stared at the housekeeper. This whole time, she'd had no idea any of this was a thing and her father had been the one smack in the middle of it. "That's where the treasure came from? My father? David Lang?"

And if she tacked one more question mark on this situation, it still wouldn't be enough.

Because of course that's what all of this would come down to. A legacy of pain perpetuated by Sophia's father, who couldn't be bothered to act like one, but could certainly find the energy to tromp through sweltering jungles for a couple of decades in search of almighty gold.

Jenny shrugged. "That's what your grandpa said, at least, but we didn't talk about it much. It was one more disappointment, you know? He wanted Mr. David to take over the business but your dad, he had the yellow fever. Chased after the glory of the gold. And by all accounts, he must have found something, but why he put only that one coin in the flower bed, no one knows. Lots of people looked, but the treasure is poof. Like a ghost."

Sitting down sounded like a really good option all at

once. Sophia braced a hand on the desk as she sank into her swivel chair behind it. "This is all very…"

Educational? Disturbing? Unbelievable?

All of the above. She stretched her neck as she contemplated all the ways her father had ruined her life, starting with abandoning his family and ending with allowing his daughter to inherit a piece of property that came with a legend attached.

"It's information," Ace suggested quietly with a nod. "And we appreciate it."

"Yes, of course. Thank you, Jenny." She glanced at the housekeeper, who still stood in the hall with her stack of towels, her intrigued expression roving over the situation in the office unabashedly. "Mr. Madden is helping me with a special project and the subject of the treasure came up, so the information you've given us is invaluable. Don't let us keep you from the rest of your day."

Jenny's face flatlined. She was obviously disappointed not to be involved in any more gossip. "Let me know if you have any other questions."

She vanished in the direction of the stairs to the upper floors, hopefully to do something productive like hang curtains in one of the guest bedrooms.

Sophia stared at the bottle of ibuprofen in its spot by the corner of her desk. "The rest of the treasure is still out there somewhere, isn't it?"

"That's unfortunately irrelevant," Ace said so matter-of-factly that she lifted her gaze to his in question. "The more important question is, how many people believe it is?"

The implications weren't lost on her. There was a good possibility that she'd just learned the reason Intruder Man had been rifling through her grandpa's papers. And even if it wasn't, other people could be out there with that same intent, which doubled her trouble.

She'd have to think about security way beyond what Ace could provide. Get some dogs maybe. Could dogs be trained to look for treasure while they patrolled the grounds searching for trespassers?

What about the guests? How could she keep *them* safe? This was a disaster.

"I'm literally clueless what to do next," she muttered, her head falling to her palms.

The to-do list on her phone rivaled the written one on her notepad, the decorator had left her swatches in three of the bedrooms for her final decision on the color scheme, which she should have already made, and Jonas had tried to speak to her twice today about the insurance claim on the barn.

If anything deserved her attention more than these, it was a treasure she'd unwittingly inherited from both her grandpa and her dad. The money alone… It could go a long way toward the deductible for the barn, and she could move up her agenda for the dude ranch. Offer spa services sooner, rather than later. The plans she'd looked at for the little detached bungalow that would match the house came with a steep price tag, but Maya gold could buy a lot of massage tables and aromatherapy.

It would be the one positive thing she'd ever gotten from her father.

But her life didn't work like that. Either there was no more treasure, and the rumors were wrong, or her father had hidden it someplace no one could find because he planned to come back for it himself.

"It's pretty simple, actually," Ace said as if he had no clue her brain had just fizzled. "The next steps."

"I'm glad one of us thinks so," she mumbled to her desk, which was a lovely shade of espresso covered in a beige computer mat she'd selected the day after she'd quit her job at Teller Advertising.

So optimistic. The pencil drawing of a sprig of almond blossoms gracing the edge of the mat had seemed so elegant at the time, the symbol of her rebirth as a resort owner. She still wanted to hold on to that hope. But this development would crimp things, no doubt.

"Hey," he said softly, like he had at the door when she'd been crying because all of this was too overwhelming. It was his *I care* voice and she couldn't stop herself from responding to it.

She glanced up, straight into his storm-colored eyes that practically dripped with concern. For her. Because he was a solid, dependable guy who had nothing better to do than sit here with her and figure this out. Or if he did have something better to do, he made her believe he'd picked this over everything else.

It meant more to her than she could have possibly verbalized.

"I'm okay," she said and meant it. "Tell me what you think we should do."

His lips lifted. "As long as you keep on remembering that it is indeed a *we*, things will go a lot smoother."

No, there wasn't a good chance she would forget. Not that or the sound rejection of her fake-dating idea. But it wasn't like he'd chucked that plan out the window because he didn't like spending time in her company or he wouldn't be here.

Maybe it really was as simple as his principles preventing him from crossing any lines. Which she firmly appreciated.

Next time, she wouldn't frame it as fake or hide her interest in getting to know him a little better—or a lot better—behind his white knight routine. They could talk about the challenges of acting on the blistering attraction between them like adults. Work through the issues. Determine some ground rules.

She could only dream of having that healthy of a conversation with a man. Her track record with men consisted of a few surface-level dates, then ditching him before he could do it to her.

"So, I guess you're about to advise me about the type of security system I need to install or something, right?" she asked, injecting as much levity into her voice as she could, given that Ace's suggestion would likely be a very painful hit to her bank account.

"Yeah, I'm already working on that angle in my head, definitely," he said. "But the most important thing we can do first is find that treasure."

Chapter 8

The expression on Sophia's face did not reveal a lot of confidence in Ace's idea.

"You want to look for a treasure that may or may not exist, may or may not be hidden somewhere on a six-hundred-acre ranch with a creek running through the middle, and may or may not also be the same treasure a dangerous man is looking for."

Sophia talked with her whole body, and Ace had no plans to apologize for how much he enjoyed it, even when her green eyes snapped with energy directed at him. Especially then.

"Yes," he responded simply. "That is what I'm suggesting. Even finding clues to where the treasure is—or was—is better than nothing. The more we have in our back pocket, the less someone else can get control of and use for their own gain."

She crossed her arms. "A treasure hunt is the last thing I have time for."

"It's the only thing you have time for," he corrected her and stood, holding out his hand. "Come with me. I need to show you exhibit A."

To her credit, she didn't argue. But she did slip her hand

into his, which immediately turned into something as a current the intensity of a lightning bolt forked between them. When folks talked about sparks, they clearly lacked the vocabulary to put the right name to it because this was way more than a tiny, quick-to-fizzle buzz. It was more like the kind of raw energy that could destroy a building in a second flat.

Bad move.

Because she felt it too. He could tell.

Now what was he supposed to do? It would be forever a lie if he had to deny his forceful attraction to this woman, and honestly, he wasn't sure he could do it. Hopefully she wouldn't say a word about it, or he might be forced to do something very painful, like tell her the truth.

Now would be a good time to kill the connection. And when he dropped her hand, his entire body cooled like lava meeting a frozen sea.

"Sorry, that was inappropriate," he muttered, praying he could get out of this room without embarrassing himself.

"It takes two to close a circuit," she said, her gaze so tightly focused on him that it was unlikely she'd miss a single nuance of his reaction to her.

Yeah, he was in a lot of trouble here. He cleared his throat. "And I won't do it again. I want to show you something outside, so just stick close to me."

Distance didn't end up being a problem. Sophia turned out to be a star at following his suggestion, her body a scant few inches from his back as she followed him through the house to the back door. The vibe between them thickened as he flung open the solid oak and pointed in the direction of the temporary stable the hands were building down the knoll from the splintered remains of the barn.

"See that guy there?" he asked. "In the black hat with the long-sleeved tan shirt? What's his name?"

Sophia peered around his shoulder, her coconutty hair literally right under his nose. Breathing through his mouth, he visualized a cold shower, a HALO drop in January and, finally, plunging through the ice in Alaska, which seemed to finally do the trick even though that was the one he'd never actually done.

"Rick?" she said with so many question marks attached that it was clear she'd guessed.

"Wrong. What about that other guy next to him? In the black shirt."

She glanced up at him, the green in her eyes a different color out here in the sunlight than they had been in the office, and he was hard-pressed to say which one he liked better.

Limpet, Limpet, Limpet.

"I sense there's a lesson coming about how I should know my employees' names," she said wryly. "So maybe you could just get on with it."

"It's not that you should know their names. It's that you *don't* know their names. Because they're new. They were just hired this morning. Jonas has about five more open spots to fill and pickings are slim. It's only a matter of time before he hires someone who is not just looking for a paycheck. Or someone who is not an official employee but blends in like one."

Which he well knew could be the case since he'd easily slid onto the ranch roster with fake credentials. The porous borders of the ranch sat on his nerves wrong too.

"So now I need to worry about dangerous employees

as well as random intruders? Great." Her resigned tone scraped across those already taut nerves.

Ace was failing at his job. The real one. The one he'd been paid a lot of zeros to get right, and he had no excuse. Being a cowboy didn't have a lot of skill to it, not that he'd seen so far, but protecting someone ill-equipped to do it themselves—that he had hundreds upon hundreds of hours of training and experience under his belt. He'd fought off a horde of mercenaries in a village outside Marjah single-handedly, for crying out loud, saving an Afghan family of nine who had been left behind during a sloppy evacuation.

He could manage the security protocol of a six-hundred-acre ranch and reassure the owner at the same time.

"Ms. Lang." She was eyeing the new hands, looking every bit as if she might be dutifully cataloging them in her memory, all because he'd been trying to make a point. "Sophia."

That caught her attention. She glanced up at him, worry and stress lines back around her lips, and it was not okay.

"I like it when you call me Sophia," she admitted, her voice warming.

That made two of them. And was also not the subject they needed to be discussing. "Listen to me, now. You do not have to worry about anything. I'm handling this. Trust me. The two ranch hands are Mark Dombrowski and Bobby Chavez. They both came from Rockland Farm down the way and are totally legit. They are not going to cause problems and if they do, I'll handle that too. Repeat what I just said."

Sophia's eyes were so wide, he wondered if he could actually fall into them. And whether he'd try to stop himself if he did. The draw nearly buckled his knees as it was.

"All of it?" she murmured.

"The important part."

She nodded once. "I trust you."

Ace nearly groaned. Of course she'd pick out that one statement from everything else to glom onto and dig the shiv a little deeper between his ribs. "I'm handling this. That part. You don't have to worry."

"I'm not worried. Do I look worried?"

Now her back was up, and she fairly bristled under his scrutiny. Apparently, he was not going to be good at reassuring the owner of the ranch he'd been hired to protect. "You look capable, fierce and strong. My mistake."

For some reason, that made her laugh, and he liked that too, a whole lot more than might be considered suitable under the circumstances. He busied himself with shutting the door since he'd made his point.

"You're the strangest blend of man, Ace Madden," she said, crossing her arms as she contemplated him. "I'm having a hard time figuring out what to do with you."

"Let me remind you, then. You're letting me do all the worrying. About security. New people on the ranch. Taking care of you."

That last bit had slipped out, his voice lowered a notch into a scratchy range that had nothing to do with the job and everything to do with the forbidden fruit standing within reach but so wholly off-limits that it made his teeth hurt.

With the door shut and the two of them closed off from the rest of the world, everything got a lot cozier and more intimate. Anything could happen and no one would be the wiser. It was already too late to avoid everyone else on the ranch knowing he had Sophia's ear. Her trust.

"I've never had a man take care of me before," she said and cocked her head, a flirty glint in her gaze that spelled a whole lot of danger if he didn't diffuse this situation carefully.

Limpet. Oh, who was he kidding. It would be impossible to cut the wire of this detonator. At this point, his best bet was keeping the explosion contained with as few casualties as possible.

"This is a first for me too," he countered gruffly and stuffed his hands in his pockets. "But just for the sake of clarity, I meant taking care of keeping you safe."

"Uh-huh. I got that."

She was still watching him with this intense, somewhat-heated expression that he very much wanted to understand. Before it took off a layer of his skin. "Are we aligned on searching for the treasure? You understand the importance of us getting to whatever is out there before someone else does?"

"I hear you. The point is to have something to advertise. So it gets out that we found whatever my father hid, which means bad people have no reason to bother us any longer."

He nodded, shoving his hands deeper in his pocket to stop the sudden urge he had to kiss her for being so brilliant. "Yes. Exactly. We make a big splash of it and voila, the danger is eliminated. I can go back to fixing fences and you can get busy bossing people."

"You make it sound easy." Her lips lifted in a small smile. "The treasure, if it exists at all, isn't going to be lying around waiting for us to find. What you're talking about is a full-scale search of a property I've barely started to learn. And that's if it's not in the house, which has a million hidey-holes and a pier-and-beam foundation, so it could even be under the house. That's the most logical place since the first coin was found in the flower bed. That's where we should start."

The woman's brain had chopped through all of that in the course of thirty seconds, when five minutes ago, she'd been skeptical of the plan to the point where he'd been convinced she'd never agree. "You impress me, Ms.…Sophia."

"I'll take the compliment, but please, for the love of God, do not call me Ms. Sophia. It makes me sound like a Sunday school teacher," she said with a wrinkled nose.

"What's wrong with that? Some of my favorite people are my former Sunday school teachers," he said. "Besides, it wasn't intentional. I'm still warming up to calling you something other than Ms. Lang."

Because that was step one toward bridging the gap between boss/employee and something else entirely. As soon as he relaxed the formality, it would be that much easier to take other liberties, like smoothing away the dark hair that constantly fell from her severe hairstyle.

And if he didn't stop obsessing over every tiny nuance of his employer, it was going to be a very long, painful treasure hunt indeed.

"Sunday school teachers are old. I might never see twenty-nine again, but I'm not so eager to rush up to thirty-nine and shake hands."

Since he couldn't tell her that she seemed like the kind of woman who would only get better with age, more beautiful with the experiences that she would share with someone, he kept his mouth shut. He certainly wouldn't be the person standing by her side, watching her age gracefully, endearingly.

"You aren't in the nursing home yet," he told her and

cleared his throat. "I like the idea of starting with the house. Though it might make more sense to do it after dark, so it doesn't interfere with your boss duties, and I can still scout around outside during the day when it's light. It would be pretty easy to make up some excuse to ride the property, but really be looking for clues."

Sophia skewered him again with that probing gaze. It gave him the impression she was puzzling something out in her head, and he'd already seen that she had a better-than-average analysis gene. Something told him he wasn't going to like the next bit of logic that popped out of her mouth, though.

"Why are you doing all of this?"

Yeah, there it was. She'd poked at the one flaw in all of this, the one thing he had no ready answer for. "I told you. I work for you. It's my job to do whatever you ask of me."

"I didn't ask you to save me from Intruder Man. I didn't text you and insist that you meet me for a clandestine discussion about a treasure that could be worth millions of dollars. A lot of men would have kept that kind of information to themselves. You literally just told me that you could do your own treasure hunt without anyone knowing, even me." She flipped a hand up in question. "What's your story, Ace Madden, who went to Sunday school and took the time to do a background check on my new employees?"

Ugh. This was the very last time he took a job under these kinds of pretenses. What possible benefit was there to keeping his identity a secret? But the instructions for the job had been clear. He couldn't reveal his true purpose for being on the ranch to anyone, least of all Sophia Lang, or he'd forfeit his fee plus incur a breach of contract penalty.

Then who would pay Stephanie's bills? She was just getting her feet under her after a year of being in and out of the hospital. He had to cross the finish line on this assignment.

What no one had told him was how to do this job without dropping huge clues all over the place that he wasn't a run-of-the-mill cowboy, and he'd just given her about twenty. He shuffled his feet as he tried to figure out the best way to lie without lying.

"Background check?" he scoffed, even though that's exactly what he'd done and if he'd thought Sophia was impressive before, his scale for judging that had just been knocked right off the table. "Those boys are open books. They'll tell you anything. All you have to do is say howdy and off they go, spilling their life stories to anyone who will listen. That's how I know they're good guys."

She didn't look convinced. "So you're a good guy too? Doing all of this out of the goodness of your heart."

"Not everyone is out to scam people," he told her sincerely, since this was one thing he could be completely honest about. "I have a protective streak. It's been there since I was little, when my sister got stuck in a tree and I found out how good it felt to be the one who saved her. That's all there is to it. Don't make me out to be something I'm not. I have plenty of flaws."

"Let me know when I've hit one," she said wryly. "I might need the hint."

She'd find some soon enough, of that he had no doubt. The pile of lies he'd fed her would be a great example. Also, a lot of women had accused him in the past of having a hero complex. Of manufacturing a situation where he could be the one to save the day, when they hadn't needed saving in the first place. It was a fine line and he wondered sometimes if they were right.

Was he doing that here too? Imagining the need for a treasure hunt when in reality, it was nothing more than an excuse to be close to Sophia?

Two days, he promised himself. He'd take two days to chase this wild goose and then, if nothing came from it, fade back into the woodwork to watch from afar, like he'd planned to do all along.

"Well," Sophia said and dusted her hands off. "I can't say I'm excited about the idea of taking time out of my schedule to look for a Maya treasure, of all things. But I am happy to be doing it with you."

Chapter 9

True to his word, Ace materialized at Sophia's front door at nine o'clock that night to start their first round of searching the house for gold. Or clues to where it was. Or something.

She'd lost track of what exactly Ace expected to find. Her father wasn't the type to leave a lot of himself behind. And how tragic was it that she'd actually started nursing a tiny spark of hope that they might find something of his? Something she could keep and point to when reminded that he'd abandoned his family in favor of this thing future Sophia would have found.

At least then she'd know what was so much more important than her and her sisters.

Sophia let Ace into the house without turning on the porch light, and yes, it was a little thrilling to be plunged into something so secretive with someone who set her skin on sizzle with nothing more than a stray glance or brush of his elbow as he skirted her to stand in the foyer.

"Hey," she said brilliantly, because her game was strong with this one.

"Hey," he returned as if he hadn't noticed she'd flubbed a perfectly good opportunity to dazzle him with her sparkling wit.

But then, this clandestine meeting wasn't about giving her a chance to flirt with him, as much as she'd like to practice a bit for the real thing later—when she might get up the courage to try again with expressing her interest in a calm, measured way that wouldn't result in another rejection.

Maybe she should create a spreadsheet matrix with relevant strategies, then weight them according to her existing skill level and probability of executing successfully.

Or she could stop standing there like a bump on a log and get this party moving.

"I thought we should start with the attic," she suggested.

Ace nodded. "Fine by me. This is your house and should be searched according to your rules and timetable. I'm just kind of along for the ride."

"I hope you're also along to provide expert treasure hunting advice, because I've never done anything like this before," she called over her shoulder as she led him to the first set of stairs, the wide ones that curved up from the foyer to the second floor in an impressive show of wood and grandeur she hoped would be the hallmark of advertising beauty shots of the property.

"I hate to break it to you, but this is my first treasure hunt too. We'll figure it out together."

A reference to her parting comment from earlier? He hadn't said anything after she'd told him she was happy to be in this with him. Which she'd spent a good bit of time wishing she could take back when he hadn't immediately responded in kind.

He followed her up the stairs and pulled even on the landing, his boots shushing across the gleaming hardwoods, the sound reassuring and somehow familiar, as if she'd heard it a hundred times. This old Victorian was made for a man like him, one so at home in his own skin, so solid and down-to-earth.

"Your house is beautiful," he commented, reading her thoughts, because of course he could.

"My grandpa was born here," she told him, playing the part of tour guide. "Everything is original and handcrafted, a lost art. I never thought it would be passed to me. But I love it."

Truth. She'd never considered herself anything other than a city girl, a corporate-ladder climber who would eventually get to the top one day. The top of what, she'd questioned many times during the worst part of burnout.

Here, she could breathe at least.

The stairs to the third floor weren't nearly as grand as those in the entranceway. They lay hidden behind a closed door, the narrow corridor dark and a little forbidding. She hadn't been up here since the first day when she took a long tour of the property she'd just inherited, but it seemed the most likely place for something to be hidden by either her grandpa or her father. It had been daylight the last time, though.

Cobwebs shone silver in the flashlight she switched on. She must have hesitated, or Ace was practicing his mind reading again, because he rested an encouraging hand at the small of her back. What he'd meant to encourage her to do, she wasn't sure, but it was fifty-fifty on whether she'd keep leading the way and let the monsters get her, or she turned and curled into him.

Ace took the decision out of her hands, as well as the flashlight, then maneuvered around her with sure steps so that he was in the lead. Which left her back vulnerable, and she didn't like that, either. She scurried after him, probably way too close for his comfort, but not close enough for hers.

At the top of the creaky stairs, pitch-black met absolute black in an unending sea of nothing. The tiny glow from the flashlight did nothing more than cast a reddish tint on Ace's hand. This was not going to work. She couldn't see a blessed thing and her heartbeat thumped painfully in her chest, driving her toward a mild panic attack. He reached out with his non-flashlight-holding hand, and she thought he might be about to enfold her into his embrace, which she would take all day long.

Instead, he snapped on the overhead light she hadn't realized existed.

"That's much better," she said, her breath coming a little easier now along with the deep pang of disappointment that he hadn't segued their surroundings into an excuse to get closer.

He grinned. "I thought we were starring in our own slasher movie for a second there. Expected a guy with a chain saw to appear in the corner."

"Nothing up here but a lot of junk," she said, glancing around at the hodgepodge of items that had been stored away up here for years. A faded velvet sofa with missing buttons and a dusty dresser with peeling paint sat against the far wall, along with a Shaker-style rocking chair with a broken armrest.

"Might as well dive in," he said. "I wish I knew what to tell you to look for, but I don't know. Maybe we start by trying to establish whether the treasure is still on the property or not."

Ace prowled to the left, while she took the right. As she delved deeper into the attic, Sophia came across piles of clothing and linens, musty from years of being stored away in a place with no ventilation. Toys and games were scattered throughout the space, including an old wooden train set with missing pieces, a set of tin soldiers and a few worn-out board games. Her father's? He'd grown up here.

Rusty hammers, wrenches and screwdrivers, as well as old paint cans and brushes, had been shoved over into one corner. Why that stuff hadn't been moved to the shed she'd had torn down, she'd never know. Probably her grandpa had considered them valuable. Dust covered everything, so it was hard to know if any of these things had value.

She ignored the readily identifiable stuff that sat in precarious stacks, opting to start looking through the boxes. The first one was open, full of Christmas decorations. The second had been taped shut, and since this was her first treasure hunt, she'd come unprepared.

She tugged at the tape, hoping the temperature extremes might have worn out the adhesive, but it wouldn't budge, and she couldn't get a fingernail under it. The box shredded her nail, though, an indictment of her calcium intake. She made mental note number 375 of the day to pick up a calcium supplement at the grocery store next time she made it into town.

"Let me." Ace materialized at her side, holding something black in his hand, which he thumbed with a flick, revealing a wicked-looking blade.

Wide-eyed, she watched him slice the tape on both sides. "That is some heavy hardware you're using as scissors."

Ace flicked the blade closed and pocketed the knife, his expression unreadable in the low light. "Would it make you feel better or worse to find out it's seen its share of non-box-related uses?"

Like he'd used to peel an apple or a human? Suddenly very unsure she wanted to know the answer, she shook her head. "You're just full of surprises."

"Well, one thing I don't want to surprise you with. I'm capable of using a knife in a lot of situations but I usually don't. I've got no problem defending you if it comes to it, though. Whatever it takes."

She believed him wholly in that moment. Not that his ability to keep her safe was ever in question. But it did make her feel marginally better to know that he wasn't the type to pull his knife as a first resort, even as she registered that he'd wanted her to know he had it on him, or he wouldn't have bothered with it. A guy with biceps like Ace's could have ripped the box in half without breaking a sweat. No knife needed.

So why had he made such a big show out of it?

He went back to his side of the attic, apparently oblivious to the fact that she was still watching him instead of returning to search her own designated area. The man moved like a precision machine, as if designed to have only the barest necessity of motion, and it was a pleasure to witness.

He did nothing superfluous, organizing his search methodically, and she had the impression he missed nothing. Her ranch hand's talents were ironically wasted as a cowboy, and she wondered if he had ever thought about doing something else with his life.

Military, she remembered. Former. Obviously, he'd left the service at some point. Recently? Was that why he carried the knife still? Actually, she had no idea if that kind of weapon made the list of required gear for a soldier. In her head, they all carried guns and dressed in camo after greasing their faces.

Probably he had a dress uniform too, like they did in the movies, and she'd bet every dime in her checking account that it looked incredibly hot on him. Too bad she'd never get to see it.

Sophia was so busy fantasizing about Ace, his uniform and some decidedly non-military-approved scenarios involving both that she almost missed that the box she'd just opened was full of newspaper clippings. Not the kind that you used to wrap breakables, like she'd originally thought, but full articles someone had cut from the paper deliberately.

The one on top had a photograph of a very young David Lang.

His haircut was the same as in the few printed pictures her mother kept in an album hidden in a drawer. Charli had found it once and pulled it out when their mom had gone to the store. Veronica never had cared one whit about their father. She didn't remember him at all, and refused to look at it, but Sophia had memorized his face, in case she passed him on the street. It seemed like something you should be able to do, recognize your father if you stumbled over him in public.

All the articles were about David Lang. Maybe her grandmother had cut these out and saved them before she'd passed over a decade ago. Sophia pulled out a full-page color article ripped from a magazine dated just five years ago. *After* her grandmother had passed.

It was the only one that didn't feature a picture of David Lang, but it mentioned him under a photo of what must be the Maya coin her grandpa had found. The article was from a magazine called *Ancient Treasures* as noted in the footer of the page, and as she skimmed the print, whoever had written the piece laid out in clear detail that the coin had been traced to the burial site of K'inich Janaab' Pakal, also known as Pakal the Great, one of the more noted Maya rulers. The coins—and the author felt quite certain the term should be plural—had been stolen at some point in the past, then taken by Conquistadors back to Spain.

"Holy crap," she called to Ace. "You have to come look at this."

Ace crossed the attic in a matter of seconds, his gaze flitting over the article as he stood at her elbow, then whistled as she tapped the paragraph of note. "The coin your grandpa found was worth twenty-five thousand dollars?"

"I'm starting to feel a whole lot better about that knife in your pocket," she said faintly.

If there were more of these coins on her property, Intruder Man might be the least of her concerns.

Ace kept reading. "The article says that the king of Spain returned the coins to the Mexican government in the early nineteen hundreds, but then they went missing."

He said the word with giant implied air quotes. She got it. They were dealing with something so valuable, the treasure had changed hands multiple times, likely not without its share of bloodshed in the process.

"So, if nothing else," she concluded, "we missed an opportunity to research this online instead of digging through boxes in the attic. I had no idea Grandpa's find had gotten any press."

Easily rectified. She'd spend a couple of hours in the morning reading more about the treasure, which at least they'd verified did in fact exist. And apparently her father had found it, or at least part of it.

"Is your father an archaeologist or an opportunist?" Ace

asked and when she lifted her brows, he shook his head with a laugh. "Is he Indiana Jones or the Nazis in this scenario?"

"You mean, is he interested in the history and doing the right thing, or would he rather profit?" She started to answer that her father cared about nothing, but obviously he'd spent his life dedicated to the pursuit of treasure, even past the point when he'd found what some might argue would be the cache of a lifetime. "He doesn't have any formal training that I'm aware of, but that doesn't mean he didn't pick up an appreciation for the culture. He'd likely have studied relentlessly to know where to dig."

"Well, that was my real question." Ace tapped the magazine page, which had started to curl at the edges but otherwise seemed unaffected by time and harsh environmental factors. "Whether it was likely he'd found the treasure himself hidden somewhere in a historical site or had gotten it via nefarious means. Because if it's the latter, we could be dealing with a much darker group of mercenaries than I would have assumed."

Aghast, she stared at him. "You think he might have stolen the treasure from someone who legitimately had a claim to it? Like from a museum or something?"

"Or something," Ace said grimly. "But I don't want to accuse your father of anything without more facts. We know there are more coins that appear to be unaccounted for. It's reasonable to assume that they might be hidden here at the ranch if your father came into possession of more than one. We need to thoroughly search the house for the coins, and then start on the property. Sooner rather than later, not as a side project when we have time."

The reality of the dauntless task in front of them set in. "We can't do all of that at night."

"No," he agreed readily. "I can't imagine anything I want to do less than look for a treasure in the dark, one potentially worth six figures or more that your father may have taken under less-than-legal circumstances. On property I don't know well."

Because he couldn't look for a treasure and keep her safe at the same time under those conditions. And she fully believed the latter was his top priority. Maybe she shouldn't. Maybe she should be completely wary of a guy she'd just met, who carried a knife in his pocket that he clearly had some skill wielding.

But she did trust him. That was the gist of it. Who else could she possibly turn to in this situation?

Chapter 10

Sophia and Ace spent another two-plus hours in the attic, finally emerging dusty and exhausted—at least on her part—near midnight. Obviously, Ace had a lot of experience with after-dark activities, as he didn't seem too worse for wear, despite their finding nothing else of use.

But then, nothing much affected him as far as she could tell. He never seemed flustered or unsure, plus he'd taken off his hat at some point, exposing his wheat-blond hair that he kept clipped short, which was a wholly different look on him that she liked, so it was no chore to keep studying him.

Maybe she'd discover one of those flaws he insisted he had. That was the purpose of the knife show earlier, as best she'd reasoned out in the hours of searching they'd done, during which she'd had nothing to do but think about Ace. He'd pulled out the knife to give her the impression he was a dangerous guy who'd done dangerous things with a deadly weapon. She got it. Joke was on him if he thought the idea scared her. It stood to reason that he'd witnessed unsavory scenes during combat and likely had participated in his share.

War wasn't pretty and she didn't want to know what she

didn't know about it. But she did want to know more about the man behind the knife.

"Get some sleep," he murmured on his way out the front door, pausing only for a second to meet her gaze in the low light.

A ripple passed between them, and she swayed into it, drawn to him inexplicably. But he stepped in the opposite direction, through the space into the outside, shutting the door firmly in her face.

Yeah, that's what was supposed to happen. But she didn't have to like it.

Sleep came fitfully and she dreamed about her father, who seemed to be always flipping a gold coin along the backs of his fingers like the pirates in the movies did. Near dawn, she gave up, throwing herself into the shower she'd been too tired to take before going to bed.

Ace showed up at the back door around 7:00 a.m., apparently over his clandestine approach, which made sense given the urgency of their task and the switch to daylight hours. They weren't going to be able to hide their activities too well, but she'd still like to try to avoid an uproar of the whole place if possible.

"Come in," she said and shut the door behind him with a sharp click, thumbing out a quick text to Becky.

"Did you eat breakfast?"

"I had coffee," he said with a shrug. He'd forgone the hat entirely today, his hair still damp from his own shower.

"Then let's test all of the floor joists first and see if we can find a false one that might have a hidey-hole beneath it." His brows lifted. "What? It was in a movie I saw. It could be a thing."

"It could be. That wasn't a vote of no confidence, it was an 'I'm impressed.' Am I allowed to say that?"

She grinned. "You never have to ask permission to compliment me. You can start in the dining room, and I'll take the living room."

They worked in silence, ears keen on the floor for telltale creaks or places where it sounded hollow. Occasionally one of them would call out, "Anything?" and the other would reply, "Nothing." Or a variation thereof.

They met up at the base of the wide, curved staircase in the foyer, Sophia already frustrated and bored with this approach, her to-do list growing by the second as emails and texts poured in, judging by the vibrations from her pocket. "We're never going to find anything this way."

"It's a tedious business," he agreed, shoving his hands in his pockets. "Do you think there's anything in your grandpa's papers that might be a schematic of the house? Possibly with something helpful like an arrow pointing to a hidden room behind the wood paneling in a bedroom or something?"

They'd already looked in her office once, but to be fair, she'd had no clue what to look for and her eye might have skimmed over something like house blueprints because she'd had no idea such a thing would be of value the first time.

But what were the odds that something would be easy?

She threw up her hands. "Maybe?"

"The office is the most logical place for your grandpa to have kept something like that."

She nodded because why not after the lack of progress thus far? Sophia led the way, handing him the key to the desk drawer, which he took without comment as she drifted to the far wall, contemplating. Had the twenty-five grand from the sale of the one recovered coin ended up in the account she'd inherited or had her grandpa spent it all? Or, door number three, did he have a safe hidden somewhere that she hadn't found yet because she'd never thought to look for one?

Tapping on the walls and lifting framed prints, she tried to imagine where her grandpa would have hidden something valuable that wasn't also the same place as in the last five thrillers she'd watched.

The third print she lifted must not have been secured to the wall all that well. It teetered on its nail, then crashed to the floor in a shower of shiny shards and wood.

Ace shot across the room, his arms snaking around her before she could blink. He lifted, pulling her clear from the splintered glass, and straight into a semi-embrace that sent a shiver over her entire body.

Adrenaline. And Ace. It was a heck of a one-two punch.

His gaze swept her with an assessing eye before finally landing on her face. "Are you okay?"

Given that his arms still lay snug against her waist, and they were aligned from hip to torso, she'd never been better in her life. Heat pumped from his body. It was delicious and paired nicely with the fireworks going off inside her. It took all her will to stop herself from stepping more fully into his embrace.

"Define *okay*," she murmured throatily, and that's when something flashed in his expression.

He'd registered their position too. Their gazes locked, singeing the air between them.

But he didn't drop his arms, thank goodness, though he should. They were treasure hunting partners. Strictly professional. The thing between them shouldn't feel like it was about to blaze into a fire hazard. And telling herself that didn't seem to make it fizzle.

What did it say about her love life that this was the most excitement she'd had with a man in ages?

"Oh, I'm sorry!" Becky stood at the door to Sophia's office, flinching as if she'd gotten an eyeful of something she'd rather not have seen. "I didn't mean to interrupt. I heard the crash from the front door just as I was knocking and rushed in to see what in the world had happened."

"No worries," Ace returned smoothly, stepping away from Sophia without jerking like a marionette—which was more than she could say for herself. "The picture frame fell off the wall. I was ensuring Ms. Lang hadn't been injured by the glass."

"Oh, okay." Becky eyed him curiously, not paying attention to Sophia at all, mercifully. "We haven't met. I'm Sophia's accountant, Becky."

"Ace Madden. Ranch hand," he explained with a head jerk toward the back acreage. "Currently repurposed as sweeper of glass. So I'll get to it."

Without a backward glance, Ace vanished in the direction of the kitchen, presumably in search of a broom and dustpan, which Jenny would help him locate. Sophia beelined for her chair, sliding into and swiveling around to face Becky from behind the desk, praying that she came across as calm and professional and not like she'd been about to test out the feel of Ace's lips for herself.

"That man is the definition of smoking," Becky said with eyes wider than a Texas horizon. "If you've got any more of them lying around, send one in my direction. I could use someone to sweep my glass."

"It's not like that," Sophia protested. "Stop making broken glass sound like a euphemism. Did you have a reason for dropping by?"

One that didn't involve almost catching Sophia in flagrante delicto with an employee, preferably.

Thankfully, Becky didn't comment on the snippiness in Sophia's tone and slid a sheaf of papers over the top of the desk. "Signatures. This is the loan paperwork I texted you about."

Oh, for crying out loud. She'd forgotten all about it. That's how things had gone lately. The second she'd read the message on her phone, it had exited her brain faster than water down a drain. Thankfully, it was a small slip, one Becky had covered, which was what Sophia paid her for.

But if she didn't watch herself, this treasure might end up costing her more than time.

"The interest rate came in a little higher than we were hoping," Becky said conversationally as if she hadn't just dropped a big wrench in the conversation.

"Wait. What?" Sophia paused, pen poised over the dotted line. "How much more? I can't afford even a dollar over the repayment amount we discussed with Ken on Friday."

"Well, it's complicated. The ranch isn't pulling in income yet." Becky tapped her index finger on the clause with the interest rate and the refigured monthly payment. "So it's a riskier loan for the bank. Ken said he tried to get the rate lowered but the lender wouldn't budge."

Dismayed, Sophia stared at the number. It would be lovely if a Maya treasure dropped in her lap right about now. Especially one with about six zeros attached. If she didn't take this loan, she wouldn't have the operating capital to open the doors and then she'd never have the money to pay off the loan. It was a vicious catch-22.

"I guess I don't have a choice," she muttered.

"Not unless you have some kind of collateral," Becky agreed. "And since you already told Ken you didn't have anything of value, he assumed that was still true."

"It is for now."

But maybe not for long, depending on what she and Ace found. Anything historical might work for collateral, especially if she could tie it to the treasure. Or barring that, she could just find the actual treasure and then she wouldn't need a loan. Easy.

She rolled her eyes and signed the loan paperwork with her eyes screwed shut, sincerely worried that she might start hyperventilating at any second if she stared any harder at that repayment amount.

"I'll let you get back to sweeping glass," Becky said with a sly grin that faltered a tad when Ace came back into the room with a broom in hand and a trash bag tucked into his back pocket.

He smiled politely and brushed past Becky to show off exactly how good he was with his hands, sweeping almost all the glass into the dustpan in one shot. The shards went into the trash bag, then Ace expertly picked up the larger pieces that hadn't shattered, following with the wood until every last speck of the wreckage had been cleared.

"Ma'am," he said to Becky, in a drawl that almost had the accountant tittering.

"Nice to meet you, Ace Madden, ranch hand," Becky said with a wave and gathered her paperwork to jet out of the door.

"I thought she'd never leave," Sophia muttered in a complete reversal of what should be her attitude when it came to dealing with ranch business.

What was wrong with her? The loan should have been first and foremost on her mind, instead of focusing on her embarrassment at almost being caught with a ranch hand.

Well, technically, she *had* been caught. There couldn't have been a more compromising position to be in when someone stumbled over them, and still be dressed. And what had Becky done? Leaped to the worst possible conclusion. Then asked for one of her own.

Maybe her accountant wasn't silently judging Sophia to quite the degree she'd been imagining. After all, Ace had handled the interruption like a pro—*and* cleaned up the mess without preamble. Any mortification came from the deep-seated conflict Sophia had over whether she should be mixing business with pleasure. So far, Charli and Becky seemed to be in the pro camp. Possibly even Jenny, too, which marked three people who knew she had a thing for Ace.

Three too many. But that ship had sailed. She could no sooner stuff the women's knowledge into the garbage disposal than she could make the treasure materialize on her desk.

Nor could she stop herself from wondering what it would be like to not have to jump apart if someone surprised them in a less-than-professional situation. What it would be like to have a man as principled and dedicated as this one by her side for a much bigger slice of life than treasure hunting.

Ace wouldn't bail if things got hard. She'd always worried she'd wind up attracted to the same kind of man as her mother. Or worse, that all men were like her father, and she had nothing to choose from but weak-willed, spineless men who would abandon her at the earliest opportunity.

Clearly not all men were like that.

“We should get back to work,” Ace suggested gently. “If you’re sure you’re okay.”

A hysterical laugh almost bubbled to the surface. “I wasn’t okay the first time you asked. But we’ll pretend that’s not true.”

“Since I’m guessing you don’t actually mean you cut yourself and need medical triage, I’ll step away from that very carefully,” he said with a wry twist of his lips, hands spread wide.

“If I *was* bleeding, you’d rip a bandage from your shirt and do some kind of MacGyver thing with chewing gum in place of stitches, wouldn’t you?” she grumbled, which made him laugh.

“Do I win or lose points if I say yes?” he said, throwing her a glance from under his lashes as he took a stack of files and settled on the floor to thumb through them since she hadn’t moved from her chair.

She might never move from this chair again if he kept looking at her like that. It turned her spine to jelly. “Jury is still out.”

“How about now?” he said and held up a plain white envelope, dumped it upside down and poured a key into his hand.

“Is that—”

“Safety deposit box key,” he confirmed, his grin widening. “Any chance you know where your grandpa did his banking?”

Chapter 11

Ace drove to the center of Gun Barrel City with Sophia riding shotgun in his stripped-down, late-model pickup truck. It had seemed like a good vehicle for an undercover security specialist playing the part of a cowboy, at the time anyway.

It was rough around the edges, the opposite of fancy. Not the kind of transportation a woman like Sophia would be used to. But when he'd bought the truck, never once had he imagined a woman would see the inside of it.

Especially not one he couldn't stop reacting to every time they were in close quarters together. If he'd thought being closeted in her office made it tough to ignore the pull between them, the cab of the truck made that seem like a picnic.

The scent of her fruity shampoo filled every nook and cranny. The product probably had some expensive French name, but at the end of the day, reminded him of good old-fashioned apples. Which prior to this job, had not seemed particularly sexy, but Sophia somehow kept his brain in a constant state of awareness, so pretty much everything seemed sexy when connected to her.

"This the one?" he asked her as he pulled up to the traffic light in front of what appeared to be the only bank on Main Street, at least on this side of the lake.

She nodded and held on to the armrest as he turned, wobbly on the bench seat she probably wasn't used to. "Let's just hope he didn't do something that will set us back, like drive all the way to Dallas to get a safety deposit box."

As the executor of her grandfather's estate, Sophia did in fact have a very good idea where he'd had an account, and on the drive over, she'd done a lot of grumbling to Ace about how the safety deposit box hadn't been listed on any of the documents.

"It'll be here," he promised her. He could feel it in his gut, though he didn't mention that it wasn't a good feeling. The more they uncovered, the more uneasy he got.

It was one thing to be chasing after a treasure so they could get to it first, and it was another thing entirely to actually find the treasure, whatever it was, only to have some unsavory types try to divest them of it. He had no interest in being a target or painting one on Sophia's back.

Once inside, Sophia asked to speak to the manager, and Ace braced for the long ordeal ahead. They didn't know the box number, and technically, the account was still in her grandfather's name—assuming the box was even at this bank—and the legal tangle of proving her ownership of the asset might even require a warrant or at least a notarized right of transfer.

But when the manager emerged, it was a woman of an indeterminate age wearing a knit sweater who immediately threw her arms around Sophia and fussed over how much she'd grown. Obviously, they'd met. Small town.

"And who is this young man?" the manager cooed as she turned her attention to Ace.

"This is Ace Madden, one of the ranch hands I hired," Sophia said. "Frances was my grandmother's best friend for ages."

Ah. That explained it. Something had finally gone their way.

"She's looking down now, thrilled to pieces that the ranch came to you instead of being sold off," Frances said with a nod. "What can I do for you today? Did you get your grandpa's accounts all squared away?"

"No, ma'am, we were wondering if this goes to a safety deposit box that my grandpa might have had here." Sophia held up the key.

Frances immediately brightened. "Well, he sure did. Let me look up the number for you and you can see what's in it in this room back here. Follow me."

And just like that, he found himself included in the party, no ID check required, just hey, y'all, here's this secure, tamper-proof container meant to store valuable items the owner wanted to keep inaccessible in a vault that you can peruse at your leisure. All because Sophia had connections.

No wonder no one locked their doors around here. Why bother when the homeowner might very well invite a B&E suspect to sit down and have cookies before they took off with their loot?

Frances the bank manager pulled the data from a less than top-of-the-line computer behind her desk and before he could wrap his head around it, she ushered them into the vault, indicating that number 9847 had belonged to her grandpa. The boxes weren't the overly secure kind that required two keys, just the one from the owner, so Frances gave Sophia a nod and went to stand near the door, presumably to give them some semblance of privacy.

"Moment of truth," Sophia murmured to Ace and shoved the key into the lock.

Zero resistance. She twisted and the door popped open to reveal the box inside, which she extracted easily with the small handle attached to the front. It opened with her key as well. White paper covered the whole of the interior.

Sophia groaned. "I hope this isn't just another copy of his will. The man had like twelve copies in a file at home."

But when she pulled it out, it wasn't a stapled sheaf. The paper was large, folded into quarters that Sophia quickly spread out. A drawing covered the entire surface, almost to the edges.

Not just a drawing. Ace sucked in a breath. "It's a map."

Quirking a brow, she glanced at the diagram. "It's the ranch. Look, here's the house, and the barn. Or what used to be the barn."

"This." Ace stabbed a finger at a small square deep in the woods that had a very conveniently placed X in the dead center. "What is this?"

"I don't know. Some kind of deer blind or something, maybe?" She squinted. "It's pretty far back into the woods. I haven't been out there since I was a kid."

A deer blind covered in branches might explain why he hadn't seen it during his tour of the property, but he didn't want to mention that he'd already done a pretty thorough recon job.

"We're going to assume this X meant something important or your grandpa wouldn't have put this map of his property in a safety deposit box. Right?" he probed in case she had any information that would contradict the feeling in his gut.

This was it. The thing they'd been looking for.

"I mean, yeah. Obviously, it's important." She glanced in the box, her expression softening. "Oh, look. My grandmother's ring. I thought she'd been buried with it."

She picked up the only other thing in the box and slipped the ring on her finger. It was a simple band inset with round diamonds and fit Sophia, both in size and style. She curled her hand closed, turning it to let the light flash over the stones.

The look on her face hooked a tender place inside him and he couldn't take his eyes off her. What would he give to be the one who could make her glow like that? But he wasn't the kind of guy who put rings on women's fingers and imagining doing exactly that with Sophia didn't help.

"If this is the only thing I get out of this treasure hunt, I'll be happy," she said with a misty smile. "Thank you."

That's when she decided it would be a good time to launch herself into his arms for a hug to accompany her gratitude, and apples engulfed him as he caught her. Suddenly, he had an armful of Sophia and everything else in the world drained away.

If this went along with a thank-you, maybe he could come up with some other stuff she'd feel grateful for.

"You're welcome," he said gruffly. "But you would have found that envelope eventually. It had your dad's name on it."

She pulled back enough to meet his gaze but not enough to break his hold on her, his new favorite way to have a conversation with her. "It did? I didn't even notice. Surely that means the treasure must be in that spot on the map. Maybe my grandpa was holding the map for my father."

"Maybe." Or it was a dead end because her father had already cleaned out whatever it was on the map. It wouldn't be difficult for someone to sneak onto the property the back way and vanish undetected, booty in hand. "We need to go check it out."

"Well, yes, of course. We should go immediately, before it gets dark. My to-do list will have to wait."

They thanked Frances and Sophia signed some papers to cancel the safety deposit box since she was taking the entirety of the contents with her. The woman's efficiency and attention to detail, despite the huge monkey wrench this treasure hunt must have thrown into her life, was a force to be reckoned with. And he couldn't recall ever being attracted to something like that. It was messing with his head.

"Are you hungry?" he asked her as they climbed back into his truck. "We can run through a drive-through."

"I'm starving," she admitted. "There's a Dairy Queen. But I'm buying since you drove."

Two points to Ms. Lang. He couldn't recall the last time a woman owned up to having an appetite or a time—ever—when one had willingly ponied up money. He'd been fully prepared to split it.

Apparently, they had something in common. A tendency to push toward balancing the scales. He let that sit in the same spot as his growing feelings for her, mostly because he couldn't do anything else. Everything about her worked for him and then some.

They ate cheeseburgers in the car on the drive back to the ranch, a mutual agreement since they were both eager to figure out what the X marked on their newly acquired map. By the time his truck rolled into the back lot where the hands parked their vehicles, he'd fallen into an easy silence with Sophia that he'd never experienced with a woman before. Usually, he was exhausted from whatever mission he'd just been on, mentally preparing for the next one, or just plain bored by the woman's company.

This time, none of that was true. It was different and interesting and complicated. Not to mention impossible to fully enjoy when he constantly felt like the hammer would drop at any second, as soon as he had to tell her the truth.

"Let me just change first," she said as she hopped out of the truck, before he could get his brain in gear and race around to help her down.

Obviously, she didn't need his help. At least not in that regard, but he'd take solace in all the other ways she'd let him be there for her thus far. He liked the idea of being her white knight, even if it couldn't last.

It was the one thing he could take from this relationship without an ounce of guilt.

When she returned, she'd traded her sleek dress for jeans and a T-shirt, with a sweatshirt tied around her waist. The messy bun that he'd started to think of as a permanent fixture on her crown had been replaced by a long, swingy ponytail that his fingers itched to comb through. It was the first time he'd seen her in casual wear and while he really liked her dresses, this side of her put a different hitch in his stride.

Because she suddenly seemed accessible. As if he could actually be with a woman like this, one who ate cheeseburgers in the cab of his truck and filled a pair of jeans as if they'd been custom-made for her frame.

"Come on," he told her more gruffly than he'd intended but jeez.

In the last hour, he'd thought about their relationship status more times than he'd thought about anything else, including the treasure. The answer to the question of who is totally distracted by Sophia and will soon make a mistake if he doesn't get his act together was Ace Madden.

Sophia didn't seem to notice, eagerly falling in next to him as she slung a backpack over her shoulders. At his eyebrow lift, she laughed. "It's snacks and some water bottles. Just in case. Plus the map and my cell phone. And an extra hair band in case my hair starts to annoy me, so I can put it back up in a bun."

"Why did you take it down, then, if there's a chance you'll just put it back up?" he asked, strictly to sidetrack himself from the fact that even her preparedness struck him as sexy.

"I don't know, it seemed more adventurous to do it this way," she said with a shrug, shadows falling on her face as they entered the woods near the new temporary barn the hands were building.

Which he was not helping with and probably should be. While protecting Sophia and helping her find the treasure counted as his primary objective, as well as his real job, he was still taking a paycheck from the ranch. He couldn't refuse or it would raise eyebrows, or even an inquiry into his background, neither of which he could afford at this point.

Great. So he'd found yet another thing to feel guilty about.

"I like the ponytail," he told her, despite knowing full well he shouldn't say stuff like that.

He seemed to have fallen into a rut where he'd keep doing the exact opposite of what his brain insisted was the right thing. Sometimes doing the right thing sucked. She didn't seem to mind the compliment though, her smile bordering on gleeful, which wasn't even close to the same as the look her grandmother's ring had put on her face, but he'd take it.

The ranch wasn't that big by the standard of someone who had traversed twenty miles in full gear, guerilla style, which meant staying off the main road. But he was cognizant of Sophia's lack of physical training, so he kept his pace slow as they took the main trail into the woods.

"It won't take long to get to the X," he assured her. "Maybe twenty minutes tops. Fortunately, it's on this side of the creek."

She nodded, seeming to have no trouble keeping up, which left him plenty of headspace to pay attention to their surroundings. The hands never came into the woods since they focused most of their attention on the flat acreage where the horses grazed, rotating the animals from field to field to ensure they always had enough to eat. The wooded area extended past the boundaries of Sophia's property and her grandpa hadn't fenced this section, likely due to the expense and effort to work around the creek.

It would be a lot easier for an intruder to sneak onto the property from this direction.

The dense trees blocked more of the sun the farther into the woods they walked. He'd like to say the close atmosphere was cozy. The kind of vibe that would allow him to slip an arm around his companion's waist, drawing her closer as they strolled without a care in the world.

That was not a fantasy he could afford to let scroll through his head, let alone act on.

He hadn't been this far into the trees. The last time he'd come into the woods, when he'd found the tarp, he'd been much closer to the house, around the other side of the barn to the north. He'd expected more wildlife, especially if Sophia was right about the X marking the spot of a deer blind. Birds flittered here and there, and an occasional squirrel chittered at them as they passed, but it was eerily quiet for woods.

Fortunate. That's what allowed him to hear the shush of footsteps behind them.

Someone was following them. One of the ranch hands?

Surely not. He knew all of them. A fellow cowboy would have called out for them to wait up if he thought they were off on something they'd allow him to crash.

Ace kept walking, careful to keep his pace identical so he didn't tip off whoever was behind them. His gaze darted around in 360-degree sweeps, preparing for an attack that might come from any direction. Or not. He didn't know this person's intent and it made him antsy.

When he passed a fallen tree branch, he casually hooked it with his hand, breaking off the smaller offshoot branches, then used it as a walking stick. It couldn't hurt to have a weapon.

Their tail got a little closer and a lot more cautious, staying just off the path, which was what had alerted him to the additional presence in the first place since the footsteps sounded different. This was no random person wondering what they were doing. Whoever they were had a bit of skill.

But Ace was better.

Sophia's safety was his number one concern. He had to know what he was dealing with here. The best way to do that was to put a tree between her and their tail while leaving Ace as the primary target—without alerting her to the danger. Which meant an evasive maneuver.

"Want to stop for a second?" he murmured. "Get some water from your backpack?"

Thankfully, she nodded and slipped off the pack, but she was still out in the open. There was only one way to get her up against a tree and he didn't hesitate to use it, even as his conscience screamed at him to think of something else.

The problem was that he couldn't think of anything else but advancing on her, grabbing her hips and backing her up until she aligned with the bark. Which, of course, meant she was sandwiched between the tree and Ace.

Dear Lord, did she feel good.

To anyone else, it would look like he meant to kiss her. It looked an awful lot like that to him too. She peered up at him, her lashes fluttering as she subtly adjusted so that they fit together better, and he bit back a groan.

"This was not what I expected to happen on our jaunt," she said breathlessly, which made two of them.

He didn't want to scare her by alerting her to the stalker's presence. But neither could he let her think he was the kind of guy to take advantage of a woman in the woods when there was no one around to hear her protest. Angling his head, he bent toward her ear, secretly inhaling her scent.

"There's someone back there," he whispered. "Don't flinch. Freeze exactly as you are. Act like you're enjoying my attention."

"It's not an act," she murmured.

That's when a shot rang out.

Chapter 12

Bark splintered from the tree above them, raining down on Sophia's shoulder. Her expression morphed instantly from intrigued to terrified.

Ace didn't have time to fix either one.

"Run," he said through gritted teeth and shouldered her backpack, then grabbed her hand to lead the way. Palmed his knife in the other hand, not that he could throw it with any accuracy unless he turned around. Not happening.

It was more important to get Sophia out of the line of fire. He sprinted off the path, farther into the heavy trees, hoping they would provide enough cover to allow him to put distance between her and the shooter.

Sophia kept up, her hand trembling in his. The fact that she didn't question him, just let him call the shots, went a long way toward allowing him to execute the extraction without worrying about getting her on board.

He headed toward the X, hoping that the original map artist had rendered the diagram to scale. His own skill in estimating the spatial distance he'd memorized wasn't in question, but an error on the part of someone else would be difficult to account for.

Fortunately, the map had it right and none too soon. The

faint outline of a building materialized in the section he'd earmarked in his mind's eye, right where he'd expected it. It was partially camouflaged, which was why he hadn't seen it before, but it wasn't deliberately disguised. The woods had just grown up around it so that you had to know it was there to notice the shape of the structure.

"Almost there," he called back to Sophia, who was huffing a bit and might need some encouragement.

If nothing else, they could use the building as a shield. As they rounded the backside, he hustled her flat up against the south wall. Wood. The building was a brown shed, one of the prefab kinds, larger than he'd first estimated.

Good. He'd been hoping for metal, which would be a lot better at stopping bullets than the rotting wood, but maybe they could duck inside if need be.

For now, they needed to vanish.

Finger to his lips, he hugged the wall in kind, sliding down to a crouch, then motioned for her to do the same. The ground here felt spongy, as if the soil might drain poorly due to the structure compromising the natural flow of rainwater. But the overgrowth of young trees in a ring around the place made it a much more ideal hiding place than it could have been.

A hush stole over the surrounding woods. He strained to hear sounds that would indicate the stalker had followed them, but there was nothing. Either their tail hadn't chased them, or he was holed up a few yards away, waiting for them to make themselves targets again.

That wasn't happening. He could park it here for hours without moving, no problem.

Sophia might be another story, though. She wasn't used to fleeing for her life in combat situations that required stealth maneuvers. Neither could he let her sit down and rest her thighs for a few minutes. If they had to run, she needed to be poised and ready.

Her gaze flicked to the knife in his hand, but he couldn't tell if she appreciated that he had a weapon or if the idea of being protected by a man who knew how to use one bothered her.

One thing for sure, she wasn't breathing normally, and he needed her to. If she passed out from lack of oxygen, he'd have to carry her. It would be a lot harder to defend against an attack if his hands were full of unconscious woman. But he couldn't risk making any sound to tell her to stop hyperventilating.

So he settled for running a soothing hand down her arm, nodding slowly in approval as she began breathing deeper, visibly calming.

Excellent, he mouthed, his thumb skimming over her skin in a circle. Later, he'd think about how nice it felt.

When he estimated that they'd been crouched here for a solid fifteen minutes, he duck-walked to the edge of the shed, then flattened himself to the ground so he could peer around the corner from the lowest profile possible.

Nothing. No movement, no shush of leaves. Even the wind didn't penetrate this deep into the woods. Their tail might have given up. Unlikely, though. It highly depended on the tail's reason for shooting at them. More likely, whoever it was had no small amount of patience and would wait them out.

The door to the shed lay around the other side, unfortunately. They might have to risk it. He would feel a lot better about getting Sophia inside the shelter, where she wasn't quite so exposed. Their tail could even now be climbing a tree far enough away so that Ace couldn't hear the telltale sounds but close enough to take both of them out with a long-range rifle.

That was one of the downsides to civilian security work. He had no clue what type of weaponry he might be up against. In Afghanistan, he was never at a disadvantage thanks to expert intel and a lot of experience he would not benefit from here in East Texas.

After a frustrating round of surveillance that yielded him zero useful information, he rolled to his knees and crawled back to Sophia, his finger to his lips again. She nodded, stretching her back with little side-to-side movements that weren't lost on him. Her muscles hurt. She wasn't used to holding a position so taxing on her body. This situation sucked, no two ways about it.

Just as he started devising a plan in his head to get them from this shed to the tree line where they might be able to make a run for the main house, something groaned, but it wasn't human. It sounded like pressure on wood.

The walls? The shed wasn't about to collapse, was it?

The groaning got louder, and Ace's stomach lurched as if the ground had dropped. Not unusual in an earthquake. Except this was no tremor, or he'd have braced for the shift.

Suddenly, the earth beneath them gave way and he was falling. Sophia cried out. They both hit a hard surface. Dirt and splintered wood rained down from above.

Coughing, Ace rolled to his feet instantly, knife raised, automatically moving to stand guard over Sophia as he assessed the perimeter. They were in some kind of underground shelter. A large one that extended past the area where they'd landed. But the dim light from above didn't penetrate the shadowy edges well enough to see what lurked there.

Sophia moaned, still flat on the concrete, her cheek to the ground. She shifted, a good sign. Concussion protocol scrolled through his mind, even as he tamped back a lick of panic at the thought of having to do any kind of injury triage in the midst of keeping a lookout for the shooter, should he try to ambush them from above.

"Sophia," he murmured and knelt to check her pulse, which was thankfully strong. "Did you hit your head?"

"No," she told him, her voice thick and laced with pain. "I landed on my shoulder. The one Intruder Man injured the other day."

He needed to know how bad it was. And get her out of the light. Pronto. "I'm going to help you sit up."

There wasn't time to stand on principle, not as loud as their untimely crash through the shelter roof had been. He got down and put an arm around her waist, gently lifting her from the concrete, then helped her move out of the circle of dirt and split wood pieces. Near the far wall, which was thankfully well into the shadowy recesses, he helped her sit back against it.

She slumped, drawing her knees up to rest her arm on them. "Where are we?"

"Some kind of shelter under the shed, but it seems like it might be a lot bigger area. Hard to see. It's pretty dark back in these corners."

"Here, use my phone." She fished it from her backpack, which was still slung around his shoulder. "One good thing, you didn't land on this so it's probably fine."

She switched on the flashlight app and handed it to him. Immediately, he tapped it off and pocketed the phone, opting to keep his concern about an ambush to himself for the moment. "In a minute. Talk to me about your pain level. One to ten."

"I don't know, like a five?"

She was lying. Her voice carried a fine thread of distress, and he couldn't see how bad she was hurt while they cowered in the dark, waiting for their tail to show up and shoot them like fish in a barrel.

Remorse soured his throat. She was hurt and it was his fault. If he'd led her into the shed in the first place, they might not have fallen through the spongy places that had rotted—definitely due to poor drainage based on the water-damaged pieces of roof that had hit the concrete along with them.

"I'll live, Ace," she assured him, somehow cluing into his own agony over their situation. "I just don't want to run for a few minutes. Can we just sit here and let me catch my breath?"

"It was a hard fall," he murmured, impressed that she was taking it so well. "And yes, to your question. We can sit here for a few minutes."

Or thirty. As long as it took for him to feel at least semi-confident that their tail wasn't too bright and hadn't figured out where they'd disappeared to. Ironic that he'd maneuvered her into position by the shed wall with the sole intent of hiding them both from view and had inadvertently pulled a decent vanishing act out of thin air.

They may have gotten extremely lucky.

Ace settled back against the wall next to Sophia and nearly bit his tongue when she slipped her hand into his. Okay. She was scared and probably in no small amount of shock. It made sense that she'd want human contact. He could buck up. And he might even be able to keep his brain from short-circuiting.

It was a toss-up whether he did that successfully or not.

Thankfully, the shooter did not show up to demonstrate his ability to track them to their belowground hideout or his skill with hitting a stationary target. At least not yet. Ace had held his position behind a half wall near the road to Kandahar for eight hours once, while waiting on a convoy of terrorists to motor past. When they finally did, he executed the operation with his usual expertise, despite not having moved a muscle in ages.

Patience was a higher-valued skill in stealth combat than almost anything else. And he'd exercise it here too. In more ways than one, apparently, as Sophia let her head drop onto his shoulder.

She trusted him. It was a revelation, even as it felt so easy and normal to be here like this with her, as if they'd been this close-knit team for far longer than a couple of days.

If she'd hesitated back there by the tree for even a second...if she'd questioned his directives, argued with him, the outcome might have been very different. But she hadn't. She'd followed him without question.

It was humbling. And poked at him with sharp prongs of guilt.

He had to move, to do something. To save her.

"Hold this for me," he ordered and closed her palm around the handle of his knife, pointy end raised. "Use it without hesitation if need be. I'm going to check this place out."

She nodded and shifted so he could stand.

The phone's flashlight app wasn't a strong light, but it was enough for him to prowl around the perimeter, noting more cobwebs than anything useful. Several empty barrels stood up against one wall in a line, probably used for storage at one time. An old refrigerator with a missing door sat near a pile of discarded tools, a bolt cutter and a rusted fence pole driver on top.

At the far end of the space, a rotting wooden staircase led to a door at the top. Fantastic. That would be their exit strategy after another couple of hours had passed, long enough for Sophia to recover and for him to feel confident they could run for it without picking up their tail again.

If they could make it up the stairs without the whole thing collapsing. He should test it first. After all, this shed clearly hadn't been used in a long time.

Cautiously, he crept up the stairs, placing his feet in the exact center of each board, expecting his foot to go through one at any second. He didn't touch the railing. The entire structure listed to the side and he thought it likely he'd end up in a heap of broken boards before reaching the top.

But he made it.

Which ended up not mattering in the slightest. The door was locked from the other side. He rattled the doorknob for good measure, noting the hinges were also on the other side. Of course. What fun would it be to have some mechanism available to resolve the situation?

As quickly as he could, he reversed his steps and crossed to Sophia to check on her since it had taken far longer to climb the rickety stairs than he would have liked.

"Doing okay?"

She nodded, barely discernible in the dark, which was good—it made her less of a target. "I'm just mad. Why does someone hate me?"

"I wish I knew." Crouching down, he relieved her of the

knife and closed it with a snap so he could use his hands to assess her. "Can you hold your phone with your other hand for a minute so I can check out your arm?"

"You're a trained medic, too?" she commented wryly, less a question than a statement of her disbelief.

But she held the phone as requested, so he got busy feeling along her clavicle, ignoring her implications since he wasn't sure he was at liberty to say that he had training in a lot of areas courtesy of Uncle Sam.

They didn't send fresh-faced recruits to do certain types of jobs. And an operative who knew a lot about the human body could do a great deal of damage to one.

"Does this hurt?" he asked and pressed on several spots.

"Yeah, but not more than it did a few minutes ago."

"Probably not fractured, then." He sat back on his heels. "Which is shocking, considering how far we fell. If it's bothering you, I can fashion a sling. It'll keep it stationary, which will help with the healing."

"I guess that would be wise."

An old button-up shirt he'd spied a minute ago split apart easily at the seams and in a flash, he had her arm tied up with the knot behind her neck. "It's not much and I'm sorry to say we're trapped for the time being."

He could practically feel her anxiety level ratchet up. "Trapped? As in no way to get out? How did my grandfather get all this stuff down here, then?"

"There's a staircase but the door at the top is locked. I might be able to bust it down, but it could be risky. I'll try in a little while."

After their tail gave up and left. He had no confidence that the roof collapse had escaped the shooter's notice, but if by some miracle it had, he did not want to take a chance on alerting the guy to their location via a second crash. Though whether the door or the staircase would be the cause remained to be seen. There was a better-than-average chance the staircase would give before the door.

"Ace? Thank you."

His mouth turned up automatically. "For getting you trapped in here? Sure thing. It was literally no problem. I didn't even have to try."

"I'm being serious. Everything hurts. I'm scared. It'll probably get cold in a little while when the sun goes down. But nothing seems as bad when you're here."

That hit him sideways. Then settled down inside him with warmth he didn't have the right to feel. He cleared his throat. "I didn't do anything."

"Sure you did. After all, this is the X on the map. Isn't it?"

Chapter 13

Sophia's little crush on Ace exploded into something a lot harder to deal with around the time he busted a locked cabinet into smithereens with nothing more than a pair of bolt cutters.

She could barely see from her position on the floor due to all the darkness, but it sounded impressive, and his brute strength coupled with the gentle care he'd taken with her arm did lovely, silky things to her insides. She was female enough to swoon a little over a capable man while still maintaining her own independence.

Yes, she could take care of herself. Had for a long time. But it was nice to have someone next to her who could also hold his own. And then some.

"Found a lantern," he called gleefully. "And matches."

She had a sneaking suspicion that he liked taking care of her too. It was lovely to not have to do everything for herself. To have someone to lean on occasionally. Who would have thought she'd find competence so sexy?

A snick and then the lantern glowed to life, burning the oil in its base. The underground shelter took shape in the low light. It was sparse and not as small as she'd imagined from her spot against the wall.

"If my grandfather did use this shelter, he must have forgotten about it in his later years," she said with a wrinkled nose.

"I'm surprised there are no existing residents, honestly," Ace said, rubbing the back of his neck. "I thought for sure I'd have to dispatch a rat or a snake and then lie to you about it."

Uh, yeah, that was one thing she'd happily allow him a pass on. She shuddered. "I don't want to know about either of those, dead or alive."

"Deal," he said simply and sank to the ground near her, which was quickly becoming her favorite place for him.

Sure, it was great that he'd done all the recon of the shelter, letting her sit here in misery with a busted arm, but she wasn't so keen on being by herself. Even when he'd left her his knife, it had been small comfort since she'd have to be the one to use it on someone.

Of course, now she had the vision in her head of it being a some*thing* with long teeth and diseases.

"What time is it?" she asked him since he'd long ago taken possession of her cell phone to use as a flashlight.

"Almost eight o'clock."

It had gotten dark an hour ago, then. Ace had used the flashlight sparingly, telling her he was trying to conserve the battery, but she knew he was also worried about someone figuring out they'd fallen into this shelter and coming in after them. They'd have nowhere to go and while she had absolute confidence Ace could handle himself in a close-quarters fight, he wasn't bulletproof. As far as she knew anyway. And she definitely wasn't.

"Surely whoever shot at us is gone. Right?"

He shrugged and she appreciated the simple pleasure of

being able to see the person she was talking to. Never again would she take above ground for granted. Or cell service. She'd checked for bars like forty-seven times at this point, had even sent Ace to the top of the stairs to see if reception was better there. But no. They couldn't call for help.

"You sure you're all right?" he asked her, his gaze flitting over her with concern.

It seemed she wasn't the only one who liked having the light. "I've been better, and I could use a shower. But I'll make it."

"You should eat something," he suggested and pulled out the last protein bar from her backpack, handing it to her.

"Only if you'll split it with me," she insisted and tore open the wrapper, extending it to him so he could take his half.

She didn't think he would. He hadn't eaten anything thus far, opting to give her all the food since she'd been the one to pack it. Which made a selfless sort of sense, until they'd ended up in a precarious situation, trapped for who knew how long.

"You need to keep up your strength too," she told him, and he finally conceded with a flat glance at her that she couldn't interpret as he ripped off a chunk of the bar.

The last of their food disappeared in less than a minute. They'd been conserving the water too, taking sips only every so often, which felt a little pessimistic. Surely someone would find them before too long, right? The ranch wasn't *that* big. A good bloodhound could find people in minutes, or at least they always did in movies.

"Now that we have a decent light, I'm going to search for a key," he told her and before she could protest, he'd rolled to his feet and begun a methodical search through the remaining cabinets.

"If you don't find one, you could always do the bolt-cutter tango with the door," she suggested.

"That's the plan," he confirmed. "Just not too keen on the execution of it. The stairs are pretty rickety."

As was the ladder he'd found. He'd tried to use it to climb out through the hole in the roof but there was nothing to brace it on, and he'd already nixed her idea of climbing it herself while he held it. Apparently, he didn't care for the possibility of her head being used for the shooter's target practice once she poked it up above ground level, and frankly, he'd convinced her it wasn't the brightest plan, either. Not that she thought it was okay for the reverse scenario where his head would be the vulnerable one, but she did admit that he had a bit more training at handling such a situation.

Regardless, it didn't matter. The ladder wasn't suitable for reaching the roof. Neither of them would get to play the part of the target.

So they were back to the locked-door strategy. Which she wasn't allowed to help with, given the state of her shoulder. Ace had pretty firmly insisted she sit tight and stay out of his way.

But when he didn't find a key, she could feel his frustration level climb.

He dusted off his hands as he dropped to the ground next to her, placing the lantern between their splayed legs. "Looks like I'll be trying to pry the door from the doorframe with the bolt cutter. Say a prayer that the force won't disengage whatever is holding the staircase to the wall."

"You don't have to try it, you know. We can hang out here a while longer. It's not going to kill anyone."

He shot her a look full of thinly concealed amusement. "Except you, you mean? I can tell you're dying to get back to the house so you can send a couple of emails."

"I am," she admitted readily with a smile that almost covered her grimace as she thought about the fun in store for her as she tried to work with a shoulder that had performed a rather impressive feat of slamming into concrete without shattering. "But not at the expense of you ending up in a pile of stair treads. Let it be for a while. Sit here and tell me a story to take my mind off how bad everything hurts."

That got his attention and not in a good way. "Everything hurts? Define *everything*. You swore up and down that your head felt fine."

"I don't have a concussion, Ace. Settle down. It was an expression."

He relaxed only slightly, his frame still vibrating with tension. Probably because she'd given him a challenge, then taken it away from him. Twice. She had a feeling he was still itching to have a crack at the doorframe, and he probably could very easily pry the wood from the wall, but the state of the stairs worried her and if they crumpled under his weight, he'd end up a lot worse for wear. Maybe even bleeding or unconscious. If anything happened to him, she'd never forgive herself for letting him get hurt on her account.

"You'll tell me if you start seeing double or feel any kind of pressure in your head, yes?"

She threw up three fingers and rolled her eyes. "You were a Scout, right?"

"Lucky guess," he told her, his mouth lifting up at the corners in a half smile.

"Please. No luck required. You have Boy Scout tattooed across your forehead. Tell me something about you I don't know."

The silence that fell weighed more than the dark. What? He didn't want to get personal? The whole point of her heading in this direction was to get his mind off trying to rescue her when really, she wanted to know more about the man behind the knife. Maybe she could ease him into it.

"Never mind," she said hastily as the silence started to sting a little. "I'll go first. Let's see. Once, when I was in college, I went on a date with Orien Bright."

His brow quirked up. "The rock star?"

"I was young and he hadn't made it big, yet. But yes. It was horrible." Plus, he hadn't adopted his stage name at that point, so to her, he'd always be Salvador Gonzales, the guy who lived next door to her best friend in a low-rent apartment on the wrong side of town.

"I wouldn't have pegged you for a rock star groupie."

"Trust me, it wasn't what you're thinking. We ate fast food and his car broke down on the way home. He was a hard-luck kid until he wasn't. I'm still not sure how he managed to get his career off the ground, let alone to go to become so famous."

"So that's the kind of guy college Sophia went for, huh? Flashy musicians."

He was teasing her. She didn't hate it. "He wore me down. Every time I saw him for a month, he was all, when are you letting me take you to dinner, SoLa? That was probably what did it. He was the only person in my life who had ever bothered to give me a nickname and it was kind of sweet."

Man, she hadn't thought about Salvador in ages, not since the first time she'd seen him on TV and realized it was him. The contrast between that skinny guy, the few other people she'd dated in college and the uber suits who would become her type once she started climbing the corporate ladder was stark.

Neither interested her now. No man had in a long time. Except this one.

"I confess, I'm not sure what you expected me to take from that story," Ace mused. "But I am intrigued at the idea of you being a rock star's girlfriend once upon a time."

She elbowed his arm without a lot of strength behind it, stunned at how much energy the scant movement had sapped. "We're getting to know each other. You obviously didn't want to go first, so…here we are. And he wasn't a rock star at the time. If he had been, I doubt he would have looked twice at me."

"Then he'd be missing out."

The admission hung there between them, and she caught his gaze, half-convinced he'd reel it back. But the vibe between them grew a few teeth and she wished she had a mirror for like five to ten seconds to at least make sure she didn't have a black eye or something from that fall.

"What?" she murmured as the moment stretched out and he still didn't look away. "Do I have something on my face?"

"A smudge of dirt. Near your eye." But as she lifted her hand to the presumed spot in question, he beat her to it, brushing his thumb across her cheek. "Let me."

Oh, she had zero problems with letting him do pretty

much anything he had a mind to. "Adult me is a lot different than college me. Especially this version. Ranch Sophia."

"What were you like before you were Ranch Sophia?"

Given that her cheek still tingled from his touch, she wasn't so sure she still had two brain cells to rub together, let alone enough to answer the question honestly. "I was Ad Exec Sophia, and you would have hated her."

His expression said he found that hard to believe. "I doubt you were too much different than you are now. Driven and competent with a side of wry humor. Right?"

"You make it sound like a compliment," she said with a laugh. "You're being too kind. It's okay if you call me out. It's more like stressed out and liable to make a bad joke to ease the tension and failing at all of the above."

"Don't diminish your accomplishments, Sophia," he told her quietly and there was something about the way he said her name that made her realize it was a deliberate choice to not come up with a cute nickname in that moment.

Because he wanted to differentiate himself from Salvador. As if he needed to. There was literally no contest in her mind between Ace Madden and every other man on the planet, even the ones she hadn't met yet.

The trick wasn't figuring out why she was so struck by him. It was trying to understand why they had such a strong dynamic that he didn't seem eager to explore. The boss-employee thing still stood between them, sure, but it felt like something they could work out, if they chose to.

"I'm not trying to be humble," she murmured, mesmerized by the way the lantern light played over his face. "That's how I operate. High achievers often see what they haven't done as opposed to what they have done. There's always something else to accomplish."

"The infamous to-do list."

She nodded, not so pleased all at once to be reminded of it. "It never gets shorter, only longer. And don't think for a minute that I'm not totally aware you're homing in on me to avoid your own true confession. It's your turn. Spill."

"What? You still want to hear something about me that you don't know? The list is vast. You'll have to be more specific."

It was like a wall came up between them the moment she shifted the focus back to him. Infuriating. What was the big deal? "It's a game, not rocket science. Pick anything. Your favorite color. The reason you went into the military. Why you sign your name with the little flourish at the end."

He eyed her. "How do you know I sign my name with a little flourish?"

A guilty flush crept through her cheeks, and she prayed the lantern light was dim enough to hide it. "I pulled your employment paperwork. I wasn't about to embark on a treasure hunt with someone I knew nothing about."

The reminder put a huge damper on the conversation. Also, she could have gone all night without mentioning she'd checked up on him. Great way to lighten the mood.

But he just nodded. "That was smart. That's what you should have done. You don't know me from Adam and it's only reasonable to take precautions."

Blinking, she stared at him. Somehow, confessing that she'd done her homework on him seemed to have raised her up in his estimation. "That's the whole point of this conversation. So I can get to know you. But maybe I already know everything I need to."

He glanced at her. "I doubt that."

"You're naturally authoritative without being overbearing. You're calm under pressure. Smart, but not like you could go three rounds on *Jeopardy* smart. Something totally beyond that, like you know how everything works and use that to solve every single problem you run across." She ticked the points off on her fingers, saving the most important for last. "I know you'd take a bullet for me. Every bit of that adds up to a guy who intrigues me."

Ace shut his eyes for a moment, squeezing them tight. "You shouldn't say things like that."

"Why not? It may have escaped your notice, so I'll spell it out for you. My father abandoned me when I was a teenager. I have a lot of issues with men who brush off responsibility. You're the opposite of that. Why is it so shocking that I would be attracted to you?"

Well, she couldn't have laid that on the line any more clearly. Obviously, the pain in her shoulder had caused her a bout of delirium or she'd never have been so forthright.

The admission saturated the atmosphere, sucking all the air from her lungs as she waited to see what he'd do with it.

"You want to hear something you don't know?" His voice scraped across her skin, unleashing a shiver, but she nodded. "I'm having a very hard time keeping my hands off you and you're not making it any easier."

"Good thing I don't want you to keep your hands off me," she murmured. "But I do disagree with you on one point. I can make it a lot easier."

She crawled into the space between them and kissed him.

Chapter 14

Ace had never been kissed before.

Sure, he'd participated in kisses. But he'd always been the one to initiate them. A hazard of being the tallest guy in the room. It wasn't often that a woman found herself in a position where she could lay one on him without a precursor.

Clearly, he'd deprived himself of something great by not orchestrating a scenario where a woman could take charge, because he became a huge fan as Sophia's mouth claimed his.

And that was the extent of his brain's ability to string a thought together. The kiss unfolded as she moved closer, still on her knees, still slightly above him and it didn't take much for her to set his skin on fire.

Man, was she a hot kisser. Sophia took no prisoners, and he frankly couldn't think of a better time to surrender to a woman. As if she'd sensed his hesitation fading, she shoved fingers through his hair, splaying them along his neck, urging him forward.

No more invitation needed than that. Ace touched her in kind, running the backs of his hands along her cheekbone, lifting her chin to slant his lips along hers at a deeper angle.

She tasted like sunshine and crisp fall days, and everything forbidden that he shouldn't want and couldn't stop himself from craving. Blood roaring through his veins, he lost himself in the sensations, funneling as much into this experience as he could before his conscience got wind of this.

And then it all crashed over him. *What* was he *doing*? This was not okay.

Wrenching himself free, he scuttled backward faster than a crab at high tide. "I'm sorry."

"I'm not." She tracked him with her gaze, disappointment filling her expression. "Don't you dare say you weren't into that kiss because I'll call you a liar."

Well, she should do that regardless. That would be the least of the nasty names she would be well within her rights to lob in his direction. But he wouldn't lie to her about this. "I wanted to kiss you or I wouldn't have."

"Buuuut...?" Her eyebrows winged up in invitation for him to finish the statement.

"You're tired, Sophia. Hurt. Scared. *Trapped*, most importantly. There are a lot of things swimming through your head right now that are impeding your judgment. I would rather shoot myself than take advantage of this situation."

"So this is you being noble. Noted."

The coolness in her tone said she didn't quite believe the things coming out of his mouth, which rankled since every word was 100 percent true. It just wasn't the whole truth. "I know you think you're making an informed decision about how you want things to go between us, but trust me, this is not the time to be jumping into something we can't take back."

"Wow, I really freaked you out, didn't I?" The wonder creeping over her face didn't help matters.

What was he supposed to do, contradict her? Tell her he wasn't so easy to spook, it was just that he drew a hard line at romancing a woman under false pretenses?

He tried again. "Sophia, I work for you. I'm trying to help you find a treasure your father may have buried on this ranch in some obscure location while keeping an unknown number of bad guys with nebulous agendas from killing you. The last thing you can afford is for me to be distracted. And that was already a pretty big issue before you kissed me."

Good God, could he sound like any more of a prissy coward? He could handle his job and Sophia too. If he was in any position to take control of this situation and put his hands on her the way he wanted to, she wouldn't be disappointed for very long.

But he couldn't.

Worse, his speech seemed to be sinking in. She nodded, a gleam in her eyes making him incredibly nervous.

"I get it. The timing is off. So we table it for now. But once we're out of this hole and back at the house, all bets are off," she said silkily.

Well. Not exactly what he'd been going for, but it was a far sight better than flat out rejecting her, which would only hurt her feelings and would probably sound a whole lot unconvincing anyway.

What had his life come to that he had to desperately grab onto the reprieve? "Yeah, that's so far in the future at this point that I'm pretty sure you're only going to want a hot shower and a bed by then."

"Ha, I want that now, but I definitely like the way you think. It's a date."

He stifled a groan and opted not to correct her deliberate misinterpretation of how many people would be in the shower and bed. Especially since that was all he could think about now that the idea was out there.

There was no scenario where he would even kiss her again before telling her the truth, let alone sleep with her. And if he told her the truth, he forfeited his fee. While she might be worth it to him, he had a payroll. Two other people's names sat next to his on the paperwork for his security company. Stephanie still had medical bills. The list of reasons he would not be getting naked with Sophia at any point in the future was long.

"How is your arm?" he asked gruffly, desperate to get out of his own head.

Sophia blinked at him. "As good as it can be under the circumstances, I guess."

At least she was apparently open to a subject change, a minor miracle. "That's good. Can we focus on the map for a minute or two? I'm still not sure why this place featured so prominently. Maybe whatever is hidden here is upstairs, but my money says it's down here."

Nodding, she got into the spirit, shifting slightly to pull her backpack into her lap with her left hand, and he didn't miss her wince. Yeah, she wasn't in any shape for activities of the intimate variety, which made it all the more important that he'd shut it down. As difficult as it had been.

She didn't have to know it was only one of many reasons.

Sophia spread the map on the ground near the lantern, her finger on the X. They'd been running through the woods with a shooter behind them. It was possible they might not be in the right spot and another building existed somewhere near here. But he didn't think so. There was no reason for a ranch owner to need two sheds of this variety. This one barely felt used in the first place.

Of course, that might have been by design. If David Lang had in fact hidden something here—or near here, since he didn't for a second believe anyone in their right mind would bury a treasure and then pour concrete on top of it—his father may have stopped using the shed for fear someone would discover the treasure.

That would mean they'd been in it together and he wasn't so sure that was a factor. More likely, the son had hidden the treasure and his father had found out about it after the fact.

Which didn't explain why the map had been squirreled away in a safety deposit box.

"You want to share what's going on in that head of yours?" Sophia suggested, resettling more comfortably on the floor. It might have been easier for her, but she'd leaned up against his shoulder and the contact sang through his entire body.

He'd love it if he had the latitude to sling an arm around her, letting her snuggle in. Her shoulder might feel better if she could take some weight off.

But he didn't move. Story of his life.

"I was just trying to piece together whether your grandfather knew your father had hidden something here and that's why the map was at the bank and not in his personal papers at home, or if he hadn't known about the map at all. The key was in an envelope, but you could tell that's what it was. Surely your grandfather knew about the safety deposit box. He had to have been paying for it or your grandma's friend wouldn't have readily known he had one."

Sophia shrugged. "He could have been paying for it

without knowing what was in it. Keep in mind, my dad wasn't super communicative. It wouldn't shock me to find out my dad had the only key and dropped it into my grandpa's files without telling him. You'd have to have a reason to search for it, like we did, to know it was there in the first place. I don't have a lot of answers for you. Sorry."

Unfortunately, he didn't have the luxury of letting any of this go. The sooner they put their time in this shelter to good use, the better. As much as he enjoyed spending this time with Sophia, playing get-to-know-you games and wishing he could start that kiss all over again weren't getting the job done.

And he still firmly believed the best way to protect Sophia was to find whatever the people after her were looking for. There was no way it was a coincidence that they'd found the key to the safety deposit box in the desk where Intruder Man had originally been searching.

"I'm going to look around some more," he told her and carefully eased out from under her lean, wishing he could find a pillow or something for her to use to lie down for a while.

For his second surveillance trip around the room, he snagged the lantern. The first time, he'd been forced to use Sophia's phone, which he left with her instead. The lantern cast a different, warmer glow and had a handle on top, allowing him to hold it up in the shadowy corners.

That was his only excuse for why he now saw the light switch that he'd previously missed.

Rolling his eyes at himself, he tried the switch. A purple light flicked on overhead. Instantly, the white part of his shirt began to glow.

"It's a black light," he called to Sophia.

What a weird thing to install in an underground shelter. Other naturally phosphorescent material glowed blue and green in the surrounding area, and he wished he knew more about what the colors meant, but his experience with black lights started and ended with using one to detect biological and chemical agents that signaled explosives.

"Ace," Sophia breathed. "Come look at this."

"What is it?"

"The map. It's glowing."

Hustling back over to her, he peered over her shoulder. "I don't see anything."

She shot him a look. "That's because you brought the lantern, dummy. Put it over there behind the stairs or something. Haven't you ever been to a blackout party?"

"This is my first one," he said wryly and did as she'd suggested. As soon as the light was hidden, another X with a circle around it appeared on the map in green ink.

But it wasn't here, it was another spot far from here. Of course.

"Guess we just figured out what's special about this shed," he said.

"This is where the treasure is buried," she said, excitement infusing her voice, the dirt across her forehead speckled with neon blue. "I know it. Look, here's the back fence, the one that borders Silver Acres Ranch. We have to dig here."

"As soon as I magic us a way out of this hole, you mean," he commented mildly. "You don't really think it's going to be that easy, do you?"

"Why not? We knew this map was something of note. Why else put it in the safety deposit box?"

Because nothing in life worked out like that. Nothing

was what it seemed, not even him. "Anyone could stumble over this shed. While it's out here a good ways, it's not invisible. No map needed."

"You'd have to know this shelter existed under the original shed to even use the black light to get the next clue," she argued in what was an excellent point. "The door to the underground part is locked. My grandfather probably has the key to the door on his key ring back at the house, but I would have never thought to bring it. There are a million keys on that ring."

But why go to all that trouble? Why have a map at all? Couldn't Sophia's father remember where he buried the treasure? All of the unanswered questions sat heavily with him, and he had to concede that his primary issue with this whole setup was that it felt like one. As if someone had deliberately planted these clues for them to find.

He might be leading Sophia into a slaughter if they followed this map. It had certainly been true when they pursued the trail the first time, landing them in their current predicament.

"We need to be careful," he said. "Do this next bit a little smarter than this round."

"Well, yes," she said with a twist of her lips. "I would prefer not to get trapped in a secret shelter next time."

That was the least of his concerns at the moment. Possibly they were safer down here than on the surface.

"What's the worst thing that can happen?" she continued, clearly excited about the possibilities. "We dig and find nothing. Or we dig and find something."

Sure, while making themselves stationary targets. But this was the whole reason he'd embarked on this mission, to find the treasure. He couldn't ignore the signs pointing to this being the ticket. It just felt off for reasons he couldn't put his finger on.

"Okay," he conceded. "It would be silly to have gone through all of this and then not follow through to the next set of coordinates."

Ace would have to figure out how to get a lot better at his job. His shoddy performance thus far left a lot to be desired, after all.

And that was the real reason he'd had to break off that kiss. What business did he have getting involved with a woman when the only thing he was really good at was sending terrorists off to meet their maker? None. When she found out what he was really like, under the surface where it really mattered, she'd feel a lot differently about that list of Ace's qualities.

Being calm under pressure was how you got good at killing people.

Chapter 15

A ranch dog's muzzle appeared over the edge of the hole in the roof shortly after dawn. Sophia glanced up at the scrabbling sound, never so happy in her whole life to see Jonas's face follow it.

"We're down here," she called, her voice shockingly weak.

It shouldn't have come as such a surprise given that she'd slept maybe two hours, and it felt like a demon slave driver stood behind her shoving hot pokers into her shoulder. Ace had suggested that she could sleep curled up in his arms, using his chest as her pillow, and in her delirium, she'd almost said yes.

But the first time she did that, she wanted it to be under different circumstances—because they were both enjoying being close to each other, not for survival purposes.

It would happen, she had no doubt. But first, she had to admit that Ace's point about a shower and a real bed did hold a lot of appeal, whether he planned to join her or not.

The hinges on the door were remarkably easy to remove from the other side and once their liberators pulled it off the frame, Ace carefully helped Sophia up the stairs. She hated that she needed his strength as much as she loved that he willingly gave it to her, his arm snug around her waist like he'd done it a million times and knew exactly where his hand fit.

Back above ground, it became clear that their disappearance had sparked quite the search effort. A group of cowboys stood off to the left, hands shoved in their pockets and faces eagerly turned toward the action.

The really interesting part was why anyone had thought to look for them. As many people as had seen Ace in Sophia's company, both in the house and out, it wouldn't have surprised her to learn everyone thought he'd whisked her away on a romantic overnight trip somewhere that wasn't here.

Frankly, that sounded fantastic. And completely ridiculous, given the amount of work she had to do to make up for nearly two days of treasure hunting and accomplishing zero ranch-owning tasks. She shouldn't be so thrilled at the idea of the staff gossiping about her and Ace, either.

"Thank you for rescuing us, Jonas," Sophia told him and got a head tip for her trouble.

In Jonas's world, it was practically a whole speech about how grateful he was to find her alive and mostly well.

Ace hustled her to the golf cart that someone had driven out to the shed and insisted she sit in the front, while he drove back to the house. The sun had just started peeking above the horizon, its orange glow lighting up the eastern sky.

"I'll have Jonas get a few of the guys to fix the hole in the roof of the shelter and reset that door," he said, and all she could do was slump in relief that he was taking charge. "Later today, I'll call someone to have a security system installed, the same as the one at the house. Without the map, the shed is useless to anyone looking for the treasure, but they don't know that."

She nodded, annoyed she hadn't thought of that herself. But that was the point of this partnership. She had to let him fill some of the gaps, especially when she didn't know what they were. Even if it sat funny to think of it like that. "If I haven't said this lately, I appreciate you."

He ducked his head, and it was adorable how tough it seemed for him to take her praise.

"Just doing my job."

Since they'd already been over that, she didn't remind him that his job description looked nothing like what he'd actually done over the last few days. She made a mental note to give him a raise. And maybe a promotion. Good grief, she should just flat out hire him to be her full-time bodyguard.

What rabbit hole had she fallen down that she needed one?

If she thought for a minute that she might be overreacting, she just called up the sound of a bullet exploding against the tree above her head, and that sent the notion right back into oblivion.

At the house, she let Ace satisfy himself that no one lurked in any of the shadowy corners, including the attic, and then watched him go back to the cowboys' quarters with reluctance. The alternative was to insist that she wasn't kidding about sharing that shower. Frankly, she didn't have the energy to deal with a hot cowboy anywhere near her bedroom, let alone a wet, unclothed one.

Plus, she'd have to admit that she didn't want to be alone and that felt like a precarious confession. Her emotions were all over the place and dang him for zeroing in on that, then doing the honorable thing by stepping away. She should take a lesson.

The shower went a long way toward making her feel human again, but nothing could be done about the dark area on her cheek. A gallon of concealer just made her look like she had a fake tan, so she wiped it all off and chalked it up to an easily explained war wound that no one would dare ask her about anyway.

Carefully, she tugged on a dress, wincing when she forgot for a second that she couldn't raise her arm above her head. Dressing herself took more effort than it should, and she had to catch her breath for a minute before getting started on her day. In that moment, she chose to keep the sling, despite being sure she'd ditch it today.

Panic started crowding into her head as all the undone things vied for attention. If she couldn't even get dressed without a break, how would she get through the rest of the day? How would she type? Not to mention the critical, exhausting task of tromping back into the woods at some indeterminate time to dig at the spot of the second X. Which would happen today regardless.

When she emerged from her room, Ace stood in the hallway. Waiting for her. Clearly.

Stetson back in place, he was leaned up against the wall, arms crossed, in a pose that she suspected had been totally natural for him to strike but made him look like the poster boy for a perfume commercial. Masculinity dripped from him, spilling into the hall, washing over her as his mouth tipped up in a smile that she felt to her toes.

Good Lord, the man was gorgeous.

Then his smile faded, and he unfolded from the wall, his attention on her face.

And suddenly, the hallway got a whole lot smaller as he reached out and brushed her cheek with his fingertips. "This is not okay."

"It's just a bruise. I'm fine."

Why did she sound so breathless? She'd just spent the night with the man. Granted, not in quite the fashion she'd fantasized about. But it still counted and should have gotten her *more* comfortable with him, not less.

It was him. He was too close. And not close enough. There was way too much space between them and her abused body that desperately wanted his warmth. Stupid. She could have indulged herself in that all night long if she'd accepted his offer to share his body heat.

Thank goodness she hadn't. Things needed to get back to business, pronto.

His stormy eyes met hers. "Your cheek looks a lot worse now that the sun is up."

"Thanks," she said wryly. "You do know how to turn a girl's head."

"Don't be ridiculous, Sophia. A bruise doesn't detract from the fact that you're the most beautiful woman I've ever met." He flicked his thumb down to her chin and lifted, his assessing gaze sweeping down her cheeks, its utilitarian nature not diminishing its power in the slightest. "I'm taking you to the doctor. Please don't argue."

"How did you know I was going to argue?" she countered, shocked her voice worked at all on the heels of learning Ace could sweep her off her feet with a few simple words.

That ghost of a smile flitted across his face again. "Because you have your phone in your hand and you were a millisecond away from opening your email. I know you have a lot to do, but this is nonnegotiable. We need to make sure you don't have a fractured cheekbone."

We. *We* need to make sure. He was aligning himself with her, making them into a unit, even post-shelter, when it didn't matter as much. What was she supposed to take from all of this? He was the one who had put the much-needed distance between them. She needed to keep it there.

"For your information, I checked my email before I got in the shower," she told him. "And I already sent two. Plus, I ordered wallpaper samples from a new place I found, and I scheduled an electrician to give me a quote on adding a generator. I can work and go to the doctor at the same time."

"Great, then it's a date," he said so mildly that she didn't for a second mistake it for a flirty comment. "Get your purse. I'll drive your car. It's more comfortable than my truck."

Walked into that one. "What if I don't want to go to the doctor?"

"Then we're going to find out how you'll take to being thrown over my shoulder and carted outside to be deposited in the passenger seat."

They stared at each other, and she gave in first. Though she absolutely wanted to find out if he would do it but had no desire to give that kind of show to the staff. "I'll go. But when he says I'm fine, you're going to owe me a whole day of being my lackey."

He lifted his brows. "I'm your lackey all day, every day."

"If I thought for a second that I was in charge, you'd strip me of that deluded idea immediately. Most likely with a scene exactly like this one."

"Whatever gets you in the car," he said and steered her toward the garage with a hand at the small of her back.

Why did this feel so comfortable? As if they'd done this dance a hundred times, even the part where they pushed each other to see what would happen. Was this what being married was like? For normal people anyway. She'd never seen a functional marriage up close and personal.

Maybe this was how other people did it. If so, she secretly liked the idea, especially if it meant being able to slide into a bed at the end of the day with Ace in it.

Good grief, what was wrong with her? Thinking about marriage to a man she'd literally just met and had kissed once. Even that had ended prematurely. As it should have.

She glanced at Ace in the driver's seat as he took off toward Gun Barrel City. Maybe when all of this was over, she could figure out a way to make it work. Ask him on a proper date. That would be lovely. She couldn't remember the last time she'd had a date with a guy she liked as much as this one. Actually, she couldn't remember the last time she'd had a date period. The shocking part was that she was considering breaking that streak instead of burying herself in work like she normally did.

Winding up on the business end of a gun did make a girl think. Reprioritize. What's the worst thing that could happen if she took a night off to do something for herself?

"Don't forget to tell the doctor to look at your arm too," Ace reminded her as they left the ranch property and turned right onto the road to town. He glanced at her. "What?"

"I never pegged you as a hoverer. It's sweet."

"It's not hovering. I need you functional ASAP so I can

feel better about forcing you to tromp through the woods later tonight."

Her stupid, traitorous insides danced the Macarena at the thought of spending another night in Ace's company, especially under the cover of dark. When ranch employees would be asleep and not paying attention to either of them. "Is that when we're going treasure hunting? Later tonight?"

He shrugged. "If you're available, yeah. Doing it during the daytime when we're a much bigger target feels like a risk after what happened last time. I don't like doing anything at night where it's more difficult to see a threat, but the reverse is also true."

"Makes it harder for the bad guys to see us too," she concluded. "That makes sense. The doctor is going to give me a thumbs-up. I feel fine."

That was almost true. After her shower, she did more closely resemble a human. The fact that she'd had to rest and questioned her ability to participate in future treasure hunting endeavors notwithstanding. He didn't have to know that.

"You got in the car," he said. "Obviously you recognize the wisdom in making sure."

More like she'd appreciated the excuse to spend a bit more time with him. He didn't have to know that, either.

Ace pulled into the lot of a small clinic near the bank. The waiting room was almost empty, save one tired-looking young mother with an active toddler who squirmed out of her grip four times before she gave up and let him roll around on the floor. After a few minutes, the nurse called the mom and kid to the back, then returned to call Sophia's name.

"You're not going to come with me and speak to the

doctor?" she asked Ace when he didn't stand up. Honestly, she'd expected him to.

"I do have faith in your ability to handle yourself," he countered mildly. "I'm just here to make sure you think so too."

She thought about that all the way to the examination room, where the nurse took her temperature and asked Sophia to step on the scale in the room. Which was where she learned she'd lost some weight since her last trip to the gynecologist. Maybe she'd skipped a few more meals than she'd realized in the midst of all the ranch renovations.

And perhaps Ace might want to retract his statement about her ability to handle everything. What was happening to her independence?

The doctor did an initial exam and asked her some questions about her pain level, then sent her down the hall to the radiology department where the technician scanned both her shoulder and cheek.

Forty-five minutes later, she waltzed back into the waiting room. Ace glanced up from his magazine, immediately tossing it aside in favor of sweeping her with his gaze. Even that little bit of eye contact put flutters in her belly. She was in so much trouble.

"No fractures," she told him and lifted her hands. "Now what are you going to obsess over?"

His quick grin warmed her considerably. "I'm sure you'll present me with something soon enough."

Once they were back in the car, she let the miles stretch out before she asked him, "Just out of curiosity, what were you waiting on me for? Earlier, outside my room. Because I know it wasn't to spirit me away to town."

"Strategy," he responded shortly, tapping his thumb on

the wheel. "As in we needed one, but I made an executive decision the second I saw your face. We'll dig at the second X after dark and make as little of a production out of it as we can."

She sank down in her seat a bit. "I'm a lot tougher than you seem to want to give me credit for."

"That's not the issue. I don't like the way it makes me feel to see you hurt."

The admission put a hum in her chest. "How does it make you feel?"

She shouldn't push the envelope like that, but she really wanted to hear the answer. Except the silence stretched in the car to the point of snapping. Obviously, he didn't want to explain. Because it made him feel things he didn't want to acknowledge? Things he'd already pushed aside due to bad timing?

But when he glanced at her, the storm clouds in his gaze had a lot more emotion in them than she would have expected.

"It makes me feel like breaking the person responsible in half. With my bare hands," he finally said. "I don't like it when violence is my first response."

Before she could figure out how to formulate a reply to that, he pulled onto ranch property. Across the field, she could see a red Mazda parked in the circular drive near the front porch.

Ace glanced at her. "Expecting company?"

"Not even a little bit." The car didn't seem familiar and had that generic look of a rental. "Maybe it's the decorator?"

"Stay in the car," he commanded her and threw it in Park, exiting so fast she didn't have a chance to argue.

She could have saved him the trouble as she spied the familiar dark-haired woman perched on the glider. Spilling from the car, she skirted Ace before he could pounce on Charli.

"Down, boy," she called back over her shoulder. "It's just my sister."

Chapter 16

Sophia threw her arms around Charli. And winced as pain knifed through her, praying Ace hadn't noticed. Stupid sling was supposed to prevent her from doing something dumb.

"What are you doing here?"

Her sister returned the hug enthusiastically, hitting the exact right spot on Sophia's shoulder to light her up. "I came to get in on all the fun."

Fun. Yeah, her sister's timing could be better. How in the world was Sophia going to manage treasure hunting with her sister visiting? "There's nothing but a lot of work at the moment. Maybe come back in a month when I'm closer to opening?"

Charli laughed, smoothing back her long, dark hair that never seemed to be scraggly the way Sophia's was, which was at least half the reason for the perpetual bun. "I'm really not expecting to be entertained. Maybe you could give me some of that work?"

A million things warred in Sophia's chest as she stared at her sister. The same one who had staunchly refused to participate in anything ranch related. The same one who was supposedly waiting around for the ranch to fail so she could collect her share of the profits when—if—Sophia was eventually forced to sell.

What had brought on Charli's change of heart?

"You want to help?" Sophia asked cautiously, in case none of this was what it sounded like. "You want to help. At the ranch. Where we are right now. This place."

Charli smirked. "Yes, the ranch. I…seem to be at a cross-roads and figured you were the one person who might get that."

Boy, did she. Her heart softened. There was never a scenario where she'd have denied her sister a place to stay, a job, support, whatever she needed. But there was more to this story that needed to be spelled out before Sophia would blindly dump her sister in the middle of everything going on here at the ranch.

Charli's gaze slid past Sophia to the man standing behind her, interest clearly piqued. "You must be the hot cowboy I've heard so much about."

"Shut it, Charlotte," Sophia muttered, her skin going red hot with embarrassment.

Ace, who had most certainly heard every word of the exchange, stepped up onto the porch, hand extended. "Ace Madden. Definitely a cowboy, but I'm not touching the rest with a ten-foot pole."

"Charlotte Lang, but everyone calls me Charli on account of Charlotte being a horrible name, plus it's the same one as the spider in the book about the pig and the web." She eyed him curiously. "Got any friends?"

"He's my employee," Sophia cut in fiercely. "He has coworkers."

"He could have friends who are not employed here," Charli insisted.

Thankfully, Ace just seemed marginally amused by the whole scenario, tipping his hat to Charli. "I have both coworkers and friends, and if I think of any who would likewise appreciate being labeled a hot cowboy, I will surely bring them by for an introduction."

With that cryptic comment, he vanished back to his real world, likely to seek out Jonas for an assignment. She missed him already. Inexplicably.

Charli's curious gaze had no place else to land except on Sophia. Which made her squirm for some reason. She was the older sister by three years. There was no reason she should feel both mortified and slightly guilty to have been caught in Ace's company.

"What?" she muttered. "He took me to the doctor."

"He took you to the doctor?" Charli repeated at a much higher decibel than necessary. "That is the coziest thing I've ever heard. When did it progress to the point where you're running errands together? I approve, by the way. He's everything you didn't tell me and more. And the way he charged up here, guns blazing, before you set him straight that I'm not a threat. Whoo, honey. Sizzling."

"You see this thing on my face?" She stabbed in the general direction of her cheek. "It's a bruise. I fell on a concrete slab yesterday. He drove me to the doctor strictly because he feels partially responsible."

Charli's face transformed into a scowl instantly as her body tensed to fly off the porch in the direction of the temporary barn. "How did he help your face meet a concrete slab? I swear to God if he touched you, he's going to regret the day he was—"

"Whoa, Char." Sophia threw up her hands as if that alone could temper the Valkyrie her sister had just become. "I love that you're ready to so fiercely defend me, but that's not what I meant. There are things going on around here that I need to talk to you about. Especially if you're staying for a few days. Come inside."

Once she'd gotten Charli off the porch and out of earshot of whoever might be strolling by, she led her sister to the kitchen, where she made them both a cup of tea. Sliding into a chair at the breakfast nook, the fatigue that she'd been fighting finally took over.

"Man, I needed this tea." Sophia moaned and shut her eyes for a blink, relaxing for the first time in forever. "How is it already noon?"

And more to the point, how would she make it until tonight without a nap? She wanted to be on point for the next round of treasure hunting. To be an equal partner to Ace.

Charli pulled out her own chair, whumped into it and picked up the second mug. "Start talking. Because I'm probably staying a little more than a few days."

Well, they'd see about that.

Sophia opened her eyes. "Then you should know that I got this bruise running from someone who was shooting at me. Ace was trying to protect me and pulled me around the side of an old building, I guess to use as a cover, and the ground gave way, dumping us into a secret underground shelter. With a concrete floor."

She threw up a hand near the bruise on her face, Vanna White style. Charli got the point, apparently, her brows drawing together.

"What in the world? Who was shooting at you?"

"Million-dollar question." Sophia filled her in on the rest—the treasure hunt, Intruder Man, the barn collapsing. Good gravy, saying it out loud made it sound much worse than it had in her head. "So you might want to think twice about sticking around."

"Are you kidding? You need me now more than ever." Charli sipped her tea and leaned back in her chair as if she'd landed exactly where she meant to be, despite never being the type to ride to Sophia's rescue in the past. "I had no clue any of this was going on. You should have told me."

Sophia had never been the type to tell her sister everything. So it was a little precious of Charli to act like they were buddies. Honestly, she was still a little miffed at both of her sisters for not wanting to go in on the ranch renovations with her. "I've been a little busy."

It felt like she'd been working with Ace on finding the treasure for a month straight, but in reality, it had only been a few days. Look what all had happened in just that short amount of time, though.

Now that she'd spelled out how dangerous it would be to stay, Charli should be making strides toward her rental car and driving away, very fast. Only she wasn't. It was time for a few questions of her own.

"What happened to your job at the…pet store?" It had been a minute since she could recall with absolute clarity what retail establishment her sister was working at this week.

Charli winced. "They wanted me to clean the bird cages and oh, my Lord, can those cockatiels poop like no one's business. I quit that job a few weeks ago. I've been waiting tables at Applebee's since then, but it's not my life's ambition or anything."

Must not comment, Sophia told herself sternly, biting back the multitudes of things she could say in reference to her sister's lackadaisical attitude toward gainful employment. Or worse, a comment about Charli's age, which wasn't nineteen, not that you'd know it to hear her talk.

The woman was almost thirty, for crying out loud. Sophia had gone to college and gained seven years of experience at her first career in that length of time, yet Charli acted like she had all the time in the world to figure out how to be a grown-up.

"So you came here looking for a purpose in life?" Sophia prompted hopefully. "I can give you a job but what I really need is for someone besides me to care about what happens to this ranch. Someone named Lang."

Charli sipped her tea and blinked as if contemplating. "I'm not going to lie. I have a lot of resentment toward dad and being here reminds me of him. He's the reason I can't have nice boys. I'm constantly attracted to losers who will abandon me at the drop of a hat because I have a thing for self-fulfilling prophecies."

"That's easy to fix," Sophia told her. "Stop dating. That's what I did."

But ironically not for the same reason. She'd never worried about someone abandoning her because she made sure to never give someone the chance. Just like she'd done with Ace. That was the root of her waffling with him, after all. As soon as she let herself ignore the fact that she was his boss, the real issue would come out—it didn't matter if he was the sticking sort. She didn't trust him enough to give him a chance to prove it either way.

Huh. It was a day for philosophical revelations apparently.

Oddly, sorting that out in her head gave her the will to concentrate the rest of the day as she tackled her most pressing tasks. Charli sat with her the whole time, dutifully learning the ins and outs of the operation at the ranch. Sophia still wasn't sure why her sister had shown up at the ranch in what amounted to a complete reversal on her initial refusal to set foot at the place. But she'd let herself be cautiously optimistic that this was a turning point.

"What are you calling it?" her sister asked at one point.

"Hidden Creek Ranch," she said and got goose bumps all over again. "I have a whole branding campaign planned around the logo, which will be everywhere, from the towels to the drinking glasses."

"This is going to be a real resort, isn't it?" Charli asked with a touch of wonder in her tone that Sophia tried not to find completely offensive.

"This is what I do," she said mildly. "Or I did when I worked for Teller. Now I'm doing it for me. And you, if you're in."

Charli shrugged. "I'm as in as I guess I can be at this point. I don't have anything else going on."

That was what Sophia would call about as half-hearted of a commitment as her sister could make and still call it a commitment.

"Great," she said without an ounce of irony. She deserved a cookie for it too. "The goal is to create a place that's inviting and luxurious, a place where people can relax and get back to nature."

Nodding, Charli pointed to the list of amenities the resort would offer. "I think I'd like to do something with the horses. Maybe that could be my area."

Biting her lip, Sophia counted to ten before she blurted out that Charli hadn't so much as climbed up into a saddle in almost twenty years. She honestly didn't remember her sister liking the horses that much the scant few times they'd visited as kids.

But things changed. Sophia had hated the ranch back then. She'd spent most of the time her parents forced her to visit wishing they could hurry up and go back home to Dallas. Maybe she could give her sister a break and stop trying to be a second mom.

"Sure," she said. "If that's what you see yourself doing."

And breathe. Don't mention that horses were the one area that didn't need a lick of direction from a Lang. That was Jonas's area, the main reason she'd hired him, so he could manage the livestock and the cowboys while Sophia did everything else. Which apparently would still be her lot.

"I figure we'd do daily trail rides," Sophia continued brightly. "You can think about being the coordinator and maybe lead them?"

"You know," Charli said thoughtfully, wheels turning as she glanced over the multipage document containing Sophia's painstaking plans for the ranch. "It's really curious to me that you didn't revamp the breeding program. That's what Grandpa did. Why turn this place into a resort in the first place? It's so much work."

Unclenching her teeth took more effort than she would have liked. "Because breeding was Grandpa's passion, not mine. And I want this to be something different. Something that's mine. Ours," she amended. "Wiping away what was here before might be cathartic. Don't you want to move on? Erase some of the bad memories?"

"Is that possible?" Charli asked with a sarcastic eye roll that nearly came with its own soundtrack. "Maybe you can forget that Dad was a piece of work and Grandpa was basically an enabler. It's a little tougher for me. I'm not the forgiving sort."

Well, Sophia wasn't, either. She'd carried a lot of resentment toward her father for years. But covering over the remnants of what had been here before would go a long way toward soothing her soul.

But that didn't mean it had happened yet. It was a good reminder. A cautionary tale. She wanted to find the treasure for many reasons, but getting something positive from her father remained the main one. Despite the danger. Despite the very nice bonus of spending time with Ace.

And maybe it would fill some gaps. Her childhood had sucked thanks to her dad, and to Charli's point, it had informed a lot more of her adult decisions than she'd credited. A good dose of anger flooded her heart, emotions she probably needed to feel. To work through, instead of repressing everything behind a facade of business and to-do lists.

"I haven't forgotten anything," Sophia muttered. "Once we find the treasure, then I'll think about everything else. Forgiveness wasn't my goal in all of this."

Charli perked up. "Can I help search for the treasure?"

That was one area she didn't mind playing a little closer to the vest. Since she hadn't mentioned the map yet, she kept that to herself and nodded. "Sure, you can work on the house. Check for secret panels, false floors, a safe behind a painting. That kind of thing. Ace and I are trying out another angle in the woods that we're planning to make some headway on tonight."

"Fantastic." Charli clapped like a little girl being presented with a pony for her birthday. "And I'm a huge fan of letting you do the outside part while I hang out in the place without bugs and snakes."

Yeah, that gelled with her sister's personality. And the second X on the map might only lead to another map or, worse, nothing, because the treasure had already been moved. There was nothing wrong with her sister working back through the house just in case.

It was also safer for Charli inside, where there were no people shooting at her.

Though it was a concern all at once to think of Charli being left alone while Sophia tromped through the woods with Ace. Ugh. Who was going to watch over her sister? Ace already had a full-time job with Sophia.

"Maybe if we find the treasure, we can just live here without turning the place into anything," Charli suggested, her allergy to hard work surfacing once again. "But in the meantime, I guess I'm going to need something else to do besides horses since we won't even have any guests for ages. What if I take over all the decorating?"

Relief spilled through Sophia so fast that she almost went light-headed. "That would be amazing."

Decorating—that was something Charli could do. It was dead in the center of her wheelhouse. And for the rest of the day, Sophia reveled in the fact that Charli had stepped up when she'd needed her.

Chapter 17

"We've got a problem," Ace said as soon as McKay picked up the call. "Grab Pierce and wrap up the research you've been doing. You're both about to become cowboys."

McKay didn't hesitate. "We can be there in four hours. What's the situation?"

That was why Ace had hand-selected Heath McKay and Paxton Pierce to go into the private security business with him. They were solid guys. Better than brothers. The best kind of family who had been through hell and everything else by his side.

"Get here and I'll explain once we're face-to-face."

It would be easier to do it once with both of the guys on his team in person, where they could get the lay of the land themselves. Strategize. Start filling the many gaps that had appeared like rogue bowling balls rolling through all of the pins Ace had set up, knocking his plans into oblivion.

The guys made it to the ranch in three hours.

Ace met them on the road, a mile past the turn-in to the main house, loathe to have a conversation where anyone could overhear them. Both men sat in the cab of an idling pickup truck with visible rust stains and a license plate presumably registered to some untraceable entity.

When Ace approached the driver's side door, McKay rolled the window down with a head tip, his mirrored sunglasses reflecting the light. "You sure this is out of the way enough? Two cars passed us already."

"We're about to add you to the ranch staff anyway. But in the meantime, we can have a conversation without extra ears. Thanks for getting here so fast," Ace said gruffly as a weight lifted off his shoulders instantly.

The three of them had history. There was nothing that could get through the united front of Madden, McKay and Pierce when they stood shoulder to shoulder against the evil of the world. They'd served together in Afghanistan, Iraq and Syria, ridding the world of the terrorist targets that had slithered into the cracks of those places.

When they'd gone into business as civilians, there'd never been any talk of who would be the boss. They were equal partners.

"It helped that you were so cryptic about why you needed us," Paxton Pierce called from the passenger seat. "Otherwise, we might have taken our time jetting to the middle of nowhere."

He and McKay were as different as the day was long. Both made Ace look short, a factor he appreciated after a few days of being the tallest guy around. But where Pierce was wiry with lean muscle and a clean look that he spent time meticulously maintaining, McKay was built like a bar brawler and shaved once a week if he remembered.

Pierce analyzed everything before he made a move; McKay never asked permission and never asked for forgiveness. Ace liked to think he balanced them, falling right in the middle of the extremes.

"That was your cue to start talking, amigo," McKay

prompted, smacking the perpetual stick of gum that had become as much of a habit as the cigarettes he'd given up ten years ago. "We found some good leads on David Lang, which we can continue following from here, pending the reason you pulled us in."

Well, that would have been handy if his teammates had managed to find Sophia's father. Hopefully they could still successfully track him down. If anyone could, it was these two.

"Things got messy, I'm not going to lie," Ace said and pushed his hat back on his head. "The main issue at the moment is the addition of a Lang sister to the mix."

McKay nodded once. "On it. I'm assuming incognito is still the name of the game?"

"It's a requirement." Ace lifted his hands, hating that the answer had to be yes. It was one thing to insert a single undercover operative on a ranch this size; it was another thing entirely to keep three people's professional status on the down-low. "Or we forfeit the fee. So far, I've managed to get Sophia to the point where she trusts me enough to keep a closer eye on her than I was expecting. I'm hoping you can do the same with Charlotte Lang."

McKay's brows rose above the rims of his sunglasses. "It's Sophia already, is it? Fast work."

"Shut up, McKay. It's not like that."

It was exactly like that, and he had a feeling McKay knew it. That was the one problem in working with guys who knew him as well as they knew themselves. They picked up on things you'd rather keep under wraps.

Like the driving need he constantly had to fight to pull Sophia into a corner and try that kiss again.

Pierce hooted. "Defensive much? Sounds like Ms. Lang

might be getting all sorts of preferential treatment, doesn't it, McKay?"

"That's what I heard." McKay grinned. "Maybe I'll try that same tack with the sister. Does she look like Sophia Lang? The other sisters weren't in the dossier."

"Because they weren't supposed to be here," Ace reminded them tautly, annoyed by the direction of the conversation, though why he'd thought his friends wouldn't pick up on his mixed bag of feelings for Sophia, he had no clue. "Charli Lang showed up this morning out of the blue and seems intent on staying awhile. Ergo, you're here for the duration. That's the bottom line. I can't protect two sisters at the same time."

"Is the other one planning to show up too?" Pierce asked, which was a perfectly legit question, but Ace had the distinct feeling he was thinking about staking his own claim on a Lang sister.

"This is not a singles bar," Ace said, channeling his inner calm. "Let's focus on the job."

Getting bent out of shape would only fuel their interest in why he was so bent out of shape over a simple thing like being attracted to an attractive woman. They'd all seen the pictures. He'd known going in that Sophia was easy on the eyes.

He just hadn't known how much he would want to look at her. How hard it would hit him to see that bruise on her face. How many pieces he would like to tear the person responsible into.

More importantly, he'd had no clue she would tie him up in so many knots, or that he'd continually have to remind himself that women like Sophia weren't made for men who had blood on their hands.

Yeah, he'd been talking to himself about focusing just as much as the guys.

"Can't do the job if we don't know all the complexities," McKay said mildly, his fingers drumming on the steering wheel.

Fair. "I don't know if Veronica Lang will become a factor or not. For the time being, Pierce, you're on bunkhouse duty. Slip into the ranks. Keep your ears open. We might be dealing with an infiltration and your job is to ferret that out."

Ace ran down the events of the last few days, and both McKay and Pierce sobered when he got to the part where an active shooter had chased him and Sophia through the woods.

"Assuming Charlotte sleeps occasionally, I can keep my ear to the ground too," McKay said, and Ace nodded.

"She goes by Charli in case that becomes relevant."

Hopefully, McKay wouldn't be introducing himself to Charli the same way Ace had been forced to make his presence known to Sophia—because someone had attacked her. McKay's job would be to prevent it in the first place, now that he was forewarned.

McKay's expression was unreadable. "Charli. Figures. I'll be saying Alpha Bravo in my head every time I look at her."

"As long as you're focused on the tangos, you can do that all you want," Ace said. "I still haven't figured out if the Langs are targets or potential collateral damage. The treasure is a huge draw for less savory types, sure, but how did whoever hired us know its existence would put Sophia and Charli at risk?"

"Do we know anything about the attackers? Same guy?"

Pierce asked, his big brain already whirring over the data. If anyone could uncover a connection, it would be Pierce.

"No idea," Ace admitted. "But if I was a betting man, I'd say, yeah. Or at the very least, it's two guys working together. That's the reason you're here. We need to know what we're dealing with to keep the Lang sisters safe."

The additional eyes on Ace's back helped too.

"We got it," McKay acknowledged, his body vibrating with tension over his lack of momentum. "Let's roll. We'll figure out more by wading into the thick of things than we will by standing around chatting about it."

"There are a lot of new people coming and going around the ranch," Ace cautioned them, appreciating the point about getting a move on, but determined not to send his teammates into battle any blinder than he had to. "A blessing and a curse. You'll be able to slide right into the routine without a lot of questions, but on the flip side, so can anyone else."

His friends nodded. They would be fine. Ace trusted them implicitly or he wouldn't be in business with them. But they'd never expected to be actively dropped into this assignment. It had been tapped as a one-man show from the beginning, and Ace was much more capable of blending than either McKay or Pierce. Hence his initial presence at the ranch, but his plan to lie low had been destroyed pretty much immediately.

This was plan B.

Pierce flipped open his laptop and worked through some last-minute additions to his and McKay's new fictional backgrounds, online presence and work history. Ace's time on the ranch proved to be useful, as he now knew exactly how the employment process worked. As in there wasn't much to it. Guys showed up and were hired almost immediately, then put to work doing menial labor. The attrition rate was horrible since most of the hands were drifters, and more than a couple had legal entanglements they were trying to avoid.

In short, the ranch was never not hiring.

Ace split from his friends and drove back to the ranch a few minutes ahead of Pierce and McKay, feeling a lot better about the situation now that he wasn't going this alone. The rest of the day, he kept close to the house, inventing excuses to stay within sight of the back door, which left the front exposed, a situation he didn't like but didn't have an immediate fix for.

The two new ranch hands were incorporated immediately into the ranch's ecosystem, but in a stroke of bad luck, McKay and Pierce were both put on perimeter duty, a task everyone hated, so it was often given to the new guys. Walking the fence line of a six-hundred-acre ranch wasn't for the weak and that alone was often the cause of Jonas shedding personnel.

Ace suspected he did it on purpose. It did weed out those who couldn't hack it in the physical realm of a working ranch. Two guys who had survived BUD/S training and multiple brutal deployments to places where the temperature often topped 120 degrees would eat a six-hundred-acre walk for breakfast.

But it did put them out of sight of the house, a major issue. He'd have to figure out how to get Sophia to reassign them without stepping on Jonas's toes. And without her catching a clue as to why he'd tried to finagle it.

Undercover security was not a picnic, that was for sure.

Later that night, McKay and Pierce finally back at

the bunkhouse pretending to be strung out after a day of fence duty, Ace slipped out to meet Sophia as arranged. He palmed his phone to text her as soon as he hit the circular drive in front of the house, then faded into the shadows in case any curious onlookers strolled by.

Me: Outside in the front

Limpet: Be right there

Her text message even sounded like her voice in his head, slightly breathless, a lot of warmth and laced with something he couldn't describe. It made him think about sunny days with blue skies and little puffy white clouds.

Maybe he should change her name from Limpet to Unicorn. Because she was one. The only woman who had ever kissed him. The only one he'd ever taken to the doctor or gone to the bank with. Granted, neither were banal errands they'd done together because they were a couple, but it was far too easy to forget that.

Well, if he wanted to be honest, he'd done all those things with Stephanie. Especially the doctor appointments. But she was his sister and that didn't count. What did count were the bills from those doctors, not the way Sophia made him feel.

Except when she exited the house and paused on the wide wraparound porch, light from the moon spilled over her in a silvery river, and she was so beautiful that his chest got tight.

Why did she have to be so supremely off-limits?

And he wasn't so far gone that he didn't recognize that might be part of the appeal. He'd long ago accepted that he thrived on challenges. He was built for them. It was what had led him to such an elite branch of the military and drove him into private security.

Of course, he also just really, really liked her.

Sophia peered into the dark, clearly looking for him. He didn't reveal himself right away, grateful for these scant few seconds when he could enjoy watching her without all of the other stuff weighing down the moment.

But she instinctively veered in his direction, apparently as drawn to him as he was to her. That was the only explanation for how she sensed where to find him. If he knew anything, it was how to vanish in hostile territory. You got good, or you died.

"Hey," he called softly as she approached, gratified when she lit up. She made him feel like that too.

"I was starting to think it was never going to be time," she groused good-naturedly.

"Yeah, I was pretty antsy to get to digging too," he admitted.

She stared at him for a long moment, her smile enigmatic. "I meant because I wanted to see you. But yeah, treasure hunting. That's a thing too."

"You shouldn't say stuff like that," he muttered as his stupid, greedy heart latched onto her sentiment and soared.

"Why not? We're not in the shelter any longer. That was your rule. Here we are, not trapped, and if I want to tell you I've had a hard time thinking about anything other than kissing you again, I am one hundred percent going to."

One hundred percent going to kiss him? Or tell him about how much she wanted to kiss him? He couldn't stop his mouth from curving up in pleasure regardless of which one it was, because they both sounded pretty good to his Sophia-starved soul.

This on the heels of vowing not to act on the swirling attraction between them. This woman was like a magnet, drawing him closer, even as he ordered himself to step back.

"We should be focusing on the treasure," he told her gruffly, shoving his hands in his pockets instead of reaching for her. All ten fingers tensed, curling into his palms, tingling with the effort.

"More bad timing?" she said with a frustrated laugh.

The worst. If he'd met her ten years ago, before he had so much blood on his hands, maybe then he could justify touching her. Even meeting her before going undercover might have worked. At least then he'd know he was being honest with her. He'd be able to give her a choice with all the facts.

But today? None of that was true.

"I need to concentrate on our surroundings, Sophia," he said, his hands on her upper arms before he'd scarcely registered pulling them free of his pockets. But he didn't remove them, soaking in the feel of her under his fingers like a blind man inhaling a book via Braille.

Man, he was in so much trouble here. McKay had sniffed it out instantly. Ace would do well to remember that he might be good at vanishing in the dark—specifically when Sophia wasn't around—but he was not good at keeping his emotions hidden.

And he didn't want to lead Sophia down the wrong path, the one that gave her hope for anything intimate springing up between them.

"I need to focus," he continued roughly, his voice carrying all the angst behind his breastbone at not being able to crush her into his embrace and lead her right back inside the house where they could be alone for hours. "We're already a target. Don't think for a minute that we're not being watched twenty-four/seven."

She stared at him, something a little bit dangerous swirling through the air between them. "I'm sorry I'm distracting you. I'll stop. I know you're worried about keeping me safe."

Good, she got it. Why did it feel like he'd been kicked in the stomach?

Chapter 18

Ace had been wafting back-off vibes in Sophia's direction since she'd found him in the shadows of the house earlier. But all of that dissolved when a rat scurried across her foot, and she inhaled sharply. Ace took her hand and held it firmly in his capable grip.

She wished he'd take a lot more than that. But his ultra-calm, ultra-in-control presence soothed her nerves, which had flared to life right around the time he'd earnestly told her to stop talking about kissing so he could make sure they weren't going to die out here in the woods.

It was a sobering reminder. And did nothing to diminish all the squishy things happening in her heart.

What a weird, wonderful thing to be constantly reminded that she wasn't alone.

Ace was here. He'd stand by her no matter what, even if someone started shooting at them. With real bullets. He wouldn't flee like a big coward, leaving her to face the threats alone the way her father had.

Sure, Charli had unearthed a lot of stuff Sophia had repressed, like how hard it was to trust men. How easily Sophia shed them usually, never giving any of them a chance to disappoint her. She'd let Ace into her life because she'd had no choice, but he'd passed all the tests with flying colors and then some.

His hand surrounded hers, a tactile reminder that they were in this together. She liked it. Probably far too much given the circumstances.

Ace threw a glance at her over his shoulder, the finger on his free hand to his lips in the universal *shh* sign. Duh. She hadn't made a peep in at least five minutes, despite the uneven terrain.

They'd circled through the woods past the perimeter fence that separated Hidden Creek Ranch from Silver Acres next door. It had been Sophia's idea and she was very sorry she'd opened her mouth. What didn't seem that far during the day turned into a huge slog in the dark.

She knew better than to even think the word *flashlight*, so they were picking their way through the woods at a snail's pace because while Ace moved like a cheetah through the brush, she could only describe herself as bovine at this point. A big clumsy cow who could draw a bad guy's attention in nothing flat by stepping on every fallen tree branch in existence.

Ace didn't seem to notice, though, carefully helping her over ruts in the ground that he'd somehow seen with his catlike night vision. Her contacts did a lot of things to correct her vision but helping her see in the dark was not one of them. Apparently, this was yet another aspect of Ace's impressive capabilities.

If she mentioned it though, he'd shrug it off like he wasn't anything special. After a decade of exposure to suits with inflated egos, she found Ace's humbleness one of his most attractive qualities.

An eternity later, Ace halted at the edge of a copse of

trees, just shy of stepping out into the wide-open field to their left. It felt like it should be the north pasture, one of the ones Jonas used in rotation to let the horses graze. None of the animals seemed to be in residence at the moment, so they were either in another pasture or she'd gotten completely turned around in their double-back trek through the neighbor's property.

Ace positioned her behind a tree, then held up his finger in the universal "wait here" sign. Then without warning, he vanished back into the woods, leaving her extremely alone.

Black swam through her vision, growing darker the longer he was gone. The forest nearly disappeared, swallowed by the inky night. Had to be a trick of the mind. As in, being terrified sucked light molecules out of existence. Had they done studies on this? Because it felt like a PhD subject any psychologist would be interested in.

Ace materialized at her back. Thank God.

She would recognize him anywhere, even without turning around. It helped that he'd crowded up against her, his heat setting her on fire from head to toe. The darkness switched from foe to friend instantly, binding them together in an intimacy that shouldn't feel so right.

"We weren't followed," he murmured into her ear, and she let her head fall back instinctively, her chin raised in his direction, seeking more contact from his lips, which were right there within reach.

It would have been so easy for him to wrap his arms around her, snuggling her back into his hard body. Why didn't he? She could scarcely breathe she was so aware of him. Surely, he felt it too. Especially since he hadn't stepped back after delivering the message, almost as if he'd struck this pose incidentally and liked it so much, he'd opted to stay.

Well, she liked it too. But had ideas on how it could be better.

She spun, her arms sliding effortlessly underneath his, and for one glorious moment, he engulfed her in the embrace she so desperately needed. Torso to torso, his cheek nuzzling hers in an almost kiss that she felt more deeply than a real one.

"No bad guys," she murmured. "No focus on our surroundings needed."

This time, he didn't wait for her to make the move. His mouth descended on hers hungrily, as if he'd been waiting for the gate to be lifted and once it was, the entire force of his essence sprang to life, driving forward. Into her.

Oh, dear Lord. The man was devouring her whole. Her bones turned to butter, and she wondered how she was still standing. But his sexy, sexy hands splayed across her back, and that was one mystery solved—he was holding her up. Supporting her. Keeping her in place against him in a delicious embrace that righted her topsy world in one swoop.

Then pulled the rug out from under her again as he deepened the kiss to impossible levels. A moan escaped her throat as she got lost in the sensations, the swirl of Ace that swamped her senses. It was more than a kiss, more than an expression of attraction. It was survival. Air in her lungs, blood in her veins, a song in her soul—none of which would exist without this man.

Suddenly, the music stopped. He shook his head and backed up, taking all of that lovely support with him, and she stumbled, a rag doll without anything inside but cotton candy stuffing.

"Don't you dare apologize again," she told him. "We're adults who make our own choices. Own that one."

He nodded once. "I don't seem to have a lot of self-control around you. It feels like a weakness."

Oh, man. That was not the confession she'd been expecting. He was pretty torn up over it too. She swallowed back her retort, choosing to savor the idea that she could make a guy like Ace lose control. He of the legendary calm, who seemed so unflappable. She did that to him.

Preening a little, she smiled. "I'll try to refrain from being so kissable, then."

"It would be appreciated," he said wryly. "Otherwise, we're never going to find this treasure. Plus, it's possible we might attract attention with the goings-on out here. Just because we're alone now doesn't mean it's going to stay that way. So keep your eyes and ears open."

Great. Now all the heat from that kiss had faded in the face of being totally aware of the hostility of their surroundings. Who hid stuff in the woods when there was a perfectly fine house with walls and an attic? David Lang. The worst father and treasure hunter on the planet.

Though if he had found a valuable Maya cache of gold, she'd have to amend the terrible treasure hunter part, which had been the modifier next to her father's name in her mind for almost twenty years.

Ace pointed up. "Earlier today, I hid a bunch of tools in a tree so we wouldn't have to carry them out here in the dark."

So that's what he'd meant when he texted her that he was taking care of supplies. Bless the man. He thought of everything. There might be swooning in her future.

In no time flat, Ace shimmied up the correct tree, no

confusion on his part despite the woods being dark. And scary. He found a solid perch and carefully handed down two spade-shaped shovels with long handles, and she didn't drop either one. Next came a pickax, then a long thin metal bar, a regular ax and finally a saw.

When Ace hit the ground, she held it up in question.

"In case of roots," he explained. "Sometimes you can't cut them easily with an ax."

"Uh, how many treasures have you dug up in your life?" she asked, awed that he seemed fully prepared for everything under the sun—or the moon, as the case may be—while she'd scarcely been able to select the right shoes for the occasion.

He laughed. "None. But I've done a lot of other things in my life that required me to understand what I was about to get into, so I researched what kind of soil to expect in East Texas, especially in a wooded area. The answer is roots. Lots of them. And probably some limestone, though my bet is that your father found a new spot if he hit limestone in his original hole. We'll see."

Dazed and maybe a tiny bit in love with Ace at this point, she followed him to the spot on the map. They'd only seen it under the black light, but he'd memorized the location. She'd argued they should mark the map with visible ink, an idea that was quickly shot down when he'd pointed out that anyone could steal the map, allowing their hard-won information to fall into the wrong hands.

So she'd had to trust that they both remembered the spot correctly.

When Ace was satisfied that they'd found the best place to start digging—reminding her that they didn't know how far down they'd have to go or how big of a hole they needed—he pointed her to an area a couple of feet away.

Careful not to put too much heft on her shoulder, Sophia drove the pointy part of the spade shovel into the ground, expecting it to go at least the entire length of the blade. Instead, momentum nearly knocked her off her feet when the tip barely pierced the ground more than an inch.

Blinking, she glanced at Ace and noted he was stepping on the rolled metal piece at the top of the spade. She tried that and got the shovel into the ground a whole inch more.

This sucked. Digging was a lot harder than she'd anticipated. Especially since she was favoring her shoulder. Not that she'd have had that much more oomph behind her strength if she wasn't. Ace made it look easy, just like he did with everything else.

How big of a wimp was she for not being able to pull her weight?

Resolute, she dug in, pulling some will from somewhere inside that she'd like to say gave her superhuman strength, but really only gave her enough gusto to get the spade into the ground another inch.

"Maybe I should stick to balance sheets," she muttered, drawing Ace's attention from the two-foot-by-two-foot-wide hole already formed beneath his shovel as he scooped out another mound of dirt.

He wasn't even breathing hard.

"If that's where you think your skills lie," he said, pausing to lean on his shovel as he spoke to her. "Then sure. I can dig and you can watch for Intruder Man. But if you want to dig together, you'll figure it out. I have faith in you. You're doing great."

Her heart gobbled up the sentiment, storing it away in

a place that she had no idea any man could reach. Dang it. She couldn't fail him now. Or herself.

She levered the shovel back into the ground for another shot, annoyed enough at her weakness to try again. This time, she jumped on the rolled metal pieces with both feet, driving the spade into the ground halfway this time.

Yes! She repeated the motion, jumping harder. The metal part disappeared into the dirt completely, but then she couldn't scoop the dirt out until she tried stepping on the handle, using the hard-packed earth at the lip of her brand-new hole as the fulcrum.

A big mound of dirt broke free. Sure, she almost face-planted in the middle of it when she didn't compensate for the sudden difference in force, but she didn't care. There was a hole now, barely discernible in the moonlight, but she'd taken a chunk of soil out of the ground all by herself.

"Take that, Texas," she said and kicked the dirt away from her hole.

Amused, Ace grinned. "You did good, Soph. Now do it again."

There was the nickname. Perfectly timed. So much better than SoLa, and the secret thrill over it did a number on her insides, opening the floodgates, allowing Ace to spill into every nook and cranny.

"Yeah, yeah," she groused good-naturedly.

Her shoulder sang with the next round, but she ground her teeth together and got another scoop of dirt out of the hole. Eventually, she had a hole one-tenth the size of Ace's, but it was still a hole, and she was still proud of it.

Without Ace there to encourage her, she might have quit. And he'd apparently be fine with that, based on his comment. That was the great part. He didn't see it as a shortcoming that she'd been clueless at first, but then had given her exactly what she'd needed to rise to the occasion.

She was so in over her head with him. Maybe she should just go ahead and admit she was falling for him. To herself only. Not to him. That would be ridiculous.

All at once, Ace froze. She glanced up at him. The look on his face put her pulse on overdrive.

"What?" she whispered. "Do you see someone coming? Are we in danger?"

"No," he murmured, his gaze catching hers. "Look."

She followed his line of sight to his shovel and watched as he spilled the dirt to the ground in a slow shower. A glint of gold fell along with the dark specks, moonlight reflecting off the flat surface.

A coin. She reached down to pluck it from the dirt, brushing it off.

"It's stamped with zigzag designs like the one in the magazine article," she breathed, awed at the possibilities of what she held in her hand. It was heavier than she would have expected, larger. Twice as big as a silver dollar. "A second coin. How many more are buried here?"

Chapter 19

Enthused and inspired by the find, Ace and Sophia threw themselves into digging, but an hour later, they'd found nothing else. He wasn't shocked.

Sophia was.

"I don't understand," she said, her hands on her hips, her voice low in deference to the fact that she had a coin potentially worth $25,000 in her pocket. "Why bury one coin? The effort alone is staggering, plus it doesn't make a lick of sense."

Ace shrugged. "There are a hundred reasons to bury one coin. Maybe that was all he had left. Maybe he split up the treasure on purpose in case someone came looking for it. Maybe your father isn't the one who buried it."

"You think my grandpa found more than one?" she mused.

"It's possible."

But he didn't think so. His current theory was that it had been left behind accidentally when David Lang moved the treasure, but he didn't want to say so. It might come across as his believing in a boneheaded mistake on the part of her father.

It was just as good a theory as any of the others. Because

he agreed with Sophia. It didn't make any sense, despite the plethora of reasons he could come up with.

Besides, Sophia was flagging. She wouldn't say a word, but Ace could tell. It was time to go. Her shoulder was bothering her, and they'd already pushed the limit of the amount of time he felt comfortable out here in the dark woods. McKay and Pierce were keeping watch a couple hundred yards away, both with one finger on the trigger of their long-range rifles with night-vision scopes, so he wasn't the slightest bit worried about being surprised.

But that didn't mean he wanted to answer questions about why the two new ranch hands were such good shots. Or why they were in the woods in the first place with not-quite-civilian-issue firearms. The longer they stayed here, the greater the odds he'd be doing both.

"There's nothing else here to find," he finally conceded and dropped his shovel on top of the one Sophia had already discarded. "I was hoping for at least another map or some sort of indicator of what to do next."

"It's fine," she said morosely, and he could tell she was disappointed they hadn't found the mother lode.

"Let's get back to the house and figure this out."

She nodded and let him lead her back the way they came. Pierce and McKay melted into the shadows behind them, following at a distance the way they'd done during the first trek into the woods. If they'd been any closer when he'd returned to where he'd left Sophia after getting them into position, he'd never have kissed her like that.

Actually, he shouldn't have done that in the first place. But her point about not needing to focus on keeping her alive right at that moment had been so inspired, he couldn't help himself.

Who was he kidding? He couldn't help himself regardless. She was iron to his magnet. He couldn't resist being drawn to her even if he wanted to. She made him feel like a million dollars, like he might actually be worth something. What he was going to do about it, that was the question.

Tell her the truth.

That was a given. He just couldn't quite figure out when he could do that and not have to forfeit his fee. If the danger to the Lang sisters passed, then he could reasonably say the job was over. But how would he know they were no longer in danger?

It was a maddening circle he couldn't seem to break out of.

At the house, Sophia insisted that he come inside instead of making themselves targets on the porch. Since he couldn't very well tell her that nothing would touch her when the rest of his team stood watch, he nodded and signaled over his shoulder with two fingers, first to the east, and second to the west. McKay and Pierce would get it and move into position as directed.

Yeah, he was breathing a lot easier with backup in place.

Wearily, Sophia sank into the armchair in the living room, the closest room to the front door. He had the feeling she might not have made it much past that.

Tamping down a host of reasons he shouldn't, he crossed the room to stand behind her, sliding his hands along her shoulders to begin kneading them, careful to stay away from the strained area that she'd fallen on.

"Oh, dear Lord that feels heavenly," she moaned, the sound vibrating through his gut.

Add that to the list of reasons he shouldn't have his hands on her. Because he instantly wanted to know what else he could do to make Sophia feel good if that little trill inside would be his reward.

Back off, champ.

Not shockingly, nothing south of his brain listened to that little voice, nor did he lift his hands from her neck.

Ace cleared his throat. "What do you want to do with the coin?"

"Take it to the bank," she said without hesitation. "Though I have a feeling there will be several historical societies that will want to study it or something."

"Maybe that's our best bet," he mused. "We should get it authenticated first. It might not even be real."

She glanced back over her shoulder and then immediately snapped her head forward as if afraid he might stop. No danger of that. This was the most fun he'd had since he'd kissed her at the edge of the forest, which he should regret but didn't.

"Do you think that's the reason why there was only one? It's a forgery?"

"Honestly, I have long stopped trying to form an opinion about this treasure business," he said simply. "My job is to stand between you and whoever is trying to beat you to finding it. You're the brains *and* the beauty of this partnership."

Her quick smile warmed him dangerously fast, and she hadn't even aimed it in his direction.

"I beg to differ. You're the one who brought the tools. You're the one who found the key to the safety deposit box. And you obviously haven't looked in a mirror lately if you think I'm the attractive one here."

The compliment pleased him more than it should. She wasn't the only woman who had ever commented on his looks, but she was definitely the first one to affect him this way. As if she'd reached inside and taken pieces of him each time they were together.

"I guess we'll just be two attractive people trying to solve the mystery of this treasure before someone else does," he told her, which made her laugh for some reason.

Another thing about her he appreciated. She didn't whine about things or complain that something hurt or that she was tired. If anything, she bucked up and forged ahead, no matter what, which made them more alike than he'd have guessed.

She kept doing unexpected things that made him happy to be around her. Like laughing when he mentioned the danger that she was in.

Though, he'd started to wonder if Intruder Man and his friends cared anything about Sophia. They were likely here for the treasure, not her.

"We'll authenticate the coin first," she decided. "That's a good call. We need to know what we're dealing with first."

He moved his hands to the top of her head, gently massaging her temples. "Sure thing, boss."

"How are you so good at that?" she groaned, her eyelids fluttering closed. "I barely even have a headache anymore."

After a beat, he decided it couldn't hurt to be honest. "My sister gets headaches. She's sick a lot. She has something called fibromyalgia."

Sophia went quiet. "I'm sorry. That sounds awful."

It was awful. Painful for him to watch and even worse for Stephanie to go through. The doctors did what they could to help her manage pain and other symptoms, which was why Ace had learned everything he could about massage since his sister's insurance didn't cover it as a medical necessity.

"Is that why you left the military?" she asked.

That was the other reason he couldn't stop thinking about Sophia—she picked up on things other people didn't. "Yeah. I needed to be closer to her and also have a reasonable guarantee of staying alive."

"This is what you call irony," she said with a wry twist of her lips that made him smile in kind. "You should think about moving to another ranch instead of staying at this one and getting shot at. Your sister is more important than my father's legacy of terrible treasure maps and coins of questionable value."

If he was strictly a cowboy—and a coward—another job might be wise, but since he was neither, he made a noise in his throat. "Then who would you fall into a secret shelter with? You'd have no one to harass you into going to the doctor. That would never do."

"I'm serious." She punctuated that by sliding out from under his hands and turning to face him. "This place is dangerous, and you've got someone counting on you."

The fact that Sophia didn't put herself in that category sat funny with him. He should be agreeing with her. Nodding and saying yes, Stephanie was important and had no one else to take care of her.

But he liked being Sophia's hero too. More than he should. More than was expressly necessary to keep doing his job. And that was his real problem.

This was a job. And he'd been skating a line that was at best unprofessional and, at worst, an opportunity to lose his sole source of income.

"I appreciate the sentiment," he told her, his hands hanging uselessly at his sides now that she'd unceremoniously ended the massage session that had been his sole excuse to touch her. "But I'm not going anywhere."

Relief spilled through Sophia's face. "Am I a terrible person for being so happy you said that?"

"No. You're human and terrified because someone has been trying to kill you. My sister will be okay. I hired a nurse who goes by several days a week. I'm exactly where I want to be."

She stared up at him, the vibe between them growing taut and full of emotion that he hadn't meant to put into play, but he couldn't call it back when it was the truth.

"Maybe you should think about going into the bodyguard business, then," she murmured. "It would probably pay better than wrangling horses."

Struck all at once at the truth of that—and the fact that he couldn't flat out tell her that she wasn't far off—he scrubbed the back of his neck, at a loss for how to fix this impossible situation of his own making.

"Maybe, but in the meantime, I work for you, and you have a coin that needs to be authenticated. Make some calls, figure out where you want to take it and I'll be ready to go whenever you tell me to get in the car."

She smiled. "I guess it's a given that you're going with me, huh."

It wasn't a question, and he didn't treat it like one. "I'm driving. Don't argue."

The team from the University of Texas's Mesoamerica Center came to them. Dr. Allen, a woman in her late fifties, drove up from Austin within a few hours of receiving Sophia's call. She'd managed to stuff a couple of her colleagues into her hatchback at a moment's notice, apparently, all three of the academics eager to be involved in authenticating Sophia's coin.

Ace hung around at the back of the room, eager to do nothing except stay out of the way and keep an eagle eye on the newcomers. It wasn't that he didn't trust anyone… but these people certainly hadn't earned a lick of his allegiance yet.

Dr. King, a slender man who couldn't stop oohing and aahing over the coin, sat at the kitchen table where he'd decreed the best light in the house to be. He'd parked there the second he'd introduced himself as a numismatist who specialized in ancient coins.

As soon as Ace was sure no one was paying attention to him, he surreptitiously googled *numismatist*, finally spelling it close enough on his third try to get the meaning. It was a coin expert. Why the guy couldn't say that was beyond him.

The other woman, an anthropologist named Dr. Fuentes, who had yet to say a word but had taken approximately 47,000 pictures and texted someone back at the university every single one, stood behind Dr. King. Her sharp gaze missed nothing.

Sophia sat next to Dr. King, leaning toward him occasionally to answer questions as the team asked them. No, she didn't know where the coin had come from. Yes, she was aware that her grandfather had found one, which she learned from Dr. King had been sold to a private collector. Unfortunately, her grandfather had not involved anyone with an interest in the history prior to the sale, so no one at the university had gotten a chance to see it.

"This is exquisite," Dr. King said for the fourth time as he held the coin under a magnifying glass.

He'd donned two pairs of gloves prior to picking it up. Apparently touching it with bare hands was a rookie mistake that he and Sophia had both been taken to task for.

Ace had bitten back a comment about the coin being buried in the ground for probably going on ten years. If that hadn't damaged it, a few fingerprints wouldn't, either. But this was Sophia's show, not his.

"Does that mean it's real?" Sophia asked, her gaze hopeful.

"I'm 99 percent certain," Dr. King said with a nod as he carefully set the coin on a digital scale. "The weight is consistent with what I would expect for a piece of gold this size. I'd like to test the metal composition more thoroughly in a lab, but visually, the color is good. I've assessed a lot of coins in my day, so my eye is pretty well trained."

Dr. Allen pointed with a long, thin piece of plastic, indicating an area of the design. "These markings are commonly found carved into the stones comprising the stepped pyramid of Pakal the Great's tomb in Chiapas. It's a symbol of the Temple of Inscriptions."

"That's fascinating," Sophia breathed. "So this coin came from there?"

"Well, we're not sure," Dr. Allen hedged. "The tomb was looted by the Conquistadors in the sixteenth century and we know they took some artifacts, the coin most likely included. I am not as well versed in Pakal's history as I would like to be able to say for sure. We need to bring in some other teams, particularly one from the National Museum of Anthropology in Mexico City. There are a couple of experts there who can help us trace this coin so we can understand its journey over the last eleven hundred years."

Sophia gasped. "It's that old?"

"Oh, yes, at least. Pakal lived during the Late Classic Period of Maya civilization, which lasted from about 600 to 900 CE," Dr. Fuentes chimed in. "When the archeology team found his tomb in the middle of the last century, it was largely intact, thanks to the Maya engineers who knew a few more tricks to keeping their pyramids sealed than the Egyptians. The Spaniards didn't make off with much. That's why we need to do some more research. This coin could have been part of the official excavation of the tomb. Those artifacts are currently housed in the National Museum. If so, that means it was stolen more recently."

If Ace were a betting man, that was where he'd put his money. Which would mean David Lang was less a treasure hunter and more an opportunistic thief. Crappy news for Sophia.

Sophia glanced at Ace, a wealth of things passing across her face that plucked at strings inside him that he would have preferred stay unplucked, and nodded. "I agree that it really doesn't belong to me even though it was found on my land. I would want it to go back to Mexico and the Maya descendants if it was indeed stolen from the tomb. Involve whoever you need to in order to figure that out."

Jeez. Something bright filled his chest, making it a little hard to breathe. Who was this woman? She'd spent all this time trying to find the treasure, only to offer to give it back at the drop of the hat.

If he hadn't experienced it himself, he would never have believed such a simple act could make him feel this way about another human being.

Dr. Fuentes beamed, as if Sophia had passed a very difficult test. "Bless you, this is very exciting for us and the research we do at the university. Thank you for calling us.

You had a choice, and we appreciate that you made the right one."

"And now we have another request," Dr. Allen inserted firmly, drawing everyone's gaze. "There may be other pieces here on the property. Other coins. Maybe artifacts such as jade beads, pendants, ceramics. The list is infinite, and the pieces are priceless. Would you let us bring a team here to do a proper excavation?"

"Oh, I'm sure that would be fine," Sophia said agreeably. "What does that entail?"

Ace nearly groaned. It meant a lot more people. Machines. Chaos. And that his job would get infinitely harder.

"Sophia," he ground out before anyone else could speak. "A word, please."

Chapter 20

Closeted in her office with Ace definitely topped Sophia's list of things she enjoyed. This was very different from normal, though. He was operating under a full head of steam, pacing around like a caged tiger who hadn't eaten in several days.

Energy rolled off his body in waves, prickling the hair on her arms, and she couldn't figure out why he was infinitely more beautiful when he was like this but so much less approachable. This was the authoritative side of him that she fully appreciated because it meant he would never let anyone get past him when he stood between her and the door.

But she'd grown attached to the gentler Ace, the one who told her she was the most beautiful woman he'd ever met and held her hand as they walked through the woods in the dark.

"I take it I've done something that displeased his highness," she offered wryly. "Maybe you could clue me in before you rip my head off?"

The look on his face almost made her laugh despite the coiled tension arcing through the small room.

"I'm not going to rip your head off," he muttered. "I might rip *something* apart. But it would not be you."

Well, she could think of a few things that might benefit from being torn in two, like the dress she'd changed into before the trio of doctors had arrived from Austin. The slightly dangerous, somewhat breathless vibe Ace had created the moment he'd shut the door lent itself to an out-of-the-norm fantasy, and she wouldn't apologize for thinking about it, not when she'd been dying for him to kiss her again.

And while she had to admit that she might have a soft spot for gentler Ace, caged tiger Ace put a tingle in her belly that she could not ignore. It would be a travesty to waste all that energy.

Now was probably not the opportune time for that. Shame.

She crossed her arms and sank into her desk chair, figuring it was probably wise to keep the desk between them. For now.

"I'm sensing that you're a little worked up about something," she tried again. "Are you upset that I said the coin should go back to Mexico?"

He slammed to a halt, his gaze laser sharp on her face. "What? No. That was the single most unselfish thing I have ever witnessed in my life. You'd be giving up thousands of dollars, maybe hundreds of thousands if they find more Maya stuff. Nobody else on the planet would have made that kind of decision. It was amazing."

Well. That was not the reaction she'd been expecting, and honestly she hadn't even considered a different choice. Something flared to life inside her, glowing just behind her breastbone. Either she was about to have an out-of-body experience or Ace had just touched something she hadn't even known was there.

It was terrifying. And dizzying. Wonderful at the same time. It made her smile, despite the energy, which hadn't fizzled at all after he'd stopped midstride.

"I couldn't have kept it," she murmured. "It wouldn't be right. You saw how earnest all those people are about the history. They want to find the truth, not make a bunch of assumptions about what my father did or didn't do. But if he stole one red cent from a museum, I want to know."

Ace skirted the desk, reaching for her before he'd scarcely cleared it, his palms warm on her arms as he gripped her with surprising tenderness. "Sophia, whatever he did doesn't reflect on you. You know that, right?"

She nodded, her throat tight all at once as she looked up at him. "I never really thought much about the reality of him being a treasure hunter, but if you get down to it, there's not much difference between stealing from a museum and stealing from a historical grave site of an important ruler in a people's ancient culture."

"No," he said, a lightness in his gaze that she hadn't ever noticed before. "There's not."

"I can fix that. If I can help the people of Mexico reclaim even a small piece of their past, I should."

His eyelids fluttered closed for a brief moment and when he opened them, most of the coiled energy had fled. She missed it all at once. Hopefully it was a preview of what she could expect if she got him riled up in a completely different way. That focused intensity called to her at an elemental level.

"Yeah," he muttered, releasing her in favor of perching on the edge of the desk. "That's not wrong. This request for a full-scale excavation, though… Soph, that's a disaster waiting to happen."

If Ace was still calling her Soph, nothing else mattered. She tucked that away, folding it into the glow that hadn't faded one tiny bit, and let just a bit of what she was feeling inside reflect on her face in the form of a tiny smile.

"What would you suggest instead? You keep trying to stave off the Mongol hordes of evil dudes who are going to show up the moment word of this new find gets out?"

Almost all the stubbornness melted from Ace's expression. "I hear you. It would be better to have a sanctioned team on-site who will likely bring their own security to the ranch. If we're not searching for the treasure, I can spend twenty-four/seven making sure you're safe."

"Well, I like where this is going," she murmured and the vibe in the room changed instantly to something with a lot more weight. "Is it time to change your official job title to boyfriend?"

"That's literally the opposite of what I meant." He pressed a thumb to his temple, still clearly torn over what he perceived as his duty versus his desires.

She took mercy on him and laughed, climbing to her feet since it felt like they'd made a decision to move forward with the excavation. "I'm just kidding. Sort of. Door's open any time you want to walk through it. Just saying."

The look on his face made her shiver all at once. "I hope you're not telling me you leave the doors unlocked at night."

"It's an expression, Ace. Jeez." *Mental note: make Ace a copy of the front door key.* "You do know how to make a girl feel wanted."

All at once, the coiled energy returned to his frame in a snap. He had her backed against the desk before she could blink, his mouth crashing down on hers in a kiss that detonated instantly with the force of an atomic bomb.

Oh, my, *yes*. And that was the extent of her brain's ability to processes words, ideas, thoughts. Ace drained everything from her and still kept demanding more. She gave it to him. How could she not?

This was exactly what she'd craved from the moment he'd shut them up together in this room. Oh, who was she kidding? She thought about him taking her into his arms pretty much all the time. But this… This was something else, something different. Slightly perilous, a little scandalous and absolutely delicious.

He ripped his mouth from hers well before she was ready, breathing as heavily as if he'd run a marathon, his gaze dark and searching on hers.

"In case you weren't aware," he ground out, his voice gravelly, "I always want you. Don't you dare think otherwise for a second."

"I, um…won't. Didn't." She blinked. Was that the trick to getting him to cross his made-up line? Tell him that he'd made her feel unwanted?

With what seemed to be a great deal of reluctance, he released her and stepped away, running a hand through his short, cropped hair, giving her the impression he'd been expecting to find his hat on his head.

"Let them know you agree to the excavation team coming to the property but make it clear that all personnel must have a background check," he told her and it didn't sound like a suggestion. "I can coordinate with them once they're on-site, if you want. Act as their point of contact."

"Of course I want that."

He nodded. "I'll support your decision, then. Bring on the chaos."

* * *

This was one of those times Ace wished he'd been wrong. But *chaos* didn't begin to describe what descended on the ranch after Sophia gave the UT Austin team the green light.

The academics consulted with the people at the museum in Mexico all right. All eleven of them. Who had also chosen to collaborate with the Peabody Museum of Archaeology and Ethnology at Harvard. They sent a team of nine, plus more equipment than he could identify, all of which rolled up in an RV painted with the university's logo, followed by a truck hauling two ATVs.

Last time he'd gotten a good head count, there were twenty-three people living in a makeshift campsite in the south pasture, eight vehicles parked nearby, and one of the teams had four drones that constantly flew overhead doing aerial photography.

Then the backhoe arrived. Followed by two generators and a partridge in a pear tree.

"This is insanity," he muttered to McKay in passing as they headed in opposite directions, Ace to check in with Dr. Allen, who seemed to be the leader so far, despite the team from Harvard obviously being much better funded.

"A grad student from Austin just arrived about ten minutes ago," McKay said.

McKay was acting as Ace's second set of eyes and ears, while Pierce, the wizard of the web, ran complicated searches on everyone's backgrounds and known associates using methods better left unexplained.

"On my way to check him out, then," Ace acknowledged. "Allen didn't mention him. I don't like it when new people show up unannounced."

True to his word, Ace played point for all the teams, ensuring they had access to the areas they needed, as well as looking out for the ranch's interest, particularly the horses that didn't like the machinery. Or the people. A sentiment he shared.

Ace found the grad student. Not hard to pick out when the kid was barely old enough to shave and wore shorts like they didn't have the same mosquitoes and chiggers in Austin as they did in East Texas.

"You the new guy?" Ace growled, gratified when the grad student jumped.

"Yes, sir, I'm Quentin. Mallory," he added quickly and stuck out his hand. Then dropped it when Ace eyed him.

They were all so earnest at this age. Ace crossed his arms, which had the not-so-accidental effect of highlighting his biceps. You couldn't be too careful or too untrusting, even with a skinny guy who couldn't weigh more than 125 soaking wet. "Dr. Allen is in the south pasture. You should check in, do not pass go, do not collect two hundred dollars."

Quentin Mallory shook his head, like it had been a suggestion he had the latitude to ignore. "Oh, yeah, I'll get to that. I heard from Dr. Fuentes that the aerial shots showed a promising area near the fence line that I'm—"

"Check in first," he told the kid flatly. These academics and Indiana Jones wannabes hoped to find artifacts and treasure. He got it. But this was his rodeo, not theirs. "This is a working ranch. You don't get to go wherever you please. Step out of line and you're off this project. Spoiler alert. I get to decide where the line is. Don't forget that."

Mallory nodded a bunch of times. "South pasture. Got it. Uh… Which way is south?"

If Ace rolled his eyes any harder, they'd bounce right out of his head. He pointed. The kid skedaddled, but Ace didn't give him the benefit of the doubt. He watched until Mallory hit the gate that led to the larger-than-it-should-be camping area.

When he turned back toward the house, Sophia had just stepped out onto the back porch, wearing a pair of cropped pants and a shirt that tied at her waist. The tiniest bit of skin peeked out and his mouth went dry instantly.

When would it stop feeling like a load of bricks had dropped on his chest every time he saw her across the way? The scant few times he'd managed to corner her in a place with enough shadows to cloak the fact that he just wanted to breathe her in for a minute hadn't been nearly enough.

That was the real shame in all of this. They were both so busy managing everything that they barely got a chance to say hi to each other, let alone a longer conversation. Which he definitely needed to have with her pronto. Or at least soon. Whenever it became clear the job was over.

Weren't they close? The addition of so many people should have made things easier. Better. Safer. Jonas had the hands patrolling the woods regularly to ensure the teams weren't digging up trees and knocking over fences. No intruders could be lurking out there, not without being seen pretty much immediately.

Of course, the problem was that everyone counted as an intruder right now. And no one did. It was often a challenge just to keep track of who was permitted to be on-site, let alone someone who wasn't.

Sophia caught his gaze and he felt it in his gut when she smiled. It didn't seem to matter that she was a football field away, he could almost smell her jasmine body-wash from here.

That would be even better—if he could smell it up close and personal. He'd sent the new kid off to be tagged. Maybe he could sneak a minute or two with the boss.

Apparently, she was of the same mind since she took off, headed in his direction. Meeting her in the middle worked for him and then some.

A rumble from behind him grew loud enough for him to glance away from Sophia. A backhoe rolled toward her, one of the big ones with a wicked-looking scoop on front, teeth extended.

The driver was a maniac going that fast this close to the house. They weren't even supposed to have the heavy machinery here. Annoyed, Ace shot the driver a warning glance.

Only there wasn't a driver. The backhoe kept on rolling toward Sophia unmanned.

Ace's pulse skyrocketed as time suspended, everything falling into a hazy, slow-motion quality. Sophia's gaze stayed stuck on him, her smile his favorite.

But that meant she wasn't paying attention to the backhoe. No one did anymore. There were so many odd machines roaming all over the property now that the noise of one scarcely registered.

She had no idea it was heading in her direction, on a straight path to intercept her.

"Sophia!" he called and threw his hands to the side, hoping it would somehow communicate to her that she needed to move. "Look out!"

He sprinted toward her, knowing he had no shot at getting to her before the backhoe did.

Finally, she glanced to her right, eyes widening. With

something akin to superhuman speed, she jumped just as the teeth of the bucket would have pierced her leg. But she landed right in the path of the giant tires.

Ace reached her then, snatching her into his arms and heaving himself to the ground with her on top of him. His back slammed into the dirt and then Sophia crushed his ribs. But he couldn't focus on that, rolling to be sure they'd cleared the tire tracks.

The backhoe kept going, heading for the house.

He released Sophia after taking a half second to be sure she was okay, then pumped his legs to reach the backhoe. It was difficult enough to scramble into the cab when this kind of equipment was still. Moving, it was almost impossible, but he managed it without getting his leg tangled with the tires.

A second later, he'd pulled the brake and then the key. The backhoe shuddered to a stop inches from the wrap-around porch.

Chapter 21

"It wasn't an accident," Ace told Sophia grimly for the third time as she—once again—refused to sit in the chair he'd pulled out from the kitchen table so he could get a good look at her.

"It doesn't make any sense why I would still be a target, though," she said as she stood at the sink, staring out over the back acreage from the relative safety of the house. Which had taken some doing to get her to agree to.

Sophia had brushed off the incident, dusted herself off and expected Ace to agree to let her continue with her plan to have a conversation with Jonas out in the open. Not happening.

"It doesn't have to make sense," he growled. He made that noise a lot lately and he didn't like that this situation had brought out his grumbly side. "You don't have to think about it at all. You just have to do what I say so you don't end up hamburger meat."

She laughed like any of this was funny. "Should I start calling you boss, then?"

"Yes," he told her succinctly. "That's exactly what you should do. The backhoe was the last straw. I'm officially accepting the promotion to head of your security detail. I haven't been able to focus on ranch duties in forever anyway. It's stupid to pretend I'm doing anything else other than shadowing you twenty-four/seven for the foreseeable future."

Her expression heated inexplicably, as if he'd just said he planned to sleep in her bed as a precaution. Oh, if only that was an option. He could see it in his mind's eye perfectly. It helped that he'd had this particular fantasy running in his head for several days now. The one where he used protecting her as an excuse to move into the house, her bedroom, her shower.

But the backhoe incident had brought one ugly truth to light—this was far from over. Sophia was still very much in danger. Which meant he had to keep his mouth shut about his real purpose here.

Though declaring himself her official bodyguard felt like crossing another line that wasn't keeping in the spirit of the job. What was the difference between repurposing himself away from cowboy duty and admitting to her he'd been hired by someone else, who was still nameless? Speaking of things that made no sense…

At this point, he was willing to split hairs. As long as he didn't have to cross a very large plot of land to get between her and danger ever again. If he was already standing next to her, any new threats would have to go through him.

"Have I mentioned lately that I'm a huge fan of Take-Charge Ace?" she murmured. "Which reminds me. If we're going to be spending every second together from now on, I feel compelled to ask. Why do they call you Ace? Is it your real name?"

"What?" He shook his head, baffled at the subject

change when she'd literally almost been killed not fifteen minutes ago. "What does that matter?"

"I'm curious. Indulge me."

Apparently, that was the magic wand he'd needed to get her to sit down in the chair he pulled out. Her new proximity meant she was within touching distance, her gaze avidly fixed on him as if whatever he was about to impart held great significance to her.

If anyone else had asked, he'd have told them no. None of their business.

But it wasn't anyone else. It was Sophia, a woman he desperately wanted to tell everything to. Whatever she wanted to know. Since he couldn't be truthful about the most important things, at least he could tell her this little bit.

He heaved a sigh. "It's short for Andrew Christopher. During my first deployment, my XO sent me on a particularly difficult mission. Let's just say it unfolded successfully. When I returned, he called me his ace in the hole and it stuck."

"Can I call you Andy?" she said mischievously and laughed again when he gave her a withering look. "I'm just kidding. Ace suits you. I like it."

Fortunately, she didn't ask for any details about the mission, which was classified anyway. But the die had been cast and talking about his successes as a SEAL meant the scene in question crowded into his mind. Reminding him who he was.

That was the real secret. The one he couldn't tell her. And that put a wall between them that was insurmountable. She'd never look at him the same again if she knew how good he was at killing.

But she didn't know and she didn't have any issues at the

moment with standing up to crowd into his space, slipping her arms around his waist as she snuggled into his torso. Somehow it became an embrace when his stupid arms refused to stay at his side and eagerly got in on that action.

He should push her away. But she glanced up at him from under her lashes, giving him that smile that she saved strictly for him.

"Thank you for saving my life, Ace. More than once."

"You're welcome," he said gruffly into her hair as the scent of jasmine filled him to the brim. Something pinged around in his heart, looking for a place to land. And found it.

Aw, dang. He'd gone and fallen for her.

Sophia put her head in her hands as she stared at the date printed on the project plan displayed on her laptop.

Charli sat next to her, crunching her way through a bag of Doritos, content to let Sophia do the heavy lifting of the resort planning. She hadn't even asked for a desk or a workspace or anything, so when she thought about it, she showed up to Sophia's office to have an impromptu meeting about the status of things.

"That face doesn't bode well," Charli noted, her eyes on Sophia instead of the project plan they'd been going over. "Are we not going to meet the date?"

"It's less than a month away," Sophia said needlessly, or at least she hoped Charli had glanced at a calendar recently. "I can't even get a firm date out of the seven billion archaeologists in my backyard of when they can wrap up the excavation. The barn is out of commission and the temp barn is not for show. Assuming none of that is actually an issue, where does the decorating project stand?"

Shrugging, her sister glanced through some papers she'd

brought with her to Sophia's office, which weren't even in a file folder or anything. "I think the decorator said he could finish the second suite by next week. Or was it the following week?"

Sophia bit her lip and counted to ten, letting Charli dig through her data until she finally pointed at something that must have meant something to her. "Next week. Then he'll start on the small bedroom. That should take probably ten to twelve days, he thought."

"Business or calendar days?"

Eyes wide, Charli hesitated. "What, like did he include weekends or some such?" When Sophia nodded, she pursed her lips. "Well, he said the team doesn't work on Sundays, so I guess he meant they work six days a week. So, that would put us at…oh."

"Exactly," Sophia confirmed grimly. "It's too close to the launch date, and that doesn't even account for the fact that ideally, I should have opened bookings already. But I haven't because of this mess."

She flipped her fingers at the window where the bright yellow paint of the rogue backhoe stood out in relief against the woods as it chugged merrily through one of the back pastures.

"What if we don't bill it as a luxury resort?" Charli asked, all nonchalant, as if she hadn't just spoken blasphemy.

"What do you mean, don't bill it as a luxury resort? What would we bill it as? Choose your own treasure hunt adventure?" she shot back sarcastically and sucked half a smoothie up through the straw. It was supposed to be her breakfast, but it had been sitting on her desk for an hour and the fruit had started to separate from the protein powder. *Ugh.*

"Maybe it can be a Cowboy Experience instead," her sister said, warming to her subject. "Like, get the guests to move the horses from pasture to pasture. Let them throw out the feed. Clean the tack after the trail ride. Why have staff do all of that?"

Just as she opened her mouth to argue, several things hit her at once. Then no one would care how rustic the surroundings were. She could save some money on payroll. The concept grew on her so fast that she went light-headed.

"Charli," she ground out. "Where in the world did that idea come from?"

"It's not a bad idea," her sister shot back defensively. "You always do this—"

"No, it's not a bad idea. I mean it like, where in the world did that *great* idea come from? You didn't want anything to do with the ranch, and then you show up out of the blue, jump in and actually contribute. It's..." Sophia swallowed, slightly ashamed and a whole lot impressed, now that she'd checked her prejudices in favor of treating Charli like she might be an equal partner in this. "Great."

Charli beamed. "Really?"

Nodding, Sophia opened a new document, ideas pouring out of her brain faster than she could type. "We can have sessions on how to make cowboy fare, like the kind of stuff they eat on cattle drives or whatever. Roping lessons. Jonas can find some guys who can lead that. What if we could find people who wanted to help rebuild the barn?"

And best of all, as already highlighted so eloquently, the guests would be working at the ranch. Getting it in shape. Filling the gaps. And *paying* for the experience. It would be unique too. There were lots of other dude ranches who advertised authentic Western experiences, but they also had golf courses and yachts you could rent for an afternoon.

This concept was different. She could hardly keep her fingers moving fast enough as enthusiasm filled her office.

She and Charli hashed out plans until well past lunchtime. Ace had poked his head in the door no less than five times, just to make sure nothing had happened to her, which was sweet, but where would she go?

Nowhere that he wasn't, that was for sure.

She hadn't forgotten for a second that he'd camped right outside her door, giving her the space and privacy to work, but within shouting distance. Jonas hadn't been thrilled over her commandeering one of his hands, but he'd get over it, especially when she presented him with Charli's newly designed ranch offering.

Ace belonged to her now, in more ways than one. And she was pretty sure he felt the same way about her. It was time to move that forward.

After she and Charli talked for so long that they both went hoarse, she sent her sister off to think about new decorating ideas with the intent of stealing a few minutes for herself. But not alone.

When she opened the door, Ace was sitting in a hardback chair, leaning back against the wall with the front half a foot off the ground. He barely fit in the chair in the first place. It was no wonder he'd figured out a way to give his ridiculously long legs extra room.

"Hey," she murmured and crossed her arms, leaning against the doorjamb as she drank in his beautiful form. "Can I see you for a minute?"

Both front legs thumped to the floor. "Am I being called to the principal's office?"

"Something like that."

But the grin on his face told her he didn't mind so much. "I like anything that means I don't have to try to see through walls to make sure you're okay."

The moment he cleared the door, she shut it and put her back against it. Ace stood near her desk, brows cocked in question, clearly waiting for her to get to the punch line.

She didn't make him wait for it. "It feels like we've turned a corner. So I think it's time you took me on a proper date."

"What corner have we turned?" he asked, scrubbing the back of his neck in that odd, endearing way he had when he was unsure what was happening.

But she wasn't fooled. A man who kissed her the way he did surely wasn't confused about the chemistry between them. A man who protected her the way he did cared. He couldn't possibly be faking that or anything else going on between them.

"This one."

She crossed the room in one stride and pulled his head down to lay a scorching kiss on him. It took him a beat to really commit but when he did, hooooh boy. He incinerated her from the inside out, his mouth pulling responses from her she hadn't previously known she was capable of.

The kiss held all the promise she'd expected it to. Hoped for. Craved.

Breaking off the kiss, she nuzzled his cheek. "That corner. The one where we both know where this is headed and we're both on board. We're well past the point where it matters that you work for me, but if it's still an issue for you, then we can find you another job."

Ace froze, his expression that of someone who had just

walked out on a thin sheet of ice and heard the first crack. In other words, not the reaction she'd been going for.

"I can't find another job, Sophia. I have to be here, where I can make sure no one tries to take you out of the equation," he argued in what amounted to a frustrating but valid point.

"Then I guess we can wait to make it official, but is there anything wrong with giving me some sign that's where this is headed?" she prompted. When he shook his head, her heart suddenly fell out of rhythm. Now she was the one in the precarious position of wondering how she'd wandered out onto the ice. "What? What's the objection this time?"

She'd meant for it come out flirty and carefree, the way she'd managed to do the last few times she'd tried to move their relationship to a place where she felt more secure in its longevity. But this time felt different. The expression on his face felt different.

And she knew. He wasn't going to say okay. He wasn't going to take her on a date. Somehow, she'd misread his interest in her.

"Sophia," he murmured and shut his eyes for a beat. When he opened them, he seemed to realize he still had her caught up in his embrace. He let go so quickly, she stumbled.

But he didn't reach out to steady her.

That's when the first crack cleaved right down the middle of her heart. "I don't like the way you just said my name. What is going on here? You can't kiss me like that and then back off when I start talking about making things official between us. Now is the perfect time. You're my security detail. We're going to be spending a lot of time together anyway, at least as long as the excavation teams are here. How is that not what you want?"

"I do want that," he told her earnestly and she believed him. Wanted to believe him.

"Then why do you look like someone just died?" Oh, man, she was such a moron. Her hand flew to her mouth as she stared up at him. "It's not your sister, is it? Because that's a legit reason you can't commit right now. I'm sorry, I didn't even think—"

"It's not my sister." He stood there, his hand at the back of his neck, refusing to meet her gaze.

Then finally he did, and she wished he hadn't. The bleakness she saw there scared her. Chilled her to the bone. And she wanted to take back everything she'd said thus far, as long as he didn't look at her like that anymore.

He blew out a breath. "I have to tell you something before this goes any further. Though I have a feeling when I'm finished, you'll be happy it never did."

Okay, now he was *really* scaring her. "What is it, Ace? You can tell me anything."

"Except this." His brief smile had not one iota of warmth in it. "I'm not who you think I am."

Chapter 22

Oh, man, now that it was out there, Ace had expected to feel lighter, as if a weight had lifted. But all he felt was blackness and his own guilt for letting it get to this point, plus a healthy amount of self-recrimination for hurting Sophia, who looked like he'd punched her in the face.

"What do you mean?" she whispered. "Are you working for Intruder Man?"

"No," he insisted hotly. But then had to take a step back. What if he *was*? "I guess that's part of the issue. I don't know who I'm working for."

"Besides me, you mean?" Her tone had an acid underlay that made him cringe.

She'd caught on really fast. If he hadn't already been in love with her, that would have tipped the scales.

"Besides you," he admitted. "I was hired by someone to watch you and make sure nothing happened to you. But it was part of my employment agreement that I wouldn't reveal to you that I'd been hired."

"Except you're telling me now," she pointed out. "What changed?"

"You did." He ached to reach out and enfold her back into his embrace, to connect with her in the way that made him feel whole. But the vibe between them said he might pull back a bloody stump if he tried it. "You deserve to understand why I can't be with you the way you would like."

"Because you've been lying to me," she said flatly, understanding dawning in her green eyes. "So this is your heroic effort to make sure your conscience is clean before we get naked together, is that it?"

"Among other things, yes."

This conversation was going either much better than he'd been expecting or much worse. That was the rub. He couldn't read Sophia the way he normally could, and it was gutting him.

"What other things?" Her gaze narrowed.

Worse. This conversation was going much worse. He swallowed. "You didn't know I was here under false pretenses. Now you do. But you also don't know why I'm so good at what I do. You deserve to know that too."

"I do know," she snapped, then all the fight seemed to drain out of her at once. "Or I thought I did. You had me convinced you were a straight arrow. The goodest of the good. The kind of guy who was the opposite of my father, one who would stick with me through thick and thin. Only to find out you're just like him. A liar."

The direct hit hurt but not as much as the hopelessness he saw steal over her expression. He'd done that to her. Made her believe there were men out there who weren't like her father, only to prove her wrong.

"I'm sorry," he whispered. "I never meant for it to happen like this. I never meant to fall for you."

She laughed bitterly and sank into her desk chair, probably to put some distance between them. "Funny, that was exactly what I was praying to hear five minutes ago. I wanted to know if you felt even a tenth of what I was feeling for you. I figured I had a pretty good read on you, so I wasn't walking into this blind. Little did I know."

"I'm not a liar," he said and held up his hands in surrender when she shot him a black look. "It's semantics. But it was a condition of my employment that I not tell you. If it means anything, I'm pretty sure I've just nullified my contract."

"You'll forgive me if I don't have a lot of sympathy for you since that sounds pretty convenient for you." The laptop on the desk in front of her was open and she stared at the screen blankly. "Who puts that kind of stipulation on an employment contract? No one. Or rather no one I'd do business with, if it's even true. It's curious that you thought nothing of it."

Well. He had bills. Bills that he wouldn't be paying now that he'd sacrificed his fee. He'd fight to allow McKay and Pierce to keep their two-thirds, but ultimately that wasn't up to him. It was a crappy situation all the way around, but he couldn't have gone another minute without telling her the truth.

Which he still hadn't done, not fully. And wished he didn't have to, but it would be better to pull the bandage off in one shot. Now, before anything else happened.

"That's because you don't really know me," he said, the harsh words making her flinch. He bucked up under it, though. It was time to lay it all out. "I'm the ace in the hole for one reason. Because I can dispatch terrorists better, faster and more efficiently than anyone else on the planet."

It wasn't a compliment, and he didn't wear it like one. It was a burden. One he'd stood up under for a long time.

Telling her felt less like coming clean and more like he'd piled filth on top of the existing wounds.

"What are you telling me?" she asked suspiciously. "That you weren't really in the military and you were some kind of mercenary instead?"

"No, of course not." Though it wasn't far off. "I was a SEAL, working for the US government. Highly trained. Very motivated to do my job. That meant eliminating targets and I was good at it. More so than anyone else in my platoon, so guess who got the dirty work? I have blood on my hands, Sophia. So much blood."

He could never wash it off. The stain went too deep.

She shook her head. "That's your big secret? You were good at your job? Pardon me while I faint in shock."

Confused, he stared at her. "Are you listening to me? I'm a highly trained killing machine. I killed people. Lots of them. I can't ever wash that stigma away."

"It's not a stigma in war, Ace," she said, brushing it aside as if his greatest shame wasn't something to even consider, let alone worry over. "You were under orders. What would you have done instead, told your commanding officer no? Please. What does that have to do with your post-service decisions? Nothing. You walked in here, fully aware that you'd be lying to me from the outset. *That's* the issue."

"But I didn't have a choice," he explained again, realizing how it sounded, and she didn't give him an inch of grace.

"We always have choices, Ace," she countered, arms crossed over her stomach as if it hurt. "And it sounds like you made yours before we even met."

He had. He'd become a SEAL. Become the kind of man

who would take the lives of others, one who didn't deserve a woman like Sophia.

"Which I can't undo. And I'm sorry for that. But the other choice would have been to not take the job, and I did. That, I won't apologize for. If I hadn't been here, you might have been killed that first day by the man who broke into your office. Or by the sniper in the woods. The backhoe. Possibly even another threat that didn't happen because I am here."

And he'd staunchly defend the fact that he'd done his job as dictated. He'd kept her safe. That had to count for something.

She nodded. "Yeah, one could view it that way. Or Intruder Man was after the key to the safety deposit box all along and because you found it, all that other stuff was set in motion. The guy in the woods could have been shooting at you, after all."

The point wasn't lost on him, and his stomach squelched with a sickening, greasy flood.

Was that what had happened? Had he inadvertently made the threat to Sophia worse? Surely not, or he wouldn't have been hired in the first place. Someone knew she'd be in danger, though.

What if that someone knew because he was the actual threat?

That made zero sense. Ace shook his head. He refused to believe that Intruder Man, or one of his associates, hired him.

"I guess we don't really know for sure," he said. "But I firmly believe that someone had your best interests at heart and handed that job to me so I could stand between you and anything that wanted to hurt you."

Her soft laugh sounded broken. “The irony. Who was supposed to protect me from you being the one to hurt me?”

“Sophia.” His own voice broke. “What’s happening between us is real. When I kiss you, it’s like the rest of the world falls away and I’m flooded with you. There’s no employment contract. No treasure, except the one I’m holding in my arms. Focus on that.”

“Are you seriously trying to make things be okay between us? Like we’re going to pick up where we left off now that I know the truth?”

She stared at him, her gaze boring through him, and he imagined this was Advertising Executive Sophia. The one she’d insisted he would hate, and while he could never hate her, he did feel the chill in his bones.

“No, that’s not what I’m trying to say.” He could scarcely breathe around the weight on his chest. “I just…don’t want you to feel like it was fake on my side. As if you can’t trust that what I feel for you is real. I don’t want to take that from you.”

The wall above Sophia’s desk had a spot where the texture hadn’t been formed right. It was flat and hollowed out, a metaphor for how he felt. As if he’d scooped out his insides, leaving him with nothingness. It was a fitting punishment for what he’d done. What he’d always known would be in store for him in the long run.

“It doesn’t matter anyway,” he continued. “I’m not good enough for you. You’re right that I made decisions long before we met that make me who I am. I was a good SEAL, but that makes me a bad person. A man who can’t erase the sins of the past. For that, I’m truly sorry. You deserve better.”

Grimly, she set her mouth in a line, her expression, her

body language, shut like she'd locked herself away behind a concrete wall. "Everything you've ever said to me is in question now. In a lot of ways, you're worse than my father. At least he just left."

"And I'm not leaving you," he told her fiercely, circling the desk, daring to get in her space even though she had clearly wanted the barrier. "I would never abandon you."

"You did, Ace," she said in a small voice that brought him up short before he could take her hand as he'd intended to do. "From the beginning, you never gave me a chance. A real chance. In your head, it was never going to work, or you would have been honest with me way before now. That's the unforgiveable part."

He nodded. It was true. There was never a scenario where he would have made a different decision and that's what he had to live with. "I'm still your bodyguard. That hasn't changed."

"Oh, I'm aware. Regardless of how any of this transpired, the danger is real. I get it. You're going to keep doing your job and I'm going to allow it. But you can do it from that side of the door." She pointed and he recognized a dismissal when he saw one.

Ace walked through the door and shut it, the click reverberating in his heart much more loudly than he would have expected.

So that was done. The weight on his chest didn't abate even hours later, when Sophia finally emerged from her office. The icy silence between them physically hurt, but he took it as his due. She spoke to him by rote, without an ounce of the spirit and fire that he'd grown accustomed to. It was like the woman he'd spent the last few weeks with didn't exist anymore. As if her essence had been sucked out.

And maybe that's what he'd really done with his confession. Drained her of everything that mattered. He'd have to live with that too. But he'd meant what he said, and he'd never walk away, not while there was a chance that someone might threaten her. Or worse.

His conscience would be clear, no matter what.

It was everything else—his heart, his soul, his very marrow—that would bear the black mark of what had happened in her office earlier.

This went on for twenty-four excruciating hours. Sophia shut herself up in her office, sometimes with Charli, sometimes alone, but Ace was always on the outside. That left him at loose ends, running patrols past her window. Coordinating with McKay as he kept an eye on Charli. Working with the archeology teams as the point person. Essentially doing exactly what he'd been doing, but this time with a layer of frost between him and Sophia.

Now it was only a job. Before, he'd been included in the small details of her life, could be easy with her and vice versa. And being cut off from that hurt.

It also made him realize this hadn't been strictly a job from the start. He'd maybe gone into this thinking so, but the idea that he'd stay on the fringes had been eliminated as a possibility pretty much from the first moment he'd laid eyes on Sophia Lang.

She'd speared something inside instantly.

And maybe she'd clued in on that a lot faster than he had. It hit him as he watched her trek to the bunkhouse to speak with Jonas, trailing her because she didn't like it when he walked in step with her. He *had* decided in his head that they weren't meant to be—because it never occurred to him that she wouldn't care about his bloody hands. That it truly wouldn't be a factor in how she felt about him.

He'd used that as an excuse, keeping it between them, all the while pretending the job stipulations were the reason. In reality, it was an easily removed barrier.

This relationship had been doomed the moment he'd thrown up that barrier. He'd ruined anything that might have happened between them with that one simple mistake.

The moment of clarity washed through him, and he wanted to tell her. To apologize all over again. But he had to wait because she'd gone inside with Jonas to discuss ranch business.

Once upon a time, he'd have been included. She'd seen Ace as a partner, someone to share the burden of her life. That's what he wanted. With Sophia. There had to be a way to fix this, to get past his mistake.

What if it was too late?

No, he refused to accept that. She had to see that he'd done it to protect himself, but he was over that now. He wanted to lay it all bare for her and let her make her own decisions.

When she came out of the bunkhouse fifty-eight agonizingly long minutes later, he smiled at her, his face muscles protesting the movement that he hadn't made in a very long time. She didn't smile back.

"Sophia, I need to talk to you," he said without preamble. "It's important."

She blew past him. "I can't talk to you right now."

"Please." He caught up with her in two strides and made the mistake of trying to slow her down by grabbing her hand.

She yanked it free and rounded on him, fire sparking

from her gaze. "Don't. This is not working. I cannot do this with you any longer. I'll hire another bodyguard. Someone without an agenda or the history. But you can't be here anymore. You're fired."

Chapter 23

Sophia slammed the door to the house, the windowpane on the top half rattling. So much for her plan to keep pretending Andrew Madden—if that was even his real name—didn't exist. She'd held out, what, a whole day before blowing her ice princess routine to shreds.

She gave herself points for not peering through the window to see if Ace really left the ranch after she'd fired him or if he would duck back into the bunkhouse to lie low while keeping his eagle eye on everything.

Because she had a feeling she knew. The man could stick.

He'd never leave unless she forced him to, by calling the cops or something. That was the screwed-up thing about all of this. Even as she'd accused him of being just like her father, she'd recognized the problem with that comparison. He wasn't anything like David Lang.

The only thing Ace had in common with her father was that she wouldn't trust either one of them as far as she could throw him. Where her father excelled at making himself scarce, Ace was wired differently.

Or at least that's what she'd believed before his bombshell. Yeah, he wasn't who she thought, not by a long shot.

He wasn't actually her employee. Not *only* her employee, rather.

All this time, she'd worried over dating someone who worked for her. Ironic, right? He was only on her payroll in order to finagle his way into her good graces so he could... Well, she didn't exactly know what his angle was, but he had one all right.

All men did. Even that one. What an idiot she was for thinking he was different.

And she wouldn't waste a second more of her energy on him. That was how men really made you suffer, by plucking at your emotions. Well, not Sophia Lang. She'd cut her teeth on kicking men to the curb.

Too bad she hadn't done that in the first place.

One tear welled up and she let it fall. That was the extent of how much she'd cry over Andrew Christopher, especially since she scarcely knew the man. You couldn't truly be sad about the loss of something that hadn't been real in the first place.

Forge ahead. That was the new plan.

Sophia stormed to her office and did not look up until she'd spent three hours working on the new marketing campaign for the Cowboy Experience at Hidden Creek Ranch. Charli's idea. And it was a good one.

All the reasons she'd been excited after hashing this out with her sister came back to her as she pulled on her considerable expertise to tease out ways to sell the concept to a variety of audiences. Twentysomethings who wanted a sustainable vacation that gave back to the earth instead of stealing from it. Thirty-to-forty-five-ish couples with kids who didn't want to spend the equivalent of a year's college tuition on a spring break trip. Baby boomers who remembered all the great Westerns fondly. Everyone in between who wanted to brag about their unique vacation.

Twice, she glanced up, imagining she'd heard Ace in the hallway. That was the problem with spending so much time with someone. You got used to them being around and when they weren't, it felt like an arm had been cut off.

Plus, she missed him. Sometime in the last hour, she'd let herself admit that.

Despite everything, the man had this smile that she couldn't get over. When he looked at her, she felt *seen*. What was she supposed to do with this ache in her heart?

It was a good thing she had all this work to take her mind off everything else wrong in her life. And just like that, her concentration snapped.

Since the last time she'd looked out the window, the sun had set, plunging the ranch into darkness. Goodness, she'd completely forgotten about eating dinner.

Maybe Charli would like to go with her into town to the Dairy Queen. Just as she raised a hand to knock on her sister's door, she remembered that Charli had told her earlier that day that she had a date tonight. One of the new ranch hands, if she recalled, which Sophia would have warned her about if asked, but really, not everyone was here under false pretenses. This new guy was probably on the complete up and up, and her sister seemed pretty into the idea of dating a cowboy, so who was she to get in the way?

A little morose that her own cowboy experience hadn't worked out so well, she padded into the kitchen, wondering where she'd left her shoes. Jenny had gone to the market apparently, bless her. The makings of a ham sandwich and a small salad would do fine.

The food tasted like sawdust, and she ate as much of

it as she could before deciding she wasn't all that hungry, after all. Good gravy, what was wrong with her? Pre-Ace, she'd never even thought twice about being alone. Or lonely. This would pass. Eventually she'd forget how the man had lit her up inside.

She heard a sound near the front door, like scrabbling. Charli. She rolled her eyes. That girl would forget her head if it wasn't attached.

"Forget your key?" she said as she flipped on the porch light and swung the door open wide.

It wasn't Charli. A man stood on her porch, a gun in his hand, which he leveled at her.

There was a *man* on her porch holding a *gun*. Pointed at *her*.

Fear flooded her stomach in an icy, oily wave. She froze, every bit of her self-defense training sliding right out of her brain. She didn't even have her purse, so how would she grab the Mace on her keychain? Stupid.

She had just enough wits about her to realize it was Intruder Man.

"Appreciate you saving me the trouble, Ms. Lang," he drawled, a sly smile on his face.

His uncovered face. That couldn't be good. Robbers always wore masks so they couldn't be identified, right? So this guy must not care about that. Because he expected her to be dead at the end of this.

"What do you want?" she croaked. "I don't have any money."

He laughed. "Oh, but you do. Specifically, coins. The Maya variety. We're going to have a good long chat about that, Ms. Lang."

He motioned her to the side and when she didn't immediately comply, he reached out and cuffed her across the cheek.

Pain exploded along the already stressed bone where she'd hit the concrete of the shelter. She cried out involuntarily, her palm flying to cover the spot, like that would help anything.

"Move out of the doorway," he snarled, apparently done with being smiley, and grabbed her arm, hustling her to the spot that was apparently acceptable to him. "We don't want any of your watchdogs to know I'm here, now do we?"

Watch*dogs*? Did he think any of the ranch hands cared about what went on at the main house? Well, other than Ace, who probably had left after all since she hadn't seen hide nor hair of him in hours.

"How do you know my name?" she asked. As if that was the most important thing to get straight here. But he'd spoken to her like he knew her, and she most certainly did not know him outside of the incident in her study. And probably the woods—surely, he'd been the one shooting at them.

"I pay attention. That's how I know you found one of the coins. Where? Tell me."

"You mean the backhoe and drones clued you in?" she shot back sarcastically, her cheek still stinging enough to egg on her mood. "You're pretty sharp."

"Don't be mouthy or I'll use my fist on your face next time, little girl," he said, and she believed him.

He wasn't too tall, but he had a beefiness about him that said he might have a heck of a punch. She already knew he could slam a woman into a wall hard enough to leave her in pain. As much as the slap had hurt, she didn't want to find out what else he had in store for her.

Like the bullets in the chamber of that gun he still

pointed at her. He cocked the hammer and nodded once. “Now talk. Tell me where you found the coin.”

Sure, and once she did that, he’d kill her and leave her body here for Charli or Jenny to find. The blood would be impossible to get out of the carpet. And that’s how you officially figured out you were verging on hysteria, when bloodstains mattered more than being dead.

“It would be easier and faster if I showed you,” she improvised wildly. “I’m not quite sure exactly where it was. It was dark and the woods are so big.”

“That’s an even better idea,” he mused. “I was thinking of making you write it down, but this way, if you tell me the wrong area, you can still be convinced to try again.”

“Who are you?” she asked, searching for some kind of weapon in her peripheral vision. “You’re the same one who broke in here and rifled through the desk in my office.”

Something flickered through his gaze. The fact that she’d identified him didn’t sit well for some reason. Well, he hadn’t worn a mask then, either. What did he expect?

“That’s not important. I’m no one to you, other than the last face you’ll ever see on this earth if you don’t tell me what I need to know.”

“I said I’d show you,” she snapped. “I need shoes and a jacket if I’m going to be walking through the woods at gunpoint.”

“Fine,” he allowed wearily. “Make it fast. You have ten seconds. I’m counting down. Ten, nine…”

She raced to find her phone and hid it in her pocket at the same time she threw on a jacket and stepped into her slip-ons, the ones she wore outside when she didn’t want to worry about wading through horse manure. Hopefully if anyone was paying attention, they would wonder why she was wearing them at night.

Who she thought would be paying that much attention, she had no idea. Charli probably had no idea what kind of shoes Sophia wore ever, let alone if it was a weird time.

Ace would know, though. He inherently processed details. But she'd sent him away and then forgot about hiring another bodyguard.

Apparently, that would be the last in a long line of mistakes.

"Time's up," he called following her trek through the house, then manhandling her without remorse as he dragged her through the front door.

She had a moment when she thought he'd leave it open, but he shut it, ruining the idea that someone might realize she'd been taken if the door was standing wide.

"Start walking," he commanded.

She did, refusing to acknowledge how hard her legs were shaking. The last time she'd taken this route, Ace had walked alongside her, holding her hand to help her over things, his thumb rubbing over hers companionably.

The tears welled up in earnest now. This man would kill her, she had no doubt, and the last thing she'd said to Ace was *you're fired.* What she wished she'd said, she couldn't fathom, but leaving things in limbo between them wasn't sitting well with her. Not when faced with this kind of an end.

Not that she planned to go down without a fight. But she didn't imagine she'd be much match for a gun.

Moonlight lit the path well enough that she didn't stumble too much, and an eternity later she saw the fence line for the Silver Acres Ranch in the distance. "We're almost there."

"This better be the right place," he said and wagged his gun. "Or I'll shoot you in the arm so you can still walk to the place you should have started with."

"This is where we found it," she told him with a scowl. "Why would I take you to the wrong place? There's nothing else here. The excavation teams started in this area first."

The man stared at the freshly turned earth and swore. The swath extended in a long dark square, stretching more than twenty feet. It couldn't be clearer that someone had dug here recently with heavy, efficient machinery. She couldn't read the look on his face, but it was definitely not happy.

"They didn't find anything else?" he asked and then turned his displeased gaze on her once again. "You're lying. They found the st—artifacts. Someone had to have found it."

Whatever *it* was, that's what this guy was looking for. Maybe had been the whole time.

"No one found anything. Look, the teams are publishing their findings on the Harvard and UT websites. You can read for yourself exactly what they're doing. No kidnapping plot required."

He shook his head, hard, as if she wasn't making sense. Well, she hated to break it to him. There was nothing about this treasure hunt that made sense.

"There was a map," he said. "Where was the other X?"

"The other X?" she repeated carefully. "There was only one. This one. How did you know about the map?"

"Not important. I need that map." His gaze narrowed and she did not like the vibe rolling from him. Dangerous, with a side of evil. "You're going to get it for me."

"You can have the map," she said and meant it. "The

treasure belongs to the people of Mexico and there are almost two dozen scientists on-site who are doing their part to ensure that's what happens to it."

She wasn't worried about this idiot discovering anything that a bunch of really smart people hadn't already learned about the treasure.

Her captor swore again and rubbed his temple. "You've been nothing but a problem. I tried to tell him. This is not the right way."

"What's not the right way?" Who was *him*?

"Stop talking. You've got a mouth that won't quit," he sneered and grabbed her arm, shoving the short barrel between her ribs. The metal scraped against bone painfully. "Move. We're taking another walk."

"To where?" she managed to get out around her clacking teeth.

If he pulled the trigger now, he wouldn't miss. The bullet would tear through her body and there would be no coming back from that.

He didn't answer, just kept hauling her through the woods. But she recognized the shed with the hidden shelter from a hundred yards away. Apparently, he'd found it since the night she and Ace had spent there. Because she didn't for a second believe he'd known they'd been trapped there and left them alone.

The man—whose name she still didn't know—marched her into the shed and down the rickety stairs, shutting the repaired door behind them. It still locked from the other side, but she didn't think that would matter since he didn't seem intent on leaving her there by herself.

The ceiling had also been repaired. Too bad. That might have been a great vantage point for someone to discover she was being held hostage down here in the shelter. If anyone would even think to look for her.

Ace would have. If she hadn't gotten her emotions in a twist and done something stupid like tell him she didn't need his services without securing an actual backup.

He would have looked for her no matter what. Whether he was on her payroll or not. She knew exactly what the expression on his face would be as he searched. How his arms would feel when he found her and crushed her to his chest as he validated for himself that she was safe.

"You've messed everything up," her captor told her derisively. "I gave you a lot of chances to back off. To leave the ranch and never come back. I really thought the backhoe would scare you away for good. Now it's time to do this differently."

The backhoe hadn't been an accident. Ace would never let her live this down. If she got out of this and had a chance to tell him. And he was still speaking to her.

A hysterical sob rose in her throat, and she choked it back. "That's what all of this has been about? Shooting at me in the woods? If you were trying to scare me away, you did a poor job of it."

"Yeah, I'm aware," he said with a frustrated smirk. "Instead of leaving, you invited a lot more people to the party. My boss is very unhappy. So we're going to see if I can get him into a little better mood. I'm going to kill you and leave you here with a note that says your little sister is next if I don't get the map in my hand in twelve hours."

Sophia's pulse scattered. New plan. Hard to come up with one when she couldn't breathe and somehow now Charli's life was in danger. She didn't believe for a second that this still-nameless guy would let Charli live after he got the map.

"You'll never get away with this," she told him. "There are too many people around. You'll never be able to search the property without getting caught."

"Oh, good point," he said, nodding as if they were having a lovely chat. "I'll include that as a stipulation, then. Map, and everyone has to clear out or the sister dies. Thanks. I owe you one. Oh, wait, you're going to be dead, so I guess I'll never have to pay."

He levered up the gun and pointed it at her. The look on his face put a chill deep down in her bowels. He was going to kill her.

Just as the muscles in his forearm tensed to pull the trigger, someone burst from the stairway and crashed into her captor.

Ace.

Chapter 24

Ace grappled with Intruder Man for the second time. It would definitely be the last.

The gun was easy to dispatch since Ace had managed to surprise him. When he kicked it to the side, he called to Sophia, "Grab it!"

That beautiful woman sprang into action, no questions asked. He didn't have time to make sure she succeeded. During the half second Ace split his attention, Intruder Man got in a lucky swing to his jaw.

Stars exploded across his vision, but he blinked fast and shook it off, rolling up on the toes of his boots to brace for the next blow. Intruder Man didn't disappoint him, coming in low. Ace blocked him easily and went in for the kill, vising his elbow around his opponent's neck and grabbing it to use as a lever to snap his neck.

It was rote. Kill or be killed. This pile of filth had kidnapped Sophia, scared her, probably hurt her. He deserved to die.

At the last millisecond, he checked his strength. And didn't do it. He held this man's life in his hands—which Intruder Man likely didn't even realize—but this wasn't who Ace wanted to be.

This was a choice. He had choices. He didn't have to live in the shadow of the man he'd been. He could be something else if he wanted to. He could choose that right now. For himself and Sophia.

The blackness inside eased all at once. Reconciling the past might take a little longer, but for the first time he felt like he could do it. History didn't have to define his future.

Intruder Man struggled in Ace's headlock, but he wasn't going anywhere unless given permission. Ace was not in a permissive mood.

"Sophia," he called. "Cock that gun and hand it to me."

She obliged and even had the foresight to come up behind him so Intruder Man couldn't grab the gun first. His heart squeezed. Sophia Lang was everything and then some.

In a flash, he released Intruder Man and stuck the gun right at the small of his back where he could take out a kidney and his heart in one shot.

"I wouldn't tempt me if I were you," Ace advised him. "I won't spare you a second time."

"Shoot him in the arm," Sophia advised, her own arms crossed and a glare on her beautiful face. "Then he can still walk and probably won't bleed to death."

There wasn't anything funny about this, but he had to bite back the urge to laugh anyway. This woman slayed him. Even when they were still at odds. The tight band around his lungs eased a fraction, though he didn't think he'd ever get back the years taken off his life when he'd found her missing.

Intruder Man snarled at her. "Shut it, little girl. You're going to get yours, don't worry."

"I'm not worried. You should be, though. I hear Huntsville is a brutal place, but you'll get used to it," she advised him with a brittle smile. "As long as you'll be there, you'll have to."

Ace wrestled his captive up the stairs, Sophia trailing him. He wished he could spend just five seconds making sure she was okay, but he had plenty of time for that later.

Besides, she obviously still had her spirit. Neither Intruder Man nor Ace's boneheadedness had stolen that from her. Good.

The police had finally arrived sometime in the last few minutes, judging by the number of flashing red and blue lights gathered at the main house. When Ace and Sophia rolled into sight, Charli flew from the porch, catching her sister in a giant hug. Several of the scientists stood off to the side, matching smiles as they patted Sophia on the back or calling out that they were happy to see her unharmed.

Ace found one of the state troopers they'd called in just in case Intruder Man had taken Sophia across county lines. He handed over his cargo, along with the gun for evidence, and engaged in the longest conversation on record about the circumstances of his involvement, how he'd captured the assailant, as well as securing his promise to go down to the local station to submit his own prints for investigative purposes.

The last thing he wanted to do was stand here doing official business when he needed to touch Sophia to calm his racing pulse.

An eternity later, he found her standing near the back door to the house, chaffing her palms up and down on her arms as if the chill had finally gotten to her. She was alone, Charli apparently having gone inside.

"Here." He slipped his own flannel shirt around her shoulders, more than comfortable in his base-layer T-shirt.

She didn't shrug it off, a miracle. It wouldn't be shocking to find out she'd rather be cold than wear something of his.

"I thought I fired you," she said, the expression on her face unreadable.

"Well, it turns out you're not my only employer, so…" He lifted his hands. "I still had that backup job to do."

"You told me you forfeited your fee." A line appeared between her brows. "Or was that a lie too?"

"There are more things in this world that motivate me than money," he told her simply. "Making sure I got you back in one piece is a job I'd do for free over and over again."

Her eyes softened then, flooding him with something that had been missing for far too long—hope. He drank in her beautiful face and finally let himself feel the terror he'd held at bay for the long minutes it had taken him to realize where Intruder Man would have taken her.

But she was safe now and he wanted nothing more than to catch her up in his embrace so he could breathe her in. If nothing else, he knew beyond a shadow of a doubt how he felt about her. Rescuing a woman you loved from a kidnapper put a lot of things in perspective.

"How did you find me?" she asked. "Or is that a dumb question? You were still watching the house, weren't you?"

The state trooper took off with a wail of his siren, escorting Intruder Man off the premises for the last time.

"Not well enough," he muttered. "The light in the kitchen was on. I figured you were still in there since you always turn it off when you leave a room. I kept thinking it was so odd that you'd stayed in the kitchen that long and finally I kicked myself into checking. You were gone. That's when I knew something was wrong."

A smile lifted the corners of Sophia's mouth. "Of all things. My anal retentiveness is what saved me?"

"No." He let his own smile bloom. "The fact that I wouldn't have been able to live with myself if I didn't get a chance to apologize is what saved you."

"I'm listening."

Miraculously, she was. He didn't waste the opportunity, and neither could he possibly deny himself the urge to reach out. To finally touch her. When he grasped her hand, she didn't flinch. Progress.

"I'm sorry I didn't believe in us at the time when it was most important. From the beginning. Rookie mistake. You see, I've never been in love before, so I had no idea I was screwing up until it was too late."

That's when the weight lifted. He'd spilled the contents of his heart all over the ground at her feet. All he could do was pray she wouldn't stomp on it.

"That was a pretty good apology," she said, her expression still not giving away much. "But Ace, jeez. I'm still reeling. Give me time to get my feet under me."

"Of course," he interjected quickly. "What like, five, ten minutes?"

Mistake. He knew it the second it left his mouth. Her smile vanished and what felt like quicksand opened up beneath his feet.

"It's not the time for jokes. I'm sorry."

Her hand slipped from his. Along with the hope he'd let himself feel. His heart ached but he made himself nod. "Okay. What can I do?"

"I need space. Obviously, firing you isn't going to work, so just… I don't know. Don't push me right now."

He nodded, his throat tight. It wasn't an outright dismissal but it also wasn't Sophia in his arms forever like the vision in his head. But maybe he could still get there. "I can do that."

And then he had to let her walk away again. But this time, he wasn't going to sit quietly on the sidelines.

When the officer assigned to Sophia's case came by the next afternoon, Ace answered the door with Sophia's blessing and checked credentials or whatever a security specialist did when he wasn't undercover any longer.

Sophia had long lost track of what she was supposed to call the man she couldn't ignore no matter how hard she tried. There was something in the set of his shoulders as he spoke to the uniformed officer that caught and held her attention. Slightly slumped, as if he had a barbell across them with fifty pounds on it weighing him down.

Not that she was spending an inordinate amount of time studying him. The opposite. In fact, she'd say she was going out of her way to not look at him.

Except that was a lie, because her eye kept being drawn to Ace no matter what she promised herself. There was something different about him. Something missing. A… sparkle. Which sounded dumb because he was the most masculine man she'd ever met in her life. But that didn't change facts and before she'd fired him, Ace had always had some kind of je ne sais quoi that she'd found enormously attractive. Obviously.

She cleared her throat.

"Thank you for coming by," she told the officer, whose name tag read Hernandez. "Do you have an update for us?"

Automatically, she'd included Ace and he'd noticed, judging by his quick glance at her face. Well, she wasn't going to take it back. Pretending she didn't see the wisdom in trying to get back to some semblance of their former partnership would be useless. She hated that she needed him. But he was incredibly good at his job. His real job. The one someone who wasn't her had hired him to do.

That was the thing she couldn't stop puzzling over in her head. At first, she'd been convinced he was lying. Who would hire someone and make a rule that it had to be a secret? That was the dumbest thing she'd ever heard of.

But then…if he'd made that up, why? What would be the benefit of lying about being forced to protect her without her knowledge? Wasn't he doing a much better job now that all pretenses were gone?

It was maddening. And that's why she hadn't made up her mind yet on whether she could trust him. Or forgive him.

"I do have an update," the officer announced, glancing at Ace.

Sophia clasped her hands together. "Please feel free to speak candidly. Mr. Madden is head of security at the ranch."

Well. *I guess I just gave Ace his job back.* Or something. The title had just rolled off her tongue so easily. He wisely chose not to say a word, but he did throw up a questioning hand behind Officer Hernandez's back. She made a face at him, and he tipped his hat with a small smile.

For one second, she forgot that she was mad at him and everything sweet and light and wonderful flooded her heart as she soaked up the harmony between them. This was how it had been before, and she missed it.

Officer Hernandez consulted what must be notes on his phone. "The man who kidnapped you is Rodrigo Cortez. He's a known associate of Karl Davenport."

The name struck a chord inside her that rang like a gong. "That was my father's partner."

Without hesitation, Ace came to stand behind her, his presence a solid warmth at her back. He didn't say a word, but she got the message just the same. *I'm here.* Her heart soaked it up. Reveled in it. She wasn't alone and this man was making sure she knew it.

What was she supposed to do with him? He'd *lied* to her. Okay, it was more like he'd misled her. Like her father had. That made them the same.

Except even she couldn't sell that to herself any longer. She was going to have to reframe everything. She just didn't know how.

Officer Hernandez consulted his notes again. "Yes, Davenport did work with David Lang, but we don't have a lead on either of their whereabouts. We're trying to get Cortez to make a deal. Trade info for leniency, but so far he's not talking."

Ace nodded. "You'll keep us informed? Especially if he makes bail?"

"He's not making bail," Hernandez confirmed grimly. "The judge considers him a flight risk since he's a Mexican citizen."

It was over. Intruder Man finally had a name, and he wasn't a threat any longer. Her knees nearly gave out as relief flooded her. Ace and the officer ran through a few more details, none of which she heard. She was too busy trying to sort out her new normal, the one where Ace didn't have to play the part of her bodyguard any longer. Where there were no secrets between them.

What did that look like? Happily ever after, or more like Sophia kicking yet another man to the curb because they were all untrustworthy?

The next morning, Sophia spent a few hours on the new Cowboy Experience plan, doubly excited about executing it since Cortez had been arrested. It bothered her a little that her father's partner, Karl Davenport, was still at large. Hernandez had assured her that several law enforcement agencies were looking for him—and her father—for questioning regarding the coins that had been found at the ranch.

She figured she'd rather them both stay far away from her. The resentment she'd always had for her father leaving her was still there, but it wasn't as sharp. Maybe she could forgive him one day.

Pulling up her accounting software, Sophia plowed through a few dozen entries until a tinkling sound broke her concentration. It was coming from the window.

Mystified, she pushed her chair back and went to investigate, her pulse trilling a little as stray noises still managed to do for some reason despite Intruder Man being behind bars. But it wasn't a threat—at least not to her life.

Her heart, on the other hand… Ace stood outside the window throwing tiny pebbles at the glass. He had an acoustic guitar in his hand and a smile on his face that she couldn't help but respond to.

Levering up the window, she crossed her arms and called out, "What's all this?"

"This—" he gestured in a wide arc around his hips "—is

me giving you space. This—" he held up the guitar "—is my attempt to steal your heart away from Orien Bright. I'm not as good, but I've been practicing."

Ace strummed the guitar and broke into a surprisingly not-awful rendition of "Mammas Don't Let Your Babies Grow Up to be Cowboys." Anyone who had grown up in Texas knew the song, which he must know and chose deliberately.

She tried not to be affected. To call up some of the lingering anger she hadn't been able to get rid of. But all of that ceased to matter as he sang to her outside her window. As grand gestures went, it was pretty simple but so powerful that it filled her to the brim. Tears burned her eyes until she let them fall.

He broke off midverse. "Don't cry, Soph. My singing isn't *that* bad."

"It's not. It's…" *Everything.* And she was so tired of being heartsick. "Come inside before everyone on the property lines up to see what's going on."

In seconds, he'd cleared the back door and stood at the threshold of her office, hat in one hand, guitar in the other. Jeez, what a picture he made. Long, lean legs in boots and jeans, a T-shirt and an unbuttoned flannel shirt. Like every other cowboy on this ranch.

But this one was different. She'd known that from the first moment. How different, she'd had no idea.

"You really learned how to play the guitar so you could serenade me?" she murmured.

He shrugged. "I needed something to do while watching the house. I figured if nothing else I could get a few moments of your time and that was worth it to me."

Another stupid tear worked its way loose and splashed

down on her cheek. What was wrong with her? She never cried, especially over a man. Men were the enemy.

But her heart wouldn't hold on to that sentiment.

Maybe a lot of men were awful human beings. But Ace wasn't in that category. Never had been. He'd kept a secret because he was told to, which was as much of a testament to his character as anything else. He'd apologized, and she'd accepted it.

What she hadn't done was return the favor.

"Please. Come in," she whispered, and bit back the smile as he took two baby steps across the threshold. "All the way in."

When this man committed, he held nothing back. He swept into her office and propped the guitar against the wall, then perched a hip on her desk, a scant two feet from her. His presence filled the room, making her light-headed for a minute as she breathed him in. He smelled like pine and man and everything good in the world.

"I owe you an apology," she said and smiled when he quirked a brow at her.

"I think you have that backward," he suggested lightly. "Hence the serenade. This is me going big and not going home."

"Yeah. I got that. You're not going anywhere." She nodded, contemplating him and his strong fingers wrapped around the brim of his hat. That, he'd kept, and held in front of him like a shield, which stung something inside her. "That's the thing. I kept trying to paint you with a brush that wasn't working. I built up this list of sins in my head that starred you right next to my dad as members of the same club. I wanted to find a flaw so I could do what I do best—abandon you before you could do it to me. I'm sorry."

Ace goggled at her. There was no other word for it. His chest rose on a sharply sucked-in breath as he blinked and swallowed in a combo that squeezed her heart as she realized she'd rendered him speechless.

It was sweet and affecting all at once. And she wasn't finished. "I'm also giving you your job back. You're unfired."

The look on his face slayed her. Apparently, being back on the payroll had done the trick to unstick his tongue from the roof of his mouth.

"Are you sure?" he asked so earnestly, she almost rolled her eyes. And honestly, kind of smile a little. He was so adorable sometimes.

"No, I had to really think about whether to hire the best security specialist I've ever seen in action to keep my ranch safe." She did smile then. "Of course I'm sure."

His storm-colored eyes locked onto hers, so much emotion raging through them that they were almost gray. "I meant about the apology. I'm struggling to understand what you think you did wrong. I'm the one who betrayed your trust and—"

She laid two fingers over his lips. "Shh. You did what you had to do. Your honor is not in question. The issue is mine. I'll say it again. I'm sorry. I didn't believe in us at the most important time, when you needed me to forgive you for keeping a secret you weren't at liberty to divulge. I'm working on getting better at letting things go. If you're willing to stick around to find out how I do, I'm not going anywhere, either."

The storm in his gaze got a lot more heated. But he

didn't rush to sweep her into his arms like she'd expected. He did cup her hand and hold it to his cheek, effectively removing her fingers from his lips, which was a shame. She got it, though. There was a lot more to say and he deserved to hear it.

"I need you, Andrew Christopher." She let the sentiment hang there between them, not pulling it back. "Maybe more than I would like."

"Does that scare you?" he asked quietly and set his hat on her desk, leaving his middle exposed. It was as much a testament to his state of mind as anything.

She did not enjoy hard questions. But he'd probably earned the right to ask them and to be given an honest answer. "It does. In many ways. I'm not used to depending on someone else. I like being responsible for myself. It's doubly hard when I trust someone, only to find out he didn't trust me with all of himself."

To his credit, he didn't flinch. He took it in the jaw, his gaze never wavering. "I know, and I'm sorry. I would take it back if I could. It's hard for me to understand why my past isn't a problem for you. It's a problem for me."

That much was the truth. She could see the ghosts of his previous career flitting through him, even as she appreciated that he understood that was the lack of trust she'd referred to. "It shouldn't be. You have a gift. Many gifts. You used them to make Americans safe, same as you did for me. I respect that. You're one of a kind."

Ducking his head at her praise, he flashed her a tiny smile. "I do believe you might be the only person on the planet who would see it that way, but I'll try to accept that it is your viewpoint."

Something shifted between them then, with an almost palpable shimmer in the atmosphere as he rested his hands on her hips, drawing her forward until she was snug against his powerful body.

Their proximity made her breathless.

"Now, we have another issue," she murmured, the storm capturing her thoroughly as she looped her arms around his neck. "I'm officially your boss again. How do you feel about dating in the workplace? Careful. There is a wrong answer."

His mouth twitched and she realized he was fighting a smile. "That depends. Is there a rule against it? I can't stop being the kind of guy who likes to follow rules."

That, she had a very good answer for. "Since I'm the boss, I get to make the rules and the answer is no. There is not a rule."

"Then I'm a fan of it. As long as I'm the only one dating the boss," he said, his voice dropping down into a rough, gravelly range that rumbled in her belly deliciously. "That's nonnegotiable."

"Man, you drive a hard bargain. Fine." She blew out a breath as if flustered and shook her head. "You're the only hot cowboy allowed in my house. But only if you kiss me right now."

Ace tightened his grip and tipped his chin, so many things flitting through his expression. But he didn't kiss her. "I'll get to that in a minute. If we're going to do this thing differently this time, then I'm not pulling any punches. I love you, Sophia Lang. I will never betray your trust again as long as I live."

Well. He'd gone and one-upped her apology, after all. And now her eyes were stinging again. "In the spirit of true confessions, I guess I have to be honest right back. I love you too."

That's when he kissed her with all the pent-up passion that she'd known from day one lurked beneath that hat.

Epilogue

With all of the university people still on-site, Ace and Sophia didn't have much time to themselves over the next few days. And it didn't look like that would change anytime soon once the team unearthed a set of jade beads that the museum in Mexico authenticated as a piece from Pakal the Great's era, but it was not a previously cataloged find, nor was it from Pakal's tomb.

At least Sophia could rest easy that her father had not stolen anything from the museum or the pyramid. It did appear that he might have legitimately found treasure and hidden at least some of it at the ranch.

Interest exploded over what other Maya artifacts might be buried on the property. When Sophia met Heath McKay and Paxton Pierce, she felt a lot better about the security situation. Not that she didn't have full faith in Ace's abilities, but these guys were obviously cut from the same cloth as her head of security, and it couldn't hurt to have extra eyes and ears.

Plus, it was kind of nice to learn that the three men would continue to work together, even after she'd inadvertently split up their company when Ace had accepted her job offer. No one seemed to hold it against her.

Meanwhile, she and Ace stole what few moments they could together, laughing softly together under the stars and grabbing lunch on the wraparound porch if they both had a break. The Cowboy Experience would open for business in a week and a half and Sophia couldn't be more excited about the future of the ranch as she and Charli checked off the to-do list together.

The following Tuesday, her grandpa's lawyer rang the doorbell unexpectedly.

"Mr. Trask," she said as she opened the door, the latest list of facts and figures draining from her head instantly. The last time she'd received an unexpected visit from this man, he'd told her she had inherited the ranch.

Surely he didn't have more surprises in store for her.

"Ms. Lang," he said with a polite smile. "I have a few things to go over with you, if you have some time."

"Of course." She stepped aside to let him into the foyer, not at all shocked to see Ace materialize on the porch behind the lawyer, clearly having noticed the strange car on the property.

He followed Mr. Trask into the house, his gait easy but alert.

"It's fine," she murmured. "He's my grandfather's attorney. And now mine, I guess."

Ace gave her a look as he drew up beside her, always ready to get between her and anything that might cause harm, no matter what. It made her heart swell every time.

Charli came down the stairs. "Was someone at the door? Oh, hello."

"Ms. Lang. I didn't know you were here. Are you living at the ranch now?" Mr. Trask glanced at Sophia, who nodded. "Then she should hear this as well."

Sensing it would be best if everyone was comfortable, she showed Mr. Trask to the living room, still furnished with her grandmother's sofas and pretty chairs flanking the fireplace. Ace clasped her hand as he settled next to her, Charli opting for one of the chairs while Mr. Trask sat on the other sofa, spreading a few papers out next to him.

"Some events have come to my attention recently," Mr. Trask said and cleared his throat. "First off, I want to apologize if I inadvertently put you in danger, Ms. Lang. It may be my fault you were kidnapped."

"What?" Sophia gasped as Ace made a sound in his throat.

"You're going to want to qualify that really fast," Ace said.

Mr. Trask nodded, his mouth firm. "I'm the one who hired you. It was my stipulation that you remain anonymous. I thought that if Ms. Lang knew there might be trouble, it would scare her away from the ranch. It was Mr. Lang's fondest wish that she remain here and build a life."

"It was you," Sophia repeated in wonder as Ace's grip tightened around her hand.

Of all things. She hadn't needed the validation that she'd been right to trust Ace, but the lingering question of why he'd had to keep his original role here a secret had finally been answered.

Mr. Trask shuffled his papers. "Again, my apologies. I had no idea why your grandfather suspected that someone might come looking for things your father may have left behind, but Mr. Lang entrusted me with looking after you, and I made the best decision I could."

"So, it's really over." Ace rubbed the back of his neck. "I was starting to think maybe we'd never know for sure what had happened. But I don't understand why you made the final payment. It arrived in my account two days ago."

And hadn't that been a shock. He'd told her he was afraid to touch it in case it was a mistake.

"Because you earned it," Mr. Trask said decisively. "Ms. Lang is living at the ranch as Mr. Lang wanted, and her sister is here too. You have done a stellar job looking after them both and I hope I can count on you to continue."

"He's on my payroll now," Sophia said, brows raised. "Along with his partners, so there's no chance of anything getting by them."

"Then my job here is done." Mr. Trask stood. "Please do let me know if you need anything else or have any questions."

Sophia showed the lawyer to the door, her mind whirling with this new information. Oh, yes, she had questions, but they could wait a little while.

"Well, that was informative," Charli said in a way that no one could mistake for sincerity and made a face. "I thought it was Heath at the door. He owes me dinner."

Heath and Charli had hit it off apparently, and since Sophia liked Ace's former teammate, she was thrilled they seemed to be spending more time together. As long as it didn't interfere with opening day, they could get married for all she cared.

Her sister vanished back upstairs, leaving her alone with Ace for the first time in what felt like ages.

"Finally got your answers," she told him, and he grinned, pulling her into a kiss.

"Back at you." But then his smile slipped. "It's still not over, though. Your father's associate, the one Intruder Man worked for, is still at large. The archaeologists are still finding new artifacts. There's a lot going on. I haven't even had time to take you on a proper date."

"You will," she predicted. "In the meantime, I trust that we'll be facing down whatever happens next together."

This was what it looked like to finally have everything she'd ever wanted.

"I love you, Soph," he murmured. "One day, I'm going to make you mine forever."

"Too late. You're already stuck with me," she teased. "Because I love you too and I'm not ever giving you up."

* * * * *